OUR WINTER MONSTER

OUR WINTER MONSTER

Dennis Mahoney

HELL'S HUNDRED

This is a work of fiction. Names, characters, places, and incidents either are the product of the author's imagination or are used fictitiously, and any resemblance to actual persons, living or dead, businesses, companies, events, or locales is entirely coincidental.

Published by Hell's Hundred
an imprint of Soho Press
227 W 17th Street
New York, NY 10011

Library of Congress Cataloging-in-Publication Data

Names: Mahoney, Dennis, 1974- author.
Title: Our winter monster / Dennis Mahoney.
Description: New York, NY : Hell's Hundred, 2024.
Identifiers: LCCN 2024012362

ISBN 978-1-64129-633-5
eISBN 978-1-64129-634-2

Subjects: LCGFT: Horror fiction. | Thrillers (Fiction) | Novels.
Classification: LCC PS3613.A3493355 O97 2024 | DDC
813/.6—dc23/eng/20240325

Interior design by Janine Agro

Printed in the United States of America

10 9 8 7 6 5 4 3 2 1

For Coley, Jack, and Bones
My Companions in the Storm

OUR WINTER MONSTER

Chapter 1

Little car, lonely road, night. A bad combination with a blizzard coming on.

Brian's in the passenger seat, powerless and fidgety and wishing he were elsewhere. Snow falls fast, zooming at the headlights. The village must be close, he tells himself again, except there's nothing. Not a glow. Not a glimmer in the dark.

His girlfriend, Holly, drives the car like an ice road trucker. Flinty. Sharp. Acting like she always drives in blizzards. She's expressionless, her eyes stay bolted to the road, and she doesn't say a word unless Brian speaks first. They're both twenty-eight but Holly seems older. For a whole strange year, starting last winter, he's felt as if they were aging in opposite directions.

"I didn't expect our emergency vacation to be a literal emergency," he says.

"This isn't an emergency," she says. "Just relax."

Holly rolls her shoulders, trying to loosen up inside her puffy winter coat. Big breath in, big breath out. Brian follows her example but his joints feel locked. His lungs are a pair of tight frozen bottles.

He squints out the windows at the emptiness around

them. Barren fields flank the road. Beyond, rolling hills and evergreen forest. The landscape is blanketed with snow from previous storms, and everything is hazy in the vast, wintry dark as if they're somewhere, anywhere, and nowhere at once.

Brian checks his phone but the map isn't working. They haven't passed another car or road sign for miles.

"This is bad," he says.

"There's nothing we can do but keep going," Holly says. "I only wish the snow would quit messing with my eyes. I'm starting to take it personally."

"Slow down, at least."

"We're fine."

Holly seems miles away as she speeds ahead, coldly in control, as if she's piloting a military drone.

"We should be home right now," Brian says, "snuggled up with Hulu."

"Well, the time travel button on the dash doesn't work."

"Do the brakes still work?"

"The eject button might."

"How am I the only one who thinks we're being reckless?"

"You're the one who said we needed a vacation!"

He had, in fact, pressed her for a getaway trip—a chance to reconnect and stabilize a bit. They'd been struggling with each other. Petty fights. Quiet blame. Minor irritations that had deepened to infections. Not to mention they were bracing for an extra-hard winter. But every time he floated the idea of a vacation, Holly shot it down with clinical detachment. She had projects at work that needed her attention. Habits and routines she didn't want to break. And if they couldn't reconnect and stabilize at home, how would fucking in an unfamiliar bed make a difference? It felt like running away, she said. It felt like giving in.

Eventually, he asked why she was always so *unyielding*. They didn't talk the rest of the night. The following day, she booked the trip.

"I was thinking sun," he says. "I was thinking beach."

"I was thinking reasonable credit card bill."

"I'm only saying we wanted to get away from winter and instead we're going to a ski village. A place that makes its own snow when it doesn't snow enough. It's like you wanted—"

"To face it head-on? I did," she says. "I do."

The snow blows down, rushes up, and coils sideways. They might as well be driving half-blind through a corkscrew. There's less and less blacktop. More and more snow. One minute, the traction's fine, but then they slip for several seconds. Every quarter mile, the slips are getting longer. A subtle bend, the slightest wiggle—it wouldn't take much to spin them off the road.

"It's getting worse," Brian says. "A dinosaur could cross and we'd never see it coming."

"Shit, yeah," Holly says. "I've been so focused on the road, I wasn't even thinking about dinosaurs."

Brian almost laughs. Holly almost smiles.

"You know what I mean," he says. "We could crash into anything. Fallen trees."

"Giant ice sculptures. Reindeer *without* glowing noses."

"Blitzen through the windshield. But really, we should stop."

"And get us buried overnight? Hope the forecast is wrong?"

"Let our senses sharpen up. Storms have lulls. Worst case scenario, we get stuck and have to walk, what . . . two or three miles?"

"I'm gonna push through."

"Of course you are," he mumbles.

He regrets it right away.

"That's me. Hard as ice," she says.

"Holl, I didn't mean . . . I don't think you're hard."

"Nope. I'm *unyielding*."

"I never should have said that. It isn't you. It's us. We always feel—"

"Stuck," she says. "And now we're stuck together in the middle of a storm."

A storm they would have easily outrun if not for Brian. He'd wasted time at home, concerned about the weather, checking the forecast and procrastinating and second-guessing the entire vacation. Instead of leaving earlier, they'd lost a crucial hour.

He hates when his fear of something makes it come true.

"I'm sorry," Brian says. "This is all my fault."

"I didn't say that."

"Anxiety makes me stupid."

"Belittling yourself doesn't help me drive. So listen. Starting now, we're playful and excited." She smiles like a tour guide working through a headache. "First, neither one of us is crabby or resentful. All right?"

"All right."

"Second, we'll pretend we're flying in a spaceship."

Brian stares ahead, focusing his eyes on the hyperspace effect of driving through snow.

"We're lightspeed. We're making good time," Holly says. "Now tell me what we'll do as soon as we arrive."

"We'll get a drink," he says.

"Several drinks. What else?"

"We'll order dinner in a cozy, overpriced restaurant."

"And have a nice, safe walk to our little B&B," she says. "They have a big fireplace in the den."

"We'll hog it. No other guests can sit around our fire."

"We'll sip another drink."

"I'll give you a neck rub."

"And then we'll have sex in an unfamiliar bed. It'll be good."

"It will."

"We're almost there. It can't be far."

"There's a huge, gaudy Christmas tree at the edge of the village," Brian says. "It's made of metal poles, all welded together, like an art installation with holiday lights. They keep it up all year."

"So we're looking for the tree."

"We'll see it any minute."

Instead, he starts imagining they're on the wrong road, as if they missed a crucial turn twenty miles back and now they're driving into nothing, getting farther every second from the safety of the village. The snow falls heavier. The car is too constricted, the air is thick and stale, and Brian feels hot and claustrophobic in his coat.

The windshield's foggy and the wipers seem futile. Holly tries clearing off the glass with her hand.

She says, "I *think* I'm in the middle of the road. Where's the shoulder?"

Brian looks out the window with his heartbeat bumping and a weird, dark shudder at the edges of his vision.

"There's too much blowing snow," he says. "I can't see a thing."

"Stick your head outside."

"For real?"

"Just guide me for a sec."

"I'd rather be inside the car if we're about to lose control."

"I'd rather have help and *not* lose control."

He often freezes when he's caught between two opposing fears, but Holly's crisp, parental voice makes him roll down the window. He's startled by the rush of in-blown air and pops his head outside. Snow blasts his face. Up his nose. In his eyes.

"Can you see?" Holly yells.

"I think you're good!"

"Are you sure?"

The bank of snow from earlier storms is broad and inconsistent. By and large, a lumpy ridge delineates the road, but there are stretches where the shoulder and the field are almost even.

"Move a little left!" Brian shouts.

"Better?"

"Yeah!"

He cranes his neck farther out and looks for obstacles ahead. The snow is crazy and kinetic, swirling in the headlights. He feels the winter landscape sprawling out around him. The fields. The hills. The evergreen forest in the distance and the unseen mountains looming in the dark. Everything is bigger. Everything is charged. Too much air floods his lungs until he's very close to fainting, bursting into tears, or screaming at the goddamned frenzy of it all.

"I think I'm having a panic attack!"

"Breathe through your nose!" Holly says. "You're doing great!"

His eyes are drawn toward the field beside the car, where a dense swirl of snow masses in the chaos. It's thirty feet away—maybe closer, hard to tell. A strange, moving shape he doesn't understand. Is it an optical illusion from the halo of the headlights? An atmospheric oddity created by the storm? Whatever it is, the shape keeps thickening and growing, almost like an animated Rorschach blot.

"There's something out there!"

"What?"

"Something big!" Brian says.

"Is it a dinosaur?"

"I'm serious!"

He squints, zeroes in, and feels his heartbeat kick—because it isn't some illusion. It's definitely real. There's something in the dark: a giant, white shape that doesn't blow apart and almost looks solid. Almost like it's chasing him. The thing seems to swell and coalesce in his direction, and even though the car is speeding on the road, the shape moves too and keeps getting closer.

"Go! We've got to go!" he yells.

It's here. It's almost on him.

Brian jerks inside and whacks his head against the frame, and for a second every thought is jolted from his head. Snow explodes through the window and whirls around the car. It packs onto Brian, muffling his face, like an airborne avalanche that won't stop coming. He barely hears Holly shouting through the snow.

His body seems to float—is he outside the car?—and everything is dark.

Then everything is gone.

Chapter 2

It's blizzard night in Pinebuck.

The village is so compact that its entire cartoon map fits on a souvenir postcard. Pinebuck isn't a boomtown like the major resorts farther north or west, but it's popular in snowy seasons—the right-sized place for a solid, modest peak. In the summer, it's as quiet as a beach town in winter, or Salem, Massachusetts six months from Halloween.

This time of year, viewed from the slopes, Pinebuck looks as if someone built a model village, maybe for a holiday display in a New York City department store, and then magically expanded it and nestled it securely in the evergreen forest at the bottom of a mountain.

There are two roads in. Route 4—the rural highway where Holly and Brian, only minutes ago, were driving in the storm—ends at the intersection with Route 19, which runs south to Hilldeclaire or north to more populated towns.

Greeting visitors at the two roads' juncture is the Rickman property. The open plot belongs to an energetic senior named Vance Rickman, who lives at the end of a long driveway, away from traffic near the edge of the forest, in a pair of double-wide trailers he welded together. Everyone in Pinebuck knows the Rickman place because of the giant Christmas tree. Vance constructed it himself—a conical sculpture made of welded metal pipes, standing fifty feet tall and festooned with thousands of green LED lights. No one coming to Pinebuck notices the village's welcome sign. What they notice is the tree, always there, always lit, telling road-weary visitors they've finally arrived.

A quarter mile farther is the beginning of Main Street. Only four blocks long, Main Street is crammed with all the usual features and amenities of an adorable vacation village. There's a tourist center, lots of B&Bs, two cafés, a diner, restaurants, bars, a liquor store, gift shops, a pharmacy, clothes and sporting goods stores, a single-screen movie theater, and a chocolatier.

Parallel to the main drag are several blocks of residential homes, many of which double as B&Bs, and then a smattering of isolated houses at the outskirts. Almost everyone who lives in Pinebuck works in Pinebuck. The homes and yards are well-maintained, and everywhere a sense of orderliness is kept, as if an unfilled pothole or any piece of trash will not only spoil the effect of a curated theme park but directly threaten the cashflow of a village that thrives on winter charm.

Pinebuck doesn't have its own school, so its kids are bussed south to Hilldeclaire. It doesn't have a hospital, either, but there's a well-staffed medical center halfway between the village and the mountain. People with cuts, breaks, or mild concussions go to the medical center. Anyone with worse is raced down to Hilldeclaire.

Tonight, the slopes and lifts are closed, but tomorrow will be different, and everyone is ready. Pinebuck's always grateful for a walloping dose of snow. Fewer storms, fewer skiers. More storms, more dollars. Kyla Ware, the owner of Winterware Gifts & Goodies, claims she can measure her precise seasonal earnings by how many inches of snow fall between November and April, and there's a village-wide consensus that less than fifteen feet on the mountain is reason for any business owner to start sweating bullets.

The current forecast is strong, with eighteen inches expected in the village and up to three feet on the mountain. But Pinebuck's optimism is shadowed, ever so slightly, by memories of the last major snow they had in late November, seven weeks ago. That particular storm kicked off the season with a glorious base of thirty-two inches on the slopes. Rooms were booked. Shops and restaurants were flush with out-of-towners days before the anticipated snowfall. But then a newlywed couple, Mitch and Becky Skylar, vanished in the storm and were never seen again.

Their disappearance cast a pall over the town. It didn't prevent the usual influx of skiers and profits, but the weeklong search parties, the peculiar details of the couple's vanishing, and the MISSING posters all around Pinebuck—featuring a picture of the Skylars, bright and carefree—left a grim, heavy atmosphere all through December.

In the weeks after New Year's Day, they're still on people's minds. No one has to *say* the Skylars' frozen bodies might be alarmingly close. A quarter mile into the woods. Thirty feet off the side of Route 4. Hidden in a snowbank nobody's checked, right behind the Mobile Mart. But in the crannies of their thoughts, everybody knows it, and all anyone can do is wait until spring and see what the melting snow finally reveals.

But tonight, for the visiting crowd and most of the residents, the somber past gives way to the energetic present. The roads are mostly empty but the sidewalks are lively. It's after 9 P.M. and the village's overnighters arrived hours ago, beating the dangerous weather, to settle in ahead of the powder and excitement of the morning mountain. Everyone's enjoying the wind and wild snow, their delicious meals rolling into drinks and desserts, merry lights and music, socializing with strangers, and hurrying from restaurants and pubs back to cozy lodgings, with their gloves on and collars up and buzzy, warm faces laughing in the blizzard.

It's a bubble of enchantment, magical and whole, like a snow globe right before it's shattered with a brick.

Chapter 3

Sheriff Kendra Book puts her Yeti on the counter.

"Milk and sugar?" Cookie asks, picking up the travel mug and filling it with coffee.

"Sugar and cream," Kendra says.

"Half and half?"

"*Cream.*"

Kendra treats herself in winter, coping with the cold and the nerve-racking duties by indulging in a wealth of suicidal food. Sugar, cream, frosted pastries oozing fruit through the wax paper bag, and—once she makes it through another long night—buttery pancakes and bacon and a big hot chocolate, with Reddi-wip, right back here at Cookie's Village Diner. This season, ever since the night the Skylars disappeared, she's been coping even more with stimulants and sweets.

"It's not my place to say," Cookie tells her, "but it might not kill you to treat yourself better."

"You're right," Kendra says. "It's not your place to say."

"That was a folksy figure of speech. This *is* my place to say. And just because I'm selling junk doesn't mean you have to buy it."

"I heard a similar thing from a snow bunny with a coat full of Oxy."

"Fine. Haul me in for slinging Danishes," Cookie says, handing a bag of them to Kendra.

"Imagine all the bright young lives that would save."

Both women are in their forties and have lived a long time in Pinebuck.

Cookie's white, skinny as a swizzle stick, and smiles at people she doesn't even like. Three times divorced, she doesn't balk at commitment but also doesn't hesitate when it's time to cut loose. She neither loves nor hates running a diner seven days a week, including every holiday. She just runs it, spirited and steady, and rarely wastes time questioning her lot in life.

Kendra is Black, amply figured, and frowns at people she doesn't even dislike. Single most of her life, she's been extra hesitant to date—or commit to much of anything—since her girlfriend, Taz, dumped her last summer and moved to Albuquerque. She can't decide if she loves or hates being sheriff. Kendra just works, stoical and steady . . . but lately she's been frozen in a bad, hard groove.

She used to like living here. Everyone in Pinebuck had seemed to like *her*. She'd been elected to her job in a landslide win, and over the intervening years, the village was a place where being a Black lesbian cop didn't make her feel like a fabulous monstrosity. Tourists were a different story, often seeing parts of her they couldn't fit together and seeming to recoil from the parts they didn't like. But tourists came and went, and for a while there, yeah—Kendra knew who she was, the locals had her back, and the person she was dating liked everything about her.

Then Taz moved away, the Skylars disappeared, and she had personal and public wounds that wouldn't heal. People saw her differently . . . and not just tourists. Had her world changed shape, or had her own shape twisted?

Either way, she's felt increasingly and bitterly alone, as if her home is now a place where she no longer fits.

At least she has Cookie, who's become a real friend. Kendra thinks they feel enlivened by their differences. Cookie thinks they're comforted by hidden similarities. Each of them suspects that both of them are right.

"We need another crap movie night," Kendra says.

"We do," Cookie says, turning on her phone and pulling up the calendar. "Sunday ought to work."

"Whose turn is it to pick?"

"We'll each pick one and have a crap double feature."

They've been meeting every month for almost half a year to watch movies they're embarrassed to admit they adore. Second-tier romcoms. Low-budget horror. Blockbuster bombs and unloved sequels. They order food, drink beer, and laugh until they snort. Amid their running commentary, they sidle into subjects they usually avoid. They've unpacked secrets, both of them have cried, and they've often learned unexpected things about each other. Mostly, though, the two of them have good, dumb fun.

A young couple walks in, ringing the bell above the door. Cold, snowy air billows into the diner. The winter smell, the vibrant faces—everything tonight reminds Kendra of the Skylars.

Cookie greets the couple with automatic pep. "Welcome to Cookie's. I'm Cookie. We close in thirty minutes."

The couple nods and smiles, friendly and appreciative. They clap snow off their coats, notice Kendra at the counter, and slink toward a booth with surly looks and lowered voices. Maybe they don't like cops. Maybe it's something else. There's been a lot of *something else* all of Kendra's life, and the last seven weeks have only sharpened her awareness, like a mean old blade with a brand-new edge. Forty-eight days since she failed at her job. Forty-eight days of shouldering the weight. And now it's easier for everyone—herself included—to focus on a part of her they just don't like.

Kendra stares out the window, seeing how the snow is falling harder already, and it takes her half a minute to realize her gaze has drifted to another patron at the counter. Tanner is a wiry little man, muscular and short, and on nights like tonight, he's the snowplow driver. Kendra's known him for years without really knowing him, because Tanner's the kind of guy you can stare at for thirty seconds and hardly register he's there. Even weirder, he's a guy who doesn't *notice* someone staring. If he does, he doesn't care. If he cares, he doesn't show it.

Tanner dips a French fry into a blob of mayonnaise and maple syrup on his plate.

When he isn't plowing roads, he's a reliable handyman who can fix just about anything. He's quiet and polite. He keeps to himself. Kendra thinks of how he helped, day after day, during the search for the Skylars. But despite all that, her flesh creeps back as if she's looking at a jellyfish slurping up food.

Am I really this judgy when I hate being judged? she thinks. *But then again, ugh. Mayonnaise and maple.*

She pops a fresh square of nicotine gum into her mouth, pressing the older piece she's already been chewing into the now-empty blister pack. The only times she isn't chewing nicotine gum are when she's sleeping, eating, or smoking a cigarette.

Cookie watches her and says, "Do you even *have* a resting heart rate?"

"I'm staying sharp," Kendra answers. "I swear I'm the only person in Pinebuck who doesn't equate snow with problems."

"You fix the ones you can and let the rest go."

"They tend to pile up."

"Well, don't carry them around. There's always more coming."

Kendra's well aware that Cookie knows problems. In her seventeen years of working at the diner, Cookie's dealt with fistfights, property damage, debt, bad employees, pain-in-the-ass locals, and innumerable hostile, drunk, and troublemaking tourists. She's been robbed at gunpoint twice. She has three ex-husbands after harrowing divorces. She almost lost the diner last summer to a fire. When she talks about trouble, Cookie knows plenty.

She wipes ketchup off the counter for the hundred-thousandth time.

"Tanner," Cookie says. "You want a coffee for the road?"

Tanner looks spooked that someone said his name.

"I'm good," he says. "Thanks."

He's got his finger in the blob of mayonnaise and syrup, and when Cookie takes his plate, his fingertip lifts and drizzles in the air. *Don't*, Kendra thinks. But he doesn't lick it; instead, he wipes his hands with a napkin, folds it into a triangle, and slips it neatly under his mug.

Cookie stares at Tanner and says, "*You* don't focus on

problems." She holds his check out of reach as if she's holding it for ransom. "You plow the roads all night and barely keep ahead, but when you're done, you don't go home and worry about the next storm."

"I'll bet you worry now, though," Kendra says. "All that snowy road and everyone relying on you."

Tanner pauses in the spotlight, totally inert. He doesn't fidget with his hands, rub his wispy hair, or give a single hint of what he might be thinking. Kendra almost feels bad for picking on the guy right before his lonely overnight shift.

"I try to see things better than they are," he says.

"Right," Cookie says, handing him his check. "It's all about perspective."

Kendra says, "Shit, is that the big secret? I'll just chuckle at the snow like a jolly old elf."

"Good start," Cookie says.

"You'd make a lousy cop."

"That's why I run a diner."

Tanner lays his credit card on the check, pivots on his squeaky stool, and retreats to the restroom.

Cookie leaves the counter and weaves around the tables. It's a route she could navigate backward and blind. She takes the order from the couple in the booth, walks behind the counter again, and drops a pair of hamburger patties on the grill. Kendra stands near the door with her pastry bag, watching flakes fall heavily and sparkle near a streetlight. The sight is picturesque but all she sees is trouble.

"I'm going. Wish me luck," Kendra says.

"Luck," Cookie answers. "You'll be fine. It's only snow."

"It's everything that *happens* in the snow that makes me worry."

Chapter 4

The restroom smells like Lysol and months of old urine. The too-familiar odor fills Tanner's nose and suddenly, he wishes he were comfortably at home. He pees into the toilet, taking his time to make sure his bladder's absolutely empty, because once he's in the truck, he can't waste time pulling over for a pit stop. He wipes the dribble off the bowl with a wad of toilet paper. He's never understood why so many men fail to do this. *Oblivious,* he thinks. *Unaware of their effects. Why leave a mess for someone else to clean if you can leave the room better? Leave the room changed.*

He washes his hands and examines himself in the streaky mirror, staring extra hard until he sees what he wants. Someone in control. Someone totally prepared. But suddenly his *self* isn't quite right. A muscle in his shoulder spasms out of nowhere. He pinwheels his arm, hearing crackles in his joint, and feels way too tense before the long night ahead.

He faced a night like this only seven weeks earlier and made it through fine. Almost better than he hoped. But he was scared that night, and now he's feeling it again.

"You aren't scared," Tanner tells himself. "You're reasonably anxious."

The weather app says heavy snow for hours, with sustained winds of 35 mph and gusts over 50. Whiteout conditions and power outages expected. Band after band of incoming snow. He'll be plowing all night—Routes 4 and 19, Main Street, side streets, rural roads, parking lots—with everything needing multiple passes as the snow keeps falling and the drifts pile up.

There are so many variables to plan for. So much relying on split-second judgment. One false move and everything can spiral, and it's hard to hide mistakes in a truck with flashing lights.

Then again, it's amazing what people don't notice. He's lost count of all the tourists who have almost stepped in front of the plow. As if they never saw the lights or heard the rumble of the blade. Like nothing bad can happen once they're on vacation. It makes them so trusting. Only later do they wonder why they're *in* a situation. Only after do they think: *I should have seen it coming.*

Tanner rubs his arm until his spasm settles down.

"You're calm. You're in control. Now get out there," he says, "and find someone to help."

When he steps out of the restroom and walks out front, an opportunity to help magically appears.

"Tanner, that you?"

Cookie's locked herself inside the walk-in cooler. He opens up the heavy-duty stainless steel door. A rush of cold air follows Cookie out. She thanks him with a laugh and hurries to the grill, where two sizzling burgers are burned beyond hope. She spatulas both into the trash and preps another pair. Tanner picks up his credit card and puts on his coat.

"I didn't want to bang on the door and embarrass myself with strangers," Cookie says, pointing with her chin toward the couple in the booth. "Would you believe that's the second time I've trapped myself this week?"

"That shouldn't happen."

"Ha. You're telling me."

"I mean there ought to be a safety release. Like a button inside."

"Oh, that broke off months ago," Cookie says blithely, as if it's no more pressing than an old cracked mug—just another of a hundred broken items in the diner. "I replaced it with a screwdriver, but the screwdriver snapped and now there's metal in the hole. I bought a whole replacement but I haven't had time. That something you can do for me?"

Again, Tanner thinks. *The magic transformation.* He imagined being helpful, found Cookie helpless, and quick as that, she sees him as a person who can help.

"I'll do it this week," he says. "Won't take long."

Cookie turns to face him. "You're a good egg, Tanner. Don't let anybody beat you."

Is that a joke? He doesn't always know the right time to laugh. His father called him Mr. Roboto because he processed humor instead of really feeling it like everybody else. For now, he grins and nods the way other people do, and then he takes out his keys and heads toward the door.

"Be safe tonight," Cookie says. "The sheriff says there's all kinds of trouble out there."

I'm ready, Tanner thinks. *I've seen it all before.*

Chapter 5

Holly wakes up and says, "Oh, just fucking *stop.*"

She doesn't realize what she's angry at until she sits up, the offending noise ends, and she discovers she's been leaning on the steering wheel horn. The car isn't moving. The headlights illuminate a vast field of snow. She doesn't remember driving off the road or passing out. But as she checks her head for injuries, she's clear enough to think, *Nobody remembers being unconscious.*

She takes her boot off the brake and hears the wheels spin, and then she puts the car in park and turns off the engine. Facts come to her in heartbeats. It's cold. The car is snowy. Something happened, something's wrong . . .

"Brian," Holly says, looking all around the car.

He isn't in his seat or in the back. He's simply gone.

She opens her door to lunge outside and jolts against her seatbelt. Once she twists around and unclips the buckle, she stumbles getting out and flops onto the ground. Her hand's in muddy slush. There's a long, deep rut, like a half-frozen stream, and the car's front tires are jammed in tight. Holly picks herself up, shields her eyes against the blowing snow, and walks around the car. He's nowhere in sight.

"Bri!" she yells. "Briiii!"

She makes herself stop. Get control. Think clearly. He wouldn't have abandoned her, that much she knows . . . but what if he banged his head, too, and wandered off confused? Except she doesn't see footprints anywhere near the car. Did the blizzard hide his tracks? How long was she unconscious? Is it possible the crash threw him out the window?

"Bri! Brian!"

She walks toward the road through the field's old drifts. Flakes hit her sideways in thick, heavy gusts. She knows he must be close. He has a bright red coat. Even in the dark, she ought to see a shape or some trace of color in the uniform snow. She makes it to the road and runs back and forth, scanning everywhere and hollering his name nonstop, until she notices she can't see the car anymore. The storm is so dense, and she's wandered so far, she can't even locate the headlights' glow.

She breathes in through her nose and exhales heat.

Don't be scared. You can't be scared, she thinks. *Just walk along the road until you find your own prints coming from the field.*

Instead, she finds the tire tracks, muddy in the snow and easier to follow than her own soft trail. And then a thought hits her, very sharp, very clear. She's been looking all over for a glimpse of Brian's coat, but if he tumbled from the car, he'd have landed near the tire tracks. Even if he crawled or rolled, he would have left marks, and yet she doesn't find a clue the whole way back.

For a dark and sickening moment, Holly wonders if her brain was damaged in the crash. What if her memory's a mess? What if everything she *thinks* is real is only a delusion, and her mind is so whacked, she can't tell the difference? Nothing scares her more than losing who she is.

She checks her head again. There's nothing wrong—no tenderness or lumps—and then she's angry at herself for being childish and weak. It's a bad situation but it isn't a delusion. Brian's gone without a trace, and if it doesn't make sense, that only means she needs to broaden her assessment.

Holly gets back in the car, rolls up the passenger window, and restarts the engine to increase the heat. She's shivering from nerves as much as from the cold, and the roaring in her head is louder than the storm. When she takes out her phone, it has two steady bars and a seventy-percent charge. She taps Brian's number and the call goes to voicemail.

"*Hi, you've reached Brian. Please leave a message and I'll call you back. Thanks.*"

Something about the *please* and *thanks* irritates Holly. The softness and politeness. The paleness of his voice.

"Brian, what the hell," she says. "Where the fuck are you? I'm in the field, I'm off the road. Like fifty, I don't know . . . a hundred feet off the road. I don't know what happened, I don't know where you are."

She looks out the windows: front, side, back.

"I'm in the car," she says. "You can still see the tire tracks leading from the road. Find the tracks. Follow the headlights. You've got to find the car and walk to me, all right? Just call me back or find me. I'm okay. We're okay."

She ends the call and opens up the Find My app. Brian's location can't be pinned down. Presumably, the storm is interfering with the signal. He's *somewhere in the circle* but the circle is a mile wide, slightly off-center from Holly at the car. She wonders if his phone is even with him. What if it's here inside the car and she didn't hear it vibrate? She checks all over, sifting through the snow piled in the cupholders, on the passenger-side floor, and finally on his empty seat. She doesn't find his phone but discovers something else.

Brian's seatbelt is snapped in two separate places. Once along the waist band, once along the shoulder strap. The buckle of the belt is still fastened in the latch. She's alarmed by the sight. By the sheer impossibility. People have high-speed collisions on the highway and their *heads* come off before the seatbelt snaps.

She turns her phone back on.

Dials 9. Dials 1.

Then her brain seems to clench, like a fist behind her eyes, and her stomach does a somersault. She thinks about another night with snow, flashing lights, and cops who'd looked at her like nobody had looked at her before. The memory enrages her. She ought to call for help but her mind won't let her. *Ask for help*, Holly thinks, *and suddenly you're helpless.* It's a childish perspective but it's hardwired, a year-long habit that's difficult to counter. Holly kills the call and hunches in her seat, waiting for a huge wave of nausea to pass, and then she crams her phone into her pocket and jumps out of the car again, screaming Brian's name until her throat starts to burn.

She sees him in her mind, through the whiteout wind, as visceral and vivid as a strong hallucination. Brian on the ground, bleeding from his head. He's lying on his back, too scared to move, and if she doesn't act fast, he'll be gone. He'll be dead.

But what is there to do if she can't even find him? Holly glares at the car, jammed in the rut. She pounds her fist on the trunk, banging snow off the top, and repeatedly kicks the bumper with the heel of her boot. Chunks crack off. She breaks a taillight in.

Her head feels weird—full of energy, or blood, or a white-noise roar scattering her thoughts. The blizzard seems to gather and condense all around her. Something's building in the storm, like a weight about to fall. Suddenly a force barrels up behind her. She senses it and turns, furious and scared, and sees a monstrous shape swirling up toward her.

She raises both arms and opens her mouth to yell, and then her eyes and voice and everything are smothered in the snow.

Chapter 6

ONE YEAR EARLIER
Six Days Before the Bad Date

Brian walked into his neighborhood liquor store, a cozy place with colorful bottles, year-round holiday lights, and a carpet so dingy it resembled concrete.

As soon as he stepped inside, something felt wrong.

He waved to Pranav, who stood at the register with his oversized glasses and tall, narrow limbs. Pranav had the air of a brilliant grad student who couldn't afford tuition and found himself trapped behind a liquor store counter. He often looked dispirited. Tonight, he looked tense.

Three other customers moved around the shop. A man with a silver beard browsed white wine. An elderly woman carried peach brandy to the counter. The two of them, along with Pranav, seemed nervously attuned to customer number three. He was a beefy man with a Boston Celtics jacket and a crew cut, mumbling to himself and swaying in a corner. Brian couldn't see his face but thought the word *trouble*. He kept the man in his periphery, grabbed a bottle of mezcal, and followed the elderly woman up toward the register. The bearded man stepped behind Brian in the line.

The Celtic yelled, "Son of a bitch!" and everybody

jolted. It was impossible to tell what had ticked him off. He stomped across the shop, cut the line, and wobbled at the counter. The woman stepped away and hugged the brandy to her chest.

"Sir," Pranav said. "You need to wait your turn, please."

His voice was high and trembly, and his whole face wavered. Brian stood straighter, and his shoulders drew back, as if his rib cage had started to expand on its own.

"Bottle of Dew," the Celtic said.

His bloodshot eyes were angry little peepholes. He took a debit card out of his wallet and snapped it on the counter.

"Sir," Pranav said.

"Lemme point. Watch my finger. Tull-a-more *Dew*."

"It's all right," the woman told Pranav. "I don't mind waiting."

"*I* do," the Celtic said.

Brian turned to glance at the bearded man behind him. The man backed up and fiddled with his phone, apparently pretending none of this concerned him. Pranav held his ground but didn't look convincing. The Celtic lost his balance, swaying right, swaying left, until he bumped the woman hard. She almost dropped her brandy.

Brian's limbs flushed and tingled, and his breaths grew deep, the way an athlete's body generates heat.

"Sir, I'm asking you again," Pranav said.

"Sir, I'm asking . . . sir, I'm asking," the Celtic parroted. "You sound like a help line."

"I'm asking you to wait. There are other customers ahead—"

"You sound *exactly* like a help line. So help. Get the bottle, put it here, ring me up."

He slapped his hand on his debit card and shook the whole counter. The bearded man put his bottle on the floor and left the store.

"I'm calling the police," Pranav said.

"Naaaah," the Celtic said. "You don't wanna do that."

He lunged across the counter, grabbing at the phone.

"*Hey*," Brian said, bullhorn loud.

He touched the Celtic's arm, right above the elbow. The Celtic spun around and got in Brian's face.

"Putcher hand on me?!"

Brian didn't blink or lean back an inch, even when their noses almost pressed together. His adrenaline was surging but he didn't feel scared. He was sober. In the right. The better, cooler head. Honestly, he thought . . . What was the worst that could happen? A shove. A wild punch. Nothing life or death.

Preferably, his confidence would calm things down. Same as at the office, where he was the only account exec who didn't sweat bullets when the boss got pissed. Same as at home, where the upstairs tenant played music too loud and Brian marched up and knocked on the door. He was cocky sometimes and had to check his ego, but at times like this, when he needed extra guts, Brian could have stared down a *team* of drunk Celtics.

"You should go."

"I should go?" the Celtic said. "I should *go*?"

"You need to chill out."

"You gonna make that happen? Chill me out, little bitch?"

Brian met his gaze with a dead-eyed glare. "I got dumped by my girlfriend," he said. "I might lose my job.

I might get evicted. That's my week. That's my life. This bottle in my fist feels ready to explode. You understand what I'm saying?"

"I only want to buy—"

"Get out," Brian said.

"Man, I just—"

"No. Get the fuck out."

The Celtic's eyes darted side to side. His bluster lost focus when he looked around the room. He yelled at Pranav again. He pounded on the counter. He was putting on a show, as if diverting from the fact that everyone was staring and he couldn't quite remember what exactly he was mad about.

"Last chance," Brian said. "You want to get crazy?"

The Celtic looked at him and sizzled like an old, damp firework. *This is it,* Brian thought. *He'll either blow or fizzle out.*

"Fuck this place," the Celtic finally said. He turned to Pranav, pretended to dial in the air, and actually made the sound effects. "Beep, boop, boop. This help line sucks." He snatched his card off the counter, stumbled when he turned, and stomped out the door as if he'd really shown *them.*

The woman with the brandy sighed and said, "Eesh. I can't believe that other man just walked out. He didn't even put his wine bottle back."

Brian picked it off the floor and placed it on the counter. He stepped aside and let the woman check out first. His head felt buzzy and his eyes were extra sharp. Mostly, though, Brian felt perfectly himself.

Pranav finished with the woman, looking rattled but relieved. After she was gone, he said, "Thanks for helping out. I'm sorry about your girlfriend. And your job. Are you okay?"

Brian laughed. "I made that up to sound volatile," he said. "My week's been really good. I never want to explode."

Chapter 7

Brian wakes on his stomach with his face near the ground.

All he sees is blowing snow. His mind tries to process the situation blindly while his body's overwhelmed by the strong, dark wind. He's barely even sure he's actually awake.

The smell of cold pine focuses his thoughts. He rises to his knees, rubbing snow off his face, and registers the evergreen trees all around him. Last thing he knew, he was sitting in the car, and now he's here by himself and doesn't see the road. Only woods, only snow. Where's the car? *Where's Holly?*

He feels the back of his head, on the cowlick, on the scar. He isn't bleeding but he flinches at the memory of pain, and his nerves flash red as if his skin is really cut. Suddenly he's picturing a figure in the snow—hulking, indistinct—coming to attack him. His body automatically responds to the threat, and without a clear thought, he jolts off the ground and scrambles through the snow toward a nearby tree.

He bumps against the trunk, fists up in self-defense. But then his legs feel weak, so he lets himself sink and scrapes his coat along the rough, frozen bark until he's hunched.

He squints through the snow but nothing's coming. No one's there.

But he *had* seen something in the blizzard. Like a beast.

"What the hell," Brian whispers. "What the *hell.* That was real."

He checks his phone. It's totally intact and almost fully charged. There's a voicemail from Holly. The message is seven minutes old. He crams the phone against his ear and listens to her voice.

"*I'm in the car,*" Holly says. "*Find the tracks. Follow the headlights.*"

Brian stands and spins, looking for the lights, but the snowy gusts are brutal and he has to shield his eyes. He can't see much beyond the phone screen's glow. He suddenly hears a crackle and a heavy, dead thump. It might have been a branch falling in the storm . . . but it might be something else. Something violent and strange.

He thinks the word *monster* like a scared little boy. He crouches at the tree again, as small as he can get, and dims the light of his phone so it doesn't draw attention. His thoughts are far away, as if they aren't really his, and for a while Brian freezes there and argues with himself.

This is bad. You've got to move.

I can't, I can't, I can't.

Toughen up. Figure it out. Find the car, get back to Holly.

He thinks of how urgent she sounded on the phone. But she also sounded confident and sensible and sharp. He breathes until he feels more solid in his body, wishing he could make himself more like Holly with her crispness, and her wits, and her logical control.

But ever since the Bad Date last winter, anything can

turn him into Play-Doh. Critiques from his boss. Hostile drivers on the highway. Holly's tone when he comes up short or disappoints her. He's tried recovering with therapy and exercise and meds, but everything he does barely manages the symptoms of a break too deep and splintery to fix.

Now he has to grapple with a genuine emergency. He can't just melt, and he can't just freeze, so he concentrates hard and starts with what he knows.

Holly said the car was in a field. They must have crashed. He checks himself for injuries and doesn't find a thing. Nothing broken, nothing sore. Not the slightest trace of pain. How could he have blacked out and wandered here intact?

I didn't, Brian thinks. *Something pulled me from the car. It carried me and left me here. What the hell was it? How can this be real?*

He'd swear he made it up . . . except it grabbed him. Here he *is*. If he walked here himself, he would have left tracks that he could easily retrace. He makes his way back to where he first woke up and looks at the impression of his body in the snow. No other tracks lead to or from the spot—certainly not the prints of a huge creature. He searches overhead in case it's hiding in the trees, but he seems to be alone. Terribly alone.

Everywhere he looks is virtually the same. Snow . . . trees . . . endless dark without a hint of headlights. He calls Holly's phone and gets her voicemail greeting. The Find My app shows her *somewhere in the circle*, but how can he decide which direction he should go? He calls her number back. Again, she doesn't answer. Eventually, he walks and talks, just to start moving and to let her know he's still alive, on his feet, and trying.

"Holl, I got your message. I don't know what happened. I'm lost. I'm in the woods. I'm in the middle of the forest. You've got to call me back. Fuck, I wish you'd answer. Something grabbed me, I don't know. It pulled me out of the car. I swear I didn't imagine it. You must have seen it, too."

Wind coils through the trees, blowing snow in all directions. Brian stumbles over obstacles he never sees coming—roots, fallen branches, hidden bumps and dips—and tries to keep the helplessness and panic from his voice.

"I'm walking now. I'll find the car. I'm gonna find the road. Yell or honk the horn or just call me back."

He peers into the distance without hanging up. The forest and the snow have a subtle green radiance. It's eerie and peculiar. Almost otherworldly. At first, he thinks the phone's glow is messing with his eyes, but when he covers up the screen, the radiance remains.

He hears another crackle in the nearby trees and pauses when the sound is followed by a rumble, like a deep vibration all through the woods. What if it's the creature coming up behind him? Or maybe it was thunder, which can happen in a blizzard. Lightning might explain the color in the air—an atmospheric charge, like St. Elmo's fire, building in the evergreen branches overhead.

"I see something. A lot of green light. Holy shit, it's the tree. It's the goddamn tree! I'm near the Christmas tree sculpture at the border of the village. You can't be very far. Just follow the road, you're almost here. We're going to be all right. I love you! Find the tree!"

Brian hangs up and walks to where the forest ends. Drifts of heavier snow look oceanic in the clearing. Farther off, to his left, he sees an oddball structure like a pair of old trailer homes pressed up together. It's blurry in the storm but the windows are lit. Someone must be home. Someone who can help.

The giant tree is straight ahead, roughly fifty paces off. The rusted metal frame is hidden by the clinging snow, so all he really sees is a monument of light, beautiful and green and absolutely magic. He wades toward the trailer home, looking at the tree, with his legs plunging almost to his knees in the drifts.

Brian hears a blast.

That was a gun. A fucking gun!

He flops down fast on his belly in the snow. The powder on the surface puffs around his body, but whoever took the shot must have seen where he dropped. His heartbeat booms from his chest to his ears. He slowly lifts his head and sees a figure with a shotgun, right between Brian and the weird double trailer. A man, he thinks. Lean and tall. Maybe bearded.

The man looks around, swiveling the gun, and seems to spot Brian lying in the snow.

"Wait!" Brian yells. "Please don't shoot!"

"Who's that?" the man shouts.

Brian stays down. "I didn't mean to trespass! Please, I had an accident—"

"Who is that there?!"

The man tromps toward him, silhouetted in the storm, and doesn't stop until they're close enough to see each other's faces. Brian stays on his stomach, trembling in the snow, and spreads his arms the way a person might surrender to a cop.

"I need help," Brian says. "We had an accident. My girlfriend and I—"

"You all right?" the man asks. "Are you hurt? Did it get you?"

Brian slowly kneels and shows his open palms.

"Shit," the man says. "Don't be scared of *me*. Get up. Come on, get up."

He grabs Brian's hand and hauls him to his feet, and then he swings the gun up and stares toward the woods. The man is older than Brian expected, maybe seventy or eighty, but he crackles with the vigor of someone much younger. He's wearing hip waders, a sweater, and an open winter coat. With his windblown hair and thick white beard, it's difficult distinguishing his head from the snow.

"My name's Brian."

"I'm Vance."

"I didn't mean to sneak—"

BOOM! Another shot. Brian jolts as if the recoil rocked his own shoulder. The weapon is a 12-gauge, pump-action shotgun, but Brian simply sees it as a big, loud gun. Vance's eyes look fierce. He's intense. A little crazed.

"What accident?" he says.

"What?" Brian asks.

"You said you had an accident."

"Right," Brian says, trying to organize his thoughts, and then he rambles about Holly, driving in the blizzard, and waking up lost and confused in the forest.

Vance doesn't really listen. He takes another shot. Brian

sees it coming and braces for the noise, but if anything, the blast jars him even more, cutting off his words and pummeling his nerves.

"Did you see it?" Vance says. "I heard it out there, cracking down limbs. Thought it might've been the storm. But then I hiked into the woods, saw it in the distance, and hauled ass out. I think it followed me. It's close. It's right fucking *here*."

"What is it? What did you see?"

"A bear! A fucking bear!"

Brian stands next to Vance, close enough to smell the old man's scent—a warm, wooly haze of sweat and bargain beer. They stare through the snow at the dark wall of trees.

"What did it look like?" Brian asks.

"Big," Vance says.

He lifts the shotgun again and trains it left to right, looking for a target he can't possibly see in the whiteout.

"You're sure it wasn't me?" Brian says.

Vance sizes him up and says, "I'm sure it wasn't you. It wasn't Bigfoot, either. I don't believe in make-believe. Bears are bad enough."

"It wasn't a bear," Brian says, mostly to himself. "They hibernate. They don't . . . It didn't *look* like a bear."

"So you did see it, too!" Vance says. "Trust your eyes!"

"It couldn't have been a bear that pulled me out of the car. It had to be something else. Something worse. Something weirder."

Vance looks at him and smirks. His smirk looks deranged. "It pulled you out of the car?" he says. "I won't say you're lying, but you're either off your rocker or you're the luckiest son of a bitch I've ever met. I've seen a bear maul a man, close as you and me are. Close as you and me."

He's right in Brian's face with the gun jammed between them. His beard is full of snow and he puffs out vapor. Brian backs up but Vance moves toward him, looking furious and adamant and ready to explode.

"Listen," Vance says. "I was out there with Paul. We knew these woods. We knew the whole place. We never heard a thing and then the bear was *on* him." Vance clamps a hand onto Brian's shoulder. "We didn't have guns. There was nothing I could do. It almost tore his arm off, flinging him around. He was screaming so bad. He was screaming . . . then he wasn't. Of *course* I ran away. You can smell it when the claws gut a man open. You smell it like his body's inside-out."

He's scared, Brian thinks. A little drunk, a little dangerous. The bear attack, whenever it was, stayed with him deep. Brian sees it in his eyes. The memory, the fear. Whatever Vance saw tonight brought it all back—the burliness and claws, the way his friend screamed—so visceral and real, he probably even smells it.

"I'm sorry," Brian says.

Vance turns toward the woods. He shoots again at nothing, like maybe he'll get lucky, and reloads the gun with shells from his pocket.

Brian's head blares.

"If there's a bear, let's go inside."

"No," Vance says. "I'll shoot the fuckin' bear."

He finishes reloading and—*BOOM!*—takes another blind shot and—*BOOM!*—rattles Brian from his teeth to the middle of his skull. There's too much randomness and recklessness and noise. Brian suddenly remembers what he said on Holly's voicemail. *Find me at the tree.*

"You've got to stop shooting. My girlfriend's out there, maybe in the woods."

"I won't shoot your girlfriend."

"You almost shot me!"

Vance doesn't answer but he holds off shooting, at least while he stalks back and forth through the drifts, wandering away from the Christmas tree's light.

Brian's about to call Holly again when an obvious alternative finally occurs to him. He takes out his phone and dials 911. Even with the phone cupped against his ear, it's difficult to hear the dispatcher's voice.

"My name is Brian," he says. "My girlfriend and I were driving on Route 4. We had an accident, a spinout. No. I don't know. I'm not hurt. I got separated from—"

BOOM!

"What? I'm not at the car anymore, I walked . . . I'm at the tree with the—"

BOOM! BOOM!

He yells at Vance, "Stop! You've got to stop! I'm on the phone!" Back on the call, Brian says, "That's a gun. It isn't mine. This guy . . . Vance. I'm near his trailers, near the tree. The big green tree at the edge—"

"Come on and show yourself! I'm here! I'll blow your grizzly head off!"

Vance is suddenly beside him.

BOOM!

Brian jolts. He drops his phone and scrabbles in the drift around his feet, looking for the glowing screen underneath the snow. When he finds his phone and brushes it off, he accidentally cancels the emergency call. He makes a frustrated sound, like a growl through his teeth, and everything's an overwhelming, overheated roar.

"You'd better stop shooting," Brian says. "I called the cops."

"I know the cops!" Vance says.

He lifts the shotgun again and points it at the woods.

Brian pictures Holly with a bullet in her chest. He tentatively grabs Vance's arm above the elbow. The gun jerks upward at the moment of the shot and Vance looks startled, as if the weapon might have backfired, but once he understands that Brian interfered, his whole face twists in a crazy look of rage. Brian cowers and his legs barely hold him up. Vance grips the gun crosswise and shoves at Brian's chest, and then they're grappling up close with the weapon pressed between them. Vance's teeth are bared. He shoulder-checks Brian onto his back, into a drift, and then he looms overhead, panting and disheveled, with the barrel of the gun aimed at Brian's stomach.

Brian wants to plead—*I'm sorry, please, I'm sorry*—but his voice won't work. It's like the words are somewhere else. He stares up at Vance until the snow blurs his head. Even the big metal tree is hidden by the storm, and the green light dims in a huge rush of white.

Brian shuts his eyes.

When he opens them again, he gets a glimpse of Vance. He's aimed the gun higher up. He looks astonished or afraid. Whatever Vance is looking at is right behind Brian. The snow starts whipping viciously around them.

Brian doesn't think. He's out of mind and out of body. He rises off the ground as something picks him up, and then he's weightless and his feet are dangling in the air. It's here again. It's got him now and everything is smudged. Vance . . . the windy snow . . . the dark . . . the cold . . . the gun.

He hears a final *BOOM!* through the storm's wild roar, and then the whiteout snuffs and silences his thoughts.

Chapter 8

ONE YEAR EARLIER
Five Days Before the Bad Date

The Christmas decorations had been up too long.

Now, in the middle of a Northeast January, their apartment had the feel of wilted festivity. The tree was brittle. Lights had died. And there were enough greeting cards, tchotchkes, and browning garlands that cleaning up the space was going to be a chore.

Early one night, Holly got home and had the place to herself. Brian was still at the office, working late to butter up a top-tier client, and she was gloomy at the prospect of hours on her own. She'd been hoping for a cozy night, relaxing in his company. The cold, slushy grayness of the day had worn her down. Now the old decorations looked particularly drab, like a visual manifestation of deep winter blues. She wished she weren't so vulnerable to outside forces. Crummy weather or a setback at work tanked her mood. Her spirit came and went. Her luck rose and fell. What she wanted was a sense of being in control.

Tonight, she decided she would finally undecorate. At least her own living room was something she could manage. She sloughed her coat, made a cup of tea, and turned up the heat. Chilled to her ribs, she stood beside the radiator and game-planned the work until the pipes got warm.

First, she took down the lights around the windows and doors, setting the working strings aside and shoving the dead ones into the trash. The room felt gloomier without the extra glow. She proceeded with the garlands and minor decorations, some of which were junk she simply threw away.

It was lifeless work, reminding her of hours at the office, where many of her days were routine slogs. She was a front-end developer at an EdTech company. Reliable. Efficient. Steady as a clock. She was popular with colleagues and superiors alike, and yet apparently she lacked something vital for promotion. Twice, she'd applied to be a project manager. Twice, someone else had gotten the position. Now she faced another year in the same old job, with her midrange duties and midrange salary.

Together, she and Brian were financially okay. They had their share of debts and loans, but Brian earned more than Holly, and he was close to a promotion of his own very soon. Still, she would have loved the bigger pay and better work, not to mention the reversal of her bleeding sense of confidence.

Holly cinched up a garbage bag and focused on the tree. She plucked the ornaments one by one, stooping each time to stick them in a box, and when the tree was finally empty, her lower back ached. She tugged the lights off the branches in a downpour of needles. The tree was shedding everywhere. The thought of vacuuming the living room *and* the building's staircase annoyed her so much she grabbed her keys and got in the car and went to buy a tree bag.

The store had a plethora of Christmas clearance items. The stuff was priced to go. Pretty soon, all the shelves would be skeletal and empty, making way for duller, more ordinary things. Same as their apartment turning commonplace again. She wondered what exactly she was hoping to accomplish. Would she really take control of her January slump by dutifully removing holiday cheer?

Suddenly, the aisle full of lights and decorations filled her with a childlike, candyland excitement. She loaded up a cart, bought an artificial tree, and played music in the car the entire way home. She carried everything inside and laid it on the floor. Then she bagged the dead tree, hauled it outside, and put the brand-new artificial tree in its place.

There was eggnog in the fridge, not yet expired. Holly added rum and took her glass into the living room. The radiators ticked and pumped out heat, and the apartment felt warm enough to walk around barefoot. She strung the new tree with all good lights and rehung the ornaments she'd just taken down. The eggnog gave her a buzz, and she partially undressed, feeling summery and free and playful as a faerie. She tripled the lights. She rearranged the furniture for coziness. She garlanded the doorways, festooned the windows, and decorated tabletops, counters, shelves, and ledges.

Last, she hung a disco ball that hadn't been on clearance but had seemed, when she saw it, like an answer to the problem of midwinter gloom. She screwed it to a ceiling joist, ran an extension cord with wire clips, and switched on the mirror ball's miniature motor. She aimed a gooseneck lamp directly at the ball and the room came alive with bright, twirling spangles. Then she poured another glass of eggnog and settled on the couch, enjoying how much warmer the apartment had become.

When Brian got home, he stood at the door and laughed.

"I spruced us up for winter," Holly said. "Isn't it great?"

Brian walked around, dazzled by the lights, and raved about Holly's exuberant display. He joined her on the couch with his own cup of eggnog. They talked about their days. They played their favorite songs. And for the first time in weeks, Holly looked ahead and thought the year seemed bright and under her control.

In the morning, up for work, she shuffled into the living room and turned on the lights. The fake tree glowed. The mirror ball spun. But the day was dead gray, sleet pinged off the windows, and a sharp, cold draft snaked around her heels. Holly hugged herself and thought about her holiday buzz. She should have known the feeling wouldn't last overnight.

It was the same as when she spruced up her desk at the office. She could rearrange her workspace or decorate her home like disco night in Christmas Town, but the changes never moved from the outside in.

She felt unmoored. At the mercy of the moment.

She squeezed a string of lights and yanked them off the wall.

Chapter 9

At first, Holly's startled by the strange, green light.

One minute, she was kicking the bumper of her car in an empty field, and now a fifty-foot cone with thousands of lights has appeared out of nowhere. She wobbles in the snow, bewildered by the sight, until she remembers Brian talked about this. It's the giant metal sculpture at the border of the village.

But how the hell did she get here? She touches her head again, convinced more than ever that she's suffered a concussion. This is the second time she's lost consciousness tonight, and she has zero memory of leaving the car and walking through the storm. She doesn't see her own footprints anywhere around her. The snow is falling hard, but if enough time has passed for the storm to hide her tracks, she ought to feel colder than she does right now. Incredibly, her core is full of energy and warmth, as if she hasn't been exposed to the elements at all.

And yet she also feels defenseless, like a kid without her parents. Lost in an unfamiliar place, on her own, in a dangerous predicament that's out of her control. She's unprepared for this, especially with her memory impaired, and she almost starts crying. This is all too much.

But then she thinks: *No. Fuck that. Fight.*

She was unprepared for most of last year and battled through. Breadwinning. Caregiving. Managing the home. Shaking off nightmares of violence and blood. She even carried the relationship, almost single-handedly, when Brian couldn't find his own way through.

She remembers a survival rule she learned last year: she needs to keep moving. Inertia is a killer. She fights through the drifts to the big metal tree, where the light grows brighter and buoys her resolve, and then she takes out her phone and sees a voicemail from Brian.

Holly plays it back, relieved that he's alive but also annoyed again—irked by the fear and weakness in his voice. It's always on *her* to stiffen her backbone, and later she's accused of being icy and inflexible. The same thing happens at the office with her colleagues. Someone drops the ball, Holly picks it up, and then they act as if she snatched an opportunity away.

Suddenly, she thinks, *What did Brian just say?*

She starts the message over, concentrating hard to hear him in the storm.

He says something pulled him out the window of the car. She feels a cold, dark firework exploding in her brain, remembering—but not quite remembering exactly—a shape that had risen in the storm and squeezed around her. Before she has a chance to clarify the memory, Brian says he made it to the big green tree.

She puts her phone away and spins around. He's here. He must be close. And if they've both found the tree, they can't have wandered far, which also means they probably weren't unconscious very long. Everything feels safer now. The worst of it is over.

Holly hears a voice. Is it a voice? More of a moan.

"Brian!" Holly yells. "Where are you? I can hear you!"

Another, louder moan crashes her relief because it doesn't sound good. It sounds like someone suffering. She shouts Brian's name and walks around the clearing, moving farther from the tree and deeper into the dark. She sees a shape and heads toward it. The nearer Holly gets, the more she grows alarmed, because it seems to be a person lying on their back. Is it Brian? Is he hurt? She dives the last yard and lands on all fours.

It's an unknown man with a thick, snowy beard.

He stares as if to say, *Who the hell are* you*?*

His eyes are shocked and teary, his jaw looks clenched, and he grips his right shoulder tightly near his collarbone.

"What happened?" Holly says.

The man tries answering and rising simultaneously. He groans when he moves and slumps back down. Holly helps him sit and lays a hand on his back, careful to avoid the man's injured shoulder. She wonders how long he's wallowed here alone.

"My name's Holly," she says. "Can you talk? Did you get lost in the storm?"

His answer sounds agonized and garbled in the wind.

"What?" Holly says, leaning closer to his face.

"I'm Vance," he says. "I live here."

He gestures with his chin. Holly sees window lights, hazy in the blizzard, from what appears to be a trailer at the border of the forest.

"What happened to your arm?" she says.

Suddenly he's frantic, looking all around as if he's just

now remembered something dangerous is near. Holly looks, too, persuaded by his fear.

"It threw me," Vance says. "It was huge. Fucking huge! It got the other guy first, and then it grabbed my arm—"

"What other guy?" she says. "Where is he? What did he look like?"

"Where's my shotgun?"

"Hey."

"Where's my *gun*?" Vance says.

A fresh chill of fear prickles through her body. She holds his bearded chin and turns his face in her direction, making him grimace from the tension in his shoulder. She regrets being rough but needs to focus his attention.

"Look at me," she says. "Tell me what happened."

He stares at her, amazed, as if he hasn't fully processed that somebody is with him.

"You're the girlfriend."

"What?"

"I thought it was a bear. I was out here shooting and a fella came up. He saw the same thing. Said it pulled him from his car. Then it rushed us out of nowhere," he says with quiet awe. "It got him from behind. Picked him up like nothing. It grabbed me by the arm and flung me in the air."

What the hell? Holly thinks. *Everybody's nuts.* In spite of herself, she scans around, dazzled by the whiteout, and feels as if a monster might attack any second.

"My boyfriend," she says. "Where is he? Where'd he go?"

He shakes his head. "Gone."

"*Vance.* Pull your shit together. Where'd you last see him?"

"He was there, and then he wasn't. I'm telling you, he's gone."

She startles him by letting out a loud, feral sound. Part snarl, part groan—an exasperated growl. Everything enrages her. The storm. This broken man. Missing, helpless Brian needing her to save him.

"He might be in your house," she says. "Come on. We're going in."

"I gotta find my gun."

She ignores Vance's words and hauls him to his feet, jostling his injury and causing him to whimper. She slings his healthy arm around her neck to keep him up. He's out of his mind with pain, or fear, or frailty from exposure, and he lets Holly guide him through the snow toward his house.

The structure is a pair of mobile homes fused together. They enter a door into the left-hand trailer and the inside glares with stark, fluorescent light. Narrowing her eyes, Holly sees that Vance has gutted most of the trailer's original fixtures and converted the space into a cluttered workshop. The walls are lined with welding gear and tools, and there's a broad worktable heaped with scrap metal, clamps, and Natural Ice beer cans. A wood stove burns to her right. Straight ahead, there's a doorway leading to the other trailer, which is dim with softer lights—presumably his living space.

She calls Brian's name. Brian isn't here.

Vance shuffles to a chair and Holly shuts the door. He grabs an open can out of a dozen on the table and drinks the whole thing before tossing it aside. It says a lot to Holly that Vance, staggering and addled, knew exactly which can wasn't empty when he chose it.

He slumps into his chair. Snow poofs off his body.

"Get me another beer," he says.

He gestures to a fresh six-pack on the far end of the table. She tugs a can off the ring, pops the top, and hands it over. He pounds it down. The empty can crinkles in his hand.

"It was just like Paul," he says. "Nothing I could do."

"You aren't making sense. I need you to concentrate and tell me something useful. Brian's still out there."

"Forget about him."

"He's my boyfriend!" she yells.

"I know," he says. "He told me. He was worried I would shoot you."

"What exactly did you see?"

He drops the can and stares at her with big, damp eyes. Are they teary from the cold, or is he genuinely crying? Whatever he remembers seems to frighten him profoundly. She feels Vance's horror flashing on her face, as if he can't tell Holly and his memory apart.

She claps her hands to snap him back. "Hey, you're spacing out."

"I didn't run," Vance says. "I stood my ground this time."

He looks brittle and bloodless, and he holds his bad shoulder with an anxious, pained expression.

"This isn't right," Vance says. "It's like steel. I can't move it."

"You must have popped it out of its socket. It's probably numb."

He tries pulling off his coat but the pain is too much. Holly helps him slide his deadened arm out of the sleeve, and then he drops the suspender of his hip waders and tugs at his sweater.

"Leave it on," Holly says. "You need to warm up."

He keeps struggling with his sweater, belligerent and wincing. Holly tries to help but he shouts from the pain. He has the strong, musky odor of an animal in distress.

"Cut it off," he says.

"What?"

"My sweater, cut it off. There's scissors on the table. Help me out. *Please.*"

"All right," she says. "Relax."

She gets the scissors and snips through his sweater from his wrist to his neck. His hand is limp and cold. Worryingly blue. As she runs the scissors up his arm, careful not to cut him, the blade seems to scrape instead of glide over skin. When she cuts through the collar and peels away his sleeve, Vance looks confused. Holly drops the scissors. They both touch his shoulder, very gently with their fingers, and instinctively retract from the strange, icy hardness.

Holly thinks it's got to be a prosthetic limb. But no—that's his *arm*, frozen solid from his collar to his elbow. Frosted on the surface like a cold piece of stone. At his neck, halfway to his jawline, the skin is red and raw where his shoulder meets the unfrozen tissue. On the opposite end, his lower forearm and hand appear to have lost circulation. Holly's never seen anything like it. Judging by his startled eyes, Vance hasn't, either.

"How long were you out there?" she asks.

"That's where it grabbed me," Vance says. "I've got to warm it up."

"Don't jostle it. I think you ought to—"

He stands and lurches past her, heading for the wood

stove. His sweater is mostly on, hanging open with the scissored sleeve dangling to his thigh. He's a damp, bedraggled mess—confused, somewhat drunk—and Holly can't decide how to help or what to say.

Vance slips on melted snow. He almost catches himself by grabbing the worktable, but he drops to one knee, twists going down, and clangs his frozen limb against the iron wood stove.

The arm cracks off.

It thumps onto the floor in one big hunk, solid at the shoulder and soft at the hand, leaving a blank, jagged space from his neck to his armpit. He looks like a mannequin that just fell apart. A mannequin that's painfully alert and fucking terrified.

"No," Vance says, staring at his arm.

Holly stares, too. She can't get a breath.

Suddenly there's blood. A lot of blood. *Gushing.*

When his arm cracked off, it took a portion of his neck, and now the veins and arteries are pumping out blood. It shoots through the air, spattering and splashing on the floor and under the table. Blood sizzles on the stove, immediately steaming. Vance paws the wound. His hand slides down and leaves a bold red smear from his neck to his ribs. He slumps and looks at Holly with childlike horror.

"Help," he says. "Help."

Holly squats beside him, boots squeaking on the floor. Vance wobbles and she cradles him, supporting his upper body with a hand behind his back and using her other hand to put more pressure on his wound. But there's so much blood. So much open flesh. They're face-to-face, close enough to feel each other's breath. He's bleeding out fast. There's nothing she can do. He stares at her with fading eyes, reminding her of Brian on the night, last winter, when she held him, too. She's dizzy from his panic and the smell of raw meat. Her vision pixelates and everything's a hot, woozy glow.

You're gonna be okay, she wants to tell him. But she can't. Blood dribbles through her fingers and she fights back tears.

"I'm sorry," Holly says. "I don't know what to do."

Vance's open mouth takes quick little gasps. There isn't peace in his expression when he starts passing out—only terror on the wane, like a siren winding down. He slips from Holly's grasp and settles on his back. She flinches at the spurting blood and presses on his wound again. It's hard to tell exactly when the flow gets weaker, but finally the blood is nothing but an ooze.

His open eyes are different now.

He's gone, she thinks. *He's dead.*

Holly scoots back and settles on her heels.

Wind rattles the trailers, but the blankness in her head is louder than the storm, like the blare of sudden quiet after very loud music. Her hands are wet. Her coat is damp. She's stunningly alone. The stink of blood saturates her nose as if she's snorted it. Eventually she stands, walks across the room, and opens up the door for a cold blast of wind.

She plunges her hands into the snow outside the trailer and scrubs off the blood. It takes a lot of snow and leaves a lot of slush. She uses fresh snow to wipe the surface of her coat, but the body and the sleeves are almost soaked through.

She isn't really thinking when she takes out her phone, calls Brian, and gets his voicemail again. When she talks, her words are faraway and not quite *now*, as if she's acting in a movie with a speaker in her ear while another, different Holly is feeding her the lines.

Through the snow, beyond the tree, she sees colors in the distance. Flashing red and blue. The beams of moving headlights. Two police trucks are driving straight toward the trailer.

Something else is coming, too. She feels it in the storm again, same as at the car when her mind blanked out. She won't say *monster* but it's dangerous. It's real. It killed the old man, it might have gotten Brian, and it isn't some delusion she can simply wish away.

She finishes her message to Brian, crams the phone into her coat, and braces at the door.

The Christmas tree's lights blur and disappear. She freezes in the doorway, staring at the storm while it rushes up and thickens, stronger than it's been, until it's too late to hide from the huge, swirling form.

This is personal, she thinks. *This is terribly familiar.*

Chapter 10

Sheriff Kendra Book picks up the arm.

She wears disposable nitrile gloves, which are thin enough to feel both the texture and the temperature of Vance's lost limb. Her mind revolts at the sensations. The slippery blood. The rubbery hand. The frigid upper arm, frozen to the core. She knows it's solid all the way through by examining the break where his shoulder met his torso and tapping it with the end of her flashlight.

Clink, clink.

The skin, the bone, the meat—they're as solid as a ham at the bottom of a freezer. Kendra lays the arm exactly where she found it, then turns around and sees how much she's already disturbed the scene, having walked through the blood covering the floor.

The splatter, and the quiet, and the wrongness of it all make Kendra feel bottomlessly, helplessly alone. Being sheriff, she's prepared for crazy shit and awful messes, but something this grim and horribly bizarre reminds her that she's frequently as unprepared as anyone. She'd love to call the cops—except she *is* the fucking cop. The best she can get is reliable support, and even that is generally in very short supply.

She looks at Deputy Fickett, who reminds her of a pencil. Slender, long, efficient . . . but tentative, somehow. He has a smooth, soft face the shade of an eraser. At the moment, his expression is hardened into shock.

I'm on my own, Kendra thinks for the umpteenth time.

She and Fickett arrived only minutes ago, driving up to Vance's trailer in separate vehicles. Kendra led the way in her Ford F-150, a truck that's rarely failed her on an unplowed road. They were responding to a chaotic 911 call from someone named Brian. The dispatcher hadn't gotten clear details but had reported possible gunshots at the Rickman property.

Kendra and Fickett knew Vance Rickman. Everybody did. He was generally harmless, but this wouldn't have been the first time Kendra had to warn him about firing his shotgun in the vicinity of tourists.

But instead of finding Vance playing with his gun, they found a bloodbath. Kendra cleared the interior with her weapon drawn while Fickett ran outside to look around the trailers. No one else had been there. Now they're back inside again, and Kendra's still annoyed she had to *tell* Fickett to check the perimeter.

She isn't ready to take her bloody gloves off yet and says, "Reach into my coat pocket."

Fickett does and says, "There's only nicotine gum."

"That's what I want. Give me two."

He peels the pieces of gum out of their blister packs and pops them into her mouth. Kendra crunches down, feeling her thoughts sharpen up before the chemical even hits. It's hard to tell anymore if it's the nicotine, the chewing, or the all-day habit she relies on the most.

She squats again and delicately probes Vance's wound, examining the surface of the raw, soft flesh. The arm alone is frozen. The rest of him is warm.

"How the hell does this happen?"

When Fickett doesn't answer, Kendra makes a fist. She asked a similar question almost word for word the day her girlfriend, Taz, loaded a U-Haul to move out of Pinebuck. They'd been solidly together. *How the hell did this happen?*

Taz had responded with the same blank look that Fickett is displaying right this second. Kendra felt alone then and feels alone now, as if her questions and emotions don't merit a reply.

Kendra snaps her fingers to get his attention. She winces when the snap speckles blood across her cheek.

"He must have been outside a long time," Fickett finally says. "Maybe he got hung up on his tree somehow."

"Except his body isn't cold. He isn't even windburned. Look at this wound."

She works her jaws hard, trying to fight the queasy smell with her Fruit Freeze gum. It tastes like chewing on a fruity piece of gristle.

"Vance was always welding and playing around with metal," Fickett finally says. "You ever seen *Terminator 2*?"

Now it's Kendra's turn to give the blank stare.

"What's that stuff?" he says. "Liquid nitrogen. Maybe he was using that for metal somehow, spilled some on his arm, and cracked it right off."

"Damn," she says. "Maybe he was actually a robot."

Fickett looks abashed. She instantly regrets mocking his suggestion, but she can't help wishing he were more than her subordinate. Someone she could lean on. Someone like a partner. She turns the conversation to harder, simpler facts.

"Tell me again about that 911 call."

"Dispatcher said it was hard to hear. Windy, like an outside call. The caller identified himself as Brian. Said he and his girlfriend spun off Route 4 and got separated. Said he was here at the tree and Vance was shooting. The dispatcher heard shots."

"I don't see his gun," Kendra says. "Shooting one minute, attacked shortly after. He wouldn't have put it away."

"It must be outside."

"That or someone took it."

She reexamines the prints on the floor. It's easy to identify hers and Fickett's. Vance's boots are clean because he apparently fell where they found him and never walked through his own blood. But there's a third set of prints—also boots, slightly smaller—that lead away from Vance toward the trailer door. Kendra opens the door and tucks her chin against the wind, looking down at the threshold where the footprints stop and overlap themselves, as if whoever wore the boots stood there a while.

Outside, several tracks lead toward the trailer—she can tell the direction by the way the snow's been shoved forward—including hers and Fickett's, along with some partially snowed-over tracks that must have happened earlier. There's a lot of red slush, like someone cleaned their hands. But she doesn't see evidence that someone walked *away*.

Only an hour after dark, with the whole storm ahead,

and she's already had to hold a dead man's arm. It pisses Kendra off. The trouble never ends.

There's always more coming, Cookie had told her in the diner. *Fix what you can and let the rest go.*

But what if nothing gets fixed and I can't let go?

Kendra's known cops who totally unravel from the bad, slow spiral of an unsolved case. They blame themselves. They second-guess everything they do. And then eventually, they start to bobble unrelated cases, feeling more and more futile and incompetent and angry. Kendra feels the same about the Skylars' disappearance. She even feels the same about Taz taking off. Neither problem solved. Neither loss let go. And now tonight, with the blood squeaking underneath her boots, her confidence is shot.

She's suddenly ashamed to be pitying herself with poor Vance Rickman savaged on the floor.

"What are you thinking?" Fickett asks.

"I'm thinking about the bear that killed Paul Whittington. Vance never quit obsessing over that. He looked for bears, shot at bears, talked about bears. He always seemed terrified a bear would get *him*."

"You think a bear did this?"

"No. But something came and got him, so I guess his fears were justified."

A loner, Kendra thinks, *who couldn't make it on his own.*

She snaps her gloves off and says, "Get Davis over here. Then follow these tracks into the field and find exactly where they came from. After that, I want you to check Route 4 and see if there's a car off the road. Call the medical examiner, too."

"What are you going to do?"

"Look for someone covered in blood or carrying Vance's gun."

That's what she always has to do when something goes wrong: pull her shit together quick and face the worst of it alone.

Chapter 11

Gary and Oliver walk with interlocked elbows.

They're in love. They're high. They're extra in love because they're high, and because it's their four-year wedding anniversary, and because the blizzard is beautiful and wildly romantic—an invigorating chaos they're savoring on the half-mile walk from a cushy restaurant back to a snuggly firelit cabin. They have nowhere to go but directly into bed, and the painful cold will only make the bed feel warmer.

Gary passes Oliver the vape pen, holding in a lungful of Cantaloupe Haze. Oliver takes a hit and holds his, too, and then they kiss and cough and laugh into each other's mouths. They've had a very good year in what was already a very good marriage. Gary and Oliver are *that* couple, the one their friends might envy or resent if they weren't so easy and enjoyable together. When they argue, it's productive. When they get along—and they usually do—it doesn't make them lazy or predictable or dull.

Their rented cabin is far away from Main Street, nestled near the forest at the outskirts of the residential neighborhood. They could have rented a B&B or regular hotel room, but their own private cabin—more expensive, more exclusive—seemed a better way to go.

"We've earned it," Gary had said.

"Plus, we're snobs," Oliver had added.

So here they are tonight: happy, high, and warm-blooded after a dinner of roast duck with blueberry sauce. They laugh at the snow, whenever it blows, walking in a winter wonderland.

Gary is small and lean, like a tan little peanut. Oliver's a tall, muscular redhead who outweighs his husband by fifty pounds. He can bench press Gary and sometimes does. They're intellectually well-matched. Each of them makes good money. They're in their midthirties and have seriously started considering adoption.

"I want to try jai alai," Oliver says out of nowhere.

Gary snort-coughs vapor, laughing at the non sequitur but also, incredibly, at the long chain of connections, in-jokes, and shorthand references that led to Oliver's statement. It had begun with a server's mispronunciation of *puttanesca*, which had brought them to an anecdote about Oliver's sister, and now it's led to jai alai and Gary understands it. At times like these, they feel like one person.

Gary stops Oliver in the middle of the road. The street is unplowed. There's no vehicle or person in sight, and the nearest homes are set back on spacious properties, their lighted windows ghostly in the snow. There's a streetlight ahead and it's just possible to make out a reflective SNOWMOBILE CROSSING road sign.

Gary packs a snowball, curves his arm, and flings the ball like a jai alai player with a cesta. He misses the road sign by a mile. Oliver cracks up and makes his own ball. He hurls a very near miss with his bigger, stronger arm.

They try a few more times until Oliver pauses, taking his time to sculpt a perfectly round, aerodynamic snowball.

Oliver flings it at the sign in a long, gorgeous arc. Gary follows its ascent, enchanted by the flight, until the ball disappears in the dense falling snow. They listen for the *bong* when it finally hits the sign. Instead, they hear a crack, dangerous and loud, and the electric pole next to the road sign tilts to the left. Wires tug and snap, blowing sparks and shaking the power lines up and down the street. The wooden pole breaks and thumps on the road. Gary and Oliver jolt at the sound. The lights go out in the nearby houses, and even though the neighborhood hadn't seemed especially bright, everything is suddenly and startlingly darker.

"Holy shit," Gary says.

"That wasn't me," Oliver says. "That couldn't have been me."

They stand and stare, astonished by the fallen pole, until they both decide it must have been a strong gust of wind.

"You made the team," Gary says.

He belly laughs hard. Oliver laughs, too, but it's a nervous, trembly laughter. He peers through the storm, trying to see the wreckage in the road. Those are live wires, he thinks, and snow is a conductor. He remembers something about keeping both feet on the ground and shuffling to safety, but before he can suggest that to Gary, something moves near the fallen pole.

Pale. Blurry. *Big*.

"What is that?" Oliver says. "Look at that. There."

He shakes Gary's arm without taking his eyes off the thing. Is it moving? Are those *arms*? Gary's laughter sputters into coughs, and he squints and tries to focus on whatever Oliver's pointing at.

"You see it?" Oliver says.

"Is that an animal?"

"It's upright."

"A bear? But don't they hibernate?"

It broke the pole, Oliver thinks. *It's bad. It's something bad.* The Cantaloupe Haze makes him vibrate and shiver. Every falling flake is electric on his face, and his shock from all that's happening is twitching every muscle.

Gary, on the other hand, is dreamily transfixed, as if he's five years old and standing in a snow globe. *Incredible*, he thinks. *Look at the arms. Look at the size!*

"That's got to be ten feet tall," Gary says. "It took down the pole. The whole fucking pole! Is that for real? That can't be real. It's like an abominable snowman."

"We should go," Oliver says, sounding very little for a big, broad man. "Let's go. We've got to go."

"Wait!" Gary says. "It's looking at us now. It's moving. Is it moving? It's coming right toward us."

The thing remains indistinct, an enormous snowy figure in the wild, snowy dark. Gary's fascination overcomes his fear. He's also reassured—as he always is, with everything—to face the unexpected with Oliver beside him. Almost hypnotized, he watches the figure approach. He actually thinks, in some corner of his mind, about the kind of people who stare at tornados—the ones who just stand there, gazing at the funnel, for reasons they themselves never understand.

It's thirty feet away now. Twenty.

Oliver was talking. What did he say? *We've got to go.*

He turns to grab Oliver's arm . . . but Oliver is gone.

Gary spins three-sixty, looking all around, and then he's dizzy and alone and the thing is almost on him, ten feet away and coming up fast. Even this close, it's sickeningly vague—a giant, moving shape in a whirlwind of snow. There's a body. Arms and legs. A head without a face.

Gary turns, slips, and runs in one fluid motion, expecting any second he'll be smashed or flung aside. It's right behind him, he can feel it, and he bounds through the snow like an athlete pumping up and down through a tire run. His vision is a blur. His legs are burning rubber, weakening and stinging from the terrible exertion.

When he finally looks back, he doesn't see the creature, which scares him even worse because it might be fucking *anywhere.*

He stumbles on a buried curb and face-plants hard, and then he rolls onto his back and wipes the snow out of his eyes.

He left me, Gary thinks. *He left me here and ran.*

His legs and lungs ache and everything's insane—the storm, the dark, his frantic thoughts—and all that makes sense is getting up and running, yelling, "Oliver!" and "Oliver!" and "*Oliver!*" again.

Chapter 12

ONE YEAR EARLIER
Four Days Before the Bad Date

Brian woke before dawn and made a terrible mistake.

He started his days earlier than Holly, who couldn't bear to leave the bed until the sun was fully up. Even then, she always tried ignoring the anemic winter light and kept her eyes shut until she *had* to wake up.

So Brian was alone from five to seven every morning. Drinking coffee. Doing dishes. Revving up the day. Lately, he'd been worrying a lot about Holly. Her mood had seemed low ever since Christmas, and although her extra decorations had briefly raised her spirits, he feared she might be slumping into full-blown depression.

He wished he could share his own happiness and pep. Today, he had a little idea to cheer her up. They'd lived in their apartment for months but still had some unpacked boxes in the closet—the kind you plan to sort through but gradually forget. One of them contained several pictures Holly liked. Brian took them out to hang them on the walls, knowing she'd be pleasantly surprised to see them up. His power drill was new and relatively quiet. If things went well, she would sleep through the noise.

He drilled starter holes, pressed in drywall anchors, and hand-drove screws for the wires on the frames. He decided to hang one of the pictures in the bathroom, right bedside the mirror, and that was when Brian made his terrible mistake. The drill bit encountered some resistance in the wall. He assumed he'd hit a stud and gave it more pressure. The bit popped forward. Brian heard a hiss. When he pulled the drill away, water dribbled from the hole.

"Ohhh," he said. "Shit."

Judging by the sound, it was likely a supply line. He wondered how much water spurted from a pipe, minute after minute, with a 3/16-inch hole. Lots, Brian thought. A horrible amount.

He didn't want to wake the landlord up. *Sorry to call this early, but I drilled through a pipe.* But Brian knew the basics from his DIY parents. He visualized the work step by step and hurried to the closet for a utility knife and duct tape.

Ideally, there'd be two of him—a few different things had to happen right away—but the thought of waking Holly felt all wrong. Had she ever done plumbing? Could she find the right supplies? She was smart, and Brian figured she could pick it up quick, but if he had to walk her through it, that would only waste time.

And the goal had been to cheer her up, not stress her out. She looked exhausted every morning, fragile from the season and a rough patch at work. He didn't want to wake her up to deal with an emergency. Jolted into action, startled and confused—why put her through it? This was his dumb fault.

By the time he finished thinking, he'd already cut the drywall to access the pipe. The unobstructed water arced to the floor, where he laid down towels to mitigate the mess. He wrapped the pipe with duct tape to buy a little time, turned the sink's faucet on, and let the water run. Then he put his coat and shoes on, grabbed his keys and wallet, and hurried to the basement. Halfway down the stairs, he wished he'd left a note in case Holly woke up and found the wreckage on her own. Instead of going back, he chose to rush forward. He'd simply get it done, like a challenge or a race.

In the basement, he shut off the service line and opened the slop sink's tap; with the faucet on upstairs, the pipes would drain clear. He ran outside, started the car, and sped to Home Depot, which opened for the day right as he arrived. Straight to plumbing for a tube cutter, a length of PEX, and push-fit couplings. Self-checkout. Back in the car. Home in record time.

Just as he had hoped, Holly wasn't up. He went to the bathroom, removed the duct tape, and found the pipe had stopped spurting with the line turned off. Using the hand-twist cutter, he removed the punctured section of the pipe, and then he cut the PEX to length and fit the new tube into place with the couplings. He turned off the sink's faucet, put the wet towels from the floor into the bathtub, and stuffed the drywall debris and old pipe into the trash. He returned to the basement, shut the slop sink off, and turned the service line on. Back upstairs, he cleared the air from the faucets and checked the new pipe.

It was perfect. Not a dribble. Job well done.

He was paper-toweling the floor when Holly appeared behind him. She had rumpled hair, marshmallow eyes, and the stunned expression of someone who'd shuffled out of a dream into a ripped-up bathroom.

"What happened to the wall!?" she said.

He laughed and told her everything, from his Curly Stooge moment of rupturing the pipe to fixing the mistake all by himself.

"You didn't get me up?" she said.

"There really wasn't much you could have done," Brian said. "I thought you needed sleep more than waking up to this."

"I've had a bad month. I'm not completely useless."

"Holl, I never said—"

"I could have turned the water off. I could have used *tape*."

"Whoa," he said. "This didn't have anything to do with you. *I'm* the one who screwed up and drilled through a pipe."

She stared at the damp, ragged hole in the drywall.

"Why were you drilling in the first place?"

"I was hanging up your pictures. You know the ones we buried in the closet?"

"You dragged out a box and started hanging pictures? At five in the morning?"

"I thought they'd cheer you up."

"Because this didn't have anything to do with me," she said.

She left him in the bathroom and went into the kitchen. The wet paper towel dripped from his hand. He felt as if he'd poked through another hidden line, and now he'd have to start again and fix that, too.

Chapter 13

Brian wakes and everything is horribly the same.

He's still disoriented in the storm, he still doesn't remember how he got here, and he still doesn't know what to do next. But he's progressed from totally bewildered fear to only partially bewildered fear. This is the second time he's blacked out and woken up alone, and while his panic hasn't faded, at least it feels familiar.

He looks around. The big metal Christmas tree is gone. There's no trace of the green lights—or any other lights, for that matter—and his surroundings are almost as dark as the forest had been. He scrapes his boot on the ground, reveals a patch of pavement, and thinks he must be standing on an unplowed road.

Again, his own footprints are nowhere in sight. Like something had picked him up and placed him right here. He remembers being lifted, way above Vance, and hopes the old man isn't crumpled up or dead. But his own body's fine. Nothing bruised, nothing broken. He wonders why the creature, which is definitely real, keeps hauling him around and leaving him intact.

Whatever the explanation, he's got to get moving. His body feels warm—much warmer than it ought to be—but now the frigid wind is cutting through his coat. His hat and gloves were in the car, his hair is getting wet, and his fingertips and ears are stinging in the cold. At least he's on a road instead of in the woods. Whichever way he walks, he's bound to find something.

It doesn't take long. He follows the edge of the road, where the bank from earlier storms is taller than the new-fallen snow, and starts to see peculiar moving lights in the distance. They look like flashlights or lanterns of differing intensities, seemingly confined to small rectangular boxes. He walks another minute toward the brightest light until a gust parts the snow and the mystery resolves itself.

He's looking at the parlor window of a ranch house, fifty feet ahead, and somebody inside is carrying a light. The illumination shifts but it's always in the frame. He must be in the residential neighborhood on the outskirts of Pinebuck. The blizzard knocked the power out and everyone's fumbling in their darkened homes with temporary lights.

People, Brian thinks, buoyant with relief.

He'll ring a doorbell. He'll try to look unthreatening and small. They'll let him in—a hard-luck tourist in the storm—and everything will start feeling sensible again. But before he gets closer to the ranch house lights, he hears a man's voice calling in the dark.

"Oliver! Oliver!"

Brian listens hard, trying to isolate the sound, until he notices a figure running on a side street.

"Hey!" Brian yells. "Over here! Hey!" He waves his arm overhead in big, sweeping arcs. The figure stops and looks, seeming curious but wary. Brian jogs toward him, waving both arms now. "Here! I'm lost, I need your help!"

The man runs to meet him, battling the snow, and when they finally come together, Brian sees a kindred spirit. Someone cold, someone scared. Desperate in the storm. Brian feels deflated. What he wanted was a *rescuer*. The man grabs his arm and pulls him in close.

"There's something out there," he says, puffing steam in Brian's face. "It's big, it's really big. It's like a—"

"Monster," Brian says.

The man looks relieved and scared in equal measure, apparently consoled that he doesn't sound crazy, but terrified that yes—there's a monster out there.

"You saw it, too," the man says. "What is it, where'd it go?"

He twists and moves away, looking this way and that, and Brian worries that he'll run away and vanish in the storm. He pulls the man back and holds him by the elbow.

"What's your name?" Brian asks.

"Gary."

"I'm Brian. Do you live here?"

"What?"

"Do you have a house around here?"

"No," Gary says. "We're vacationing. My husband . . ."

Again he pulls away and turns in all directions with a gust of snowy air spiraling around him.

"We were walking," Gary says. "We saw it knock a power pole down like a stick. I was watching it, and Oliver . . . It scared him and he ran. I've got to go, I've got to find him. I can't believe he *ran*."

A deep, percussive crunch interrupts Gary's words. Like a bulldozer crackling over branches. Wind blasts around them, buffeting their ears, and it's impossible to pinpoint the direction of the sound.

"Come on," Brian says. "We need to get inside."

"Oliver—"

"I know. My girlfriend's missing, too. But we're exposed out here. We have to find help."

They hurry to the ranch house, following the glow of unsteady light. Gary's faster than Brian, maybe because he's fitter, and maybe because this is only his first adrenaline rush of the night. Brian's already peaked and crashed a couple times. His body is shot, his nerves are overcooked, and Gary pulls ahead with energy and focus. He reaches the front of the house and repeatedly jabs the doorbell. Brian catches up and joins him on the steps.

"The power's out," Brian says. "The bell won't work."

He pounds on the door, jolting Gary with the noise, and then they back away and eyeball the wide parlor window. A flashlight beam wobbles in the living room. It's held by a tall and overweight man, a shadowy giant who leans toward the glass, smooshes his nose against the pane, and redirects his light at Brian's and Gary's faces. Strangers in the dark, banging on the door—the man is understandably worried and suspicious.

"Hello!" Brian says. "We didn't mean to startle you!"

The man doesn't answer or acknowledge them at all.

"We can't weird him out," Brian says to Gary. "I'm going to have to lie."

"Do it quick," Gary says.

Brian thinks fast. He shouldn't say *attacked*, and he shouldn't say *monster*, and he shouldn't say the two of them have only just met.

"My friend and I are lost! Our cellphones are dead!"

Snow gusts hard and stings Brian's cheek. The man doesn't move. His face is hard to see.

"I sprained my ankle!" Gary says. He hops and wobbles just a bit, as if his right foot is iffy. "We're really sorry to put this on you, but can we come inside to warm ourselves up and use your phone?"

The flashlight beam swivels off their faces. Brian turns toward the door, expecting it to open.

Gary says, "You're kidding me. That gutless son of a bitch."

The man draws his curtains. A trace of light flutters through the door's frosted glass, followed by the snap of a deadbolt lock.

"Nice!" Gary yells. "Way to treat tourists! Wait till all your friends and relatives and neighbors read about your shitty hospitality on *Yelp*!"

They hear another monstrous crunch, closer than before. Brian feels a rumble underneath his boots.

"Thanks a million! I hope your pipes freeze up!"

"It's coming," Brian says. "We've got to go, we've got to hide."

He pulls Gary so hard, they almost topple over, but they stumble into a jog and hurry to the back, past the house's side windows and away from the street. Brian assumes the man inside is watching where they go. The last thing they need is someone else like Vance, brandishing a gun to safeguard his home, and so he runs until the house disappears in the snow.

"Look," Brian says. "Let's get inside that."

There's a white aluminum shed in the corner of the yard

with a mushroom of snow bulging off the roof. Brian leads the way. He ducks beneath a clothesline strung across the yard. They make it to the shed, open up the mercifully unlocked doors, and slip inside exactly as a terrifying growl vibrates the metal and the core of Brian's head.

The shed is dark and cold, but aside from the rattle of the wind on the walls, everything's immediately quieter and calmer. Brian stumbles over a lawnmower. He turns his phone light on and sees fold-up chairs, empty pots, and a garden gnome with a cracked face. Powdery snow has slithered through the gaps and settled on the floor. There's a long-dead rodent in the corner. Fur and bone.

Gary hunkers near the door and blows on his hands. The vapor of his breath intermittently obscures him. Neither of them moves. Neither of them speaks.

Brian wonders how he's come to this, cowering in a storm with less and less control over what comes next. He's felt the same at work for the whole last year, having lost so many steps he's almost fallen off the track. It's worse at home with Holly. The more she helps and cares for him, acknowledging his struggles, the more they both assume he needs her help and care. He's like a teen who's stopped washing his own clothes because his mother, sick of nagging, simply does it for him. What if leaning more on Holly is the reason he's off-balance? What if he's already reached some tipping point of failure, and nothing either one of them could do will tip him back?

All he knows for sure is that his life keeps crashing. Only an hour ago, he was sitting in the car with Holly at his side. Now he's huddled with a stranger, fighting to survive.

Brian finds an unplayed message on his phone. He puts the speaker to his ear—cold on cold—and dims the whole shed by covering the screen. Holly's voice sounds startlingly close in the dark.

"*It's me. I'm in the trailer, near the big green tree. I blacked out and woke up in the field and now I'm here. I met the old man. He told me you were with him. That you both saw . . . whatever, I don't know. He wasn't clear.*

"*And now the old man's dead. Something happened to his arm. It was frozen. Brian, Jesus . . . it was frozen to the bone. I found him that way and took him inside and then his arm cracked off. The whole fucking arm. I couldn't stop the blood and then his face . . . the way he looked at me. It made me think of you. You've got to call me back.*

"*You must have run away. You must be close. You can't be dead. We're going to be okay if we can find each other now.*

"*Wait, I think . . . there's flashing lights. Police trucks are coming. They'll help. They're here to help. They'll know I tried to save him.*

"*Wait, though. Fuck. Something else is coming. The snow looks wrong. It's messing with my eyes. Bri, you've got to call me back and tell me you're alive. Something isn't right. What the hell is happening?*"

Her message ends. He calls her back and only gets her voicemail.

"Shit!" Brian says.

This game of phone tag is maddening. It's like remembering a dream, or dreaming of a memory, while someone else is altering the plot with crazy facts. He thinks of poor Vance being lifted off the ground. He lost his arm and bled to death? And Holly's in his trailer now? He pictures her alone, soaked in Vance's blood and staring at the snow while the monster comes toward her.

He ought to leave the shed and hurry back to find her, but he's paralyzed and barely even hears Gary talking.

"What?" Brian asks.

"Can I use your phone?" Gary says. "I left mine behind. I didn't think I'd need it."

Brian hands it over without hesitation. Gary calls his husband, who immediately answers.

"It's me. Oll, it's *me*. Are you okay?" Gary says. "I'm okay . . . Where are you? . . . I'm in a shed, a metal shed. I'm hiding with a man I met. He saw the same thing . . . It's a white metal shed, off the road behind a ranch house . . . Try every fucking shed, then! Just hurry up and find me."

Gary ends the call and hands back the phone. The screen blinks off and the shed goes dark. Brian thumbs it back on and Gary looks frozen, like a man growing ice crystals inside his head.

"What did your girlfriend say?" Gary finally asks.

"It's hard to explain," Brian says. "She's in trouble, we're in trouble. I don't know what to do."

The last ten minutes race through his head, like a slideshow flashing in the pulses of a strobe light. Quickly, uncontrollably, Brian starts to laugh. He could have just as easily erupted into sobs, but once he gets laughing, it's difficult to stop.

"What?" Gary asks.

"I'm looking forward to your Yelp review."

Gary laughs, too, remembering his tirade. "I can't believe he hid. He even closed the curtains!"

Once they settle down again, Brian moves closer. "You really saw a monster?"

"I think I really did."

Gary tells his story. The jai alai snowballs, the power line falling, the giant snowy creature hulking at the road sign. Standing transfixed. Discovering Oliver had fled. Running when the monster stalked up toward him.

"It had arms and legs. A snowy head. I couldn't see its face. It reminded me . . ." Gary says with faraway eyes. "One time I almost drowned. I was scuba diving, and something happened to my regulator, and the sun was like a starburst, way overhead on the surface of the water. I thought it was last thing I'd ever get to see. The feeling I would die . . . the shape of that light . . ." Gary trails off and finally shakes his head. "I'm not making sense. Fuck, I'm really high. Maybe the vape cart was laced. I feel like I'm on acid."

"It isn't drugs," Brian says. "I saw it, too. It pulled me out of my car and left me in the woods."

"It pulled you out of your car?! And didn't take your head off?"

"I know," Brian says. "I don't get it, either. But it's definitely dangerous. It grabbed a person I was with—the guy who made the giant light-up tree. I think it ripped his arm off. My girlfriend said he's dead."

Gary looks dazed. "We've got to call the cops."

"I already did. But the monster came again and carried me away. I blacked out and woke up, and then I saw you."

"Wait," Gary says. "You got away twice? What the hell is it . . . your own trained yeti?"

No, Brian thinks. *But it's personal somehow. Maybe it's*

a good thing, protecting me from danger. The spinout on the slippery road. The shotgun blasts.

But if he's somehow responsible for summoning the monster, everybody else is suffering for *him*. Like he's some kind of lightning rod nobody should touch.

Gary falls silent with his own swirling thoughts. Probably thinking of how his husband ran away and left him. How a couple might change when one half is strong and the other half is suddenly, pathetically exposed.

Brian stares at the rodent carcass frozen in the corner. It's almost inconceivable the thing had ever lived. Wind thumps harder on the shed's flimsy walls, and the snow starts slithering and coiling through the seams. Pressure seems to build. His head begins to throb.

He and Gary hear a noise like metal being torn.

It sounds as if it's coming from the nearby house. Brian looks at Gary. Gary looks at Brian. Neither of them speaks because they're listening intently. Half a minute passes—only wind, only waiting—before they both have the same awful realization.

Gary reaches for the phone just as Brian shuts it off. The light, the fucking light. It might have glimmered through the seams.

Suddenly the shed is absolutely dark. All Brian sees is the phone's glowing afterimage, bobbing in his vision everywhere he looks. He blindly reaches out and Gary does the same. They huddle like children with their foreheads together. Brian hears nothing but his own beating heart—pulse, pulse, pulse—shushing everything away.

How long before it's safe? How long until it's over?

There's a shocking, screeching jolt and off goes the roof.

Mostly off. It's peeled and curling back, right above their heads, like a tuna can lid barely clinging to the rim. The entire shed lifts and thumps back down. Brian and Gary clunk skulls. Gary falls backward, Brian topples sideways, and the snow blows maniacally around them.

Even in the blizzard, in the dark, Brian sees.

A shape looms above them with a blank, snowy head. It grabs two walls where they're riveted together, pops them apart like a buttoned-up shirt, and folds one down until it's crumpled on the ground. The wall with the door remains bizarrely upright. The door is partly open. It's the quickest way out and Gary leaps toward it, going through the gap and flopping in a drift. Brian's right behind him, scrambling on his hands and knees and knocking into everything from pots and rusty tools to the lawnmower engine. He halfway stands and lunges through the door. His shoulder bangs the frame and he spins from the impact, tumbling out backward and landing on his ass.

The monster's out of sight, having blended with the storm, but Brian sees Gary running for his life. Back toward the ranch house, fast as he can go. Just before he's far enough to vanish in the whiteout, Gary runs straight into a clothesline pole. Brian hears *BONG*. Gary stops, Gary falls, and then he's lying on his back, having knocked himself cold.

Brian starts to run before he's really on his feet, fighting for traction as he stumbles, slips, and sprints from the shed. He reaches Gary's side and tries to pick him up. Gary's head lolls. A plum-sized bulge is rising on his forehead.

Brian holds him in his lap, cradling his neck. He has a memory of Holly holding him this way. It changes Brian's view of everything that's happening. He sees it all—the violence, the monster, and the body—like another place and time. He has the strangest sensation of being two Brians. Outside and inside. Somewhere else. Here.

The monster reappears as a dark white blur between Brian and the shed.

Its figure starts dissolving, growing smudgier and fainter, like the image of a movie projected onto fog, while the fog thins out and softly disappears. It's less and less solid. Less and less real. The dense, bristling snow that seems to constitute its body scatters into all the other flakes of the blizzard.

Brian sees Holly where the monstrous shape had been.

She's upright, supported by a whirlwind gust, and then she slumps to her knees when the storm lets her go. It shouldn't make sense. It doesn't make sense. But Brian understands what he sees. Brian knows.

Holly was the monster. Like she summoned it or gathered it, embodying the storm, with her body as a focal point of all the blizzard's violence. The thing had coalesced with Holly at the core. Maybe conscious. Maybe not. Either way, it was her.

She looks at him—disoriented, free of the possession, twenty feet away and tiny in the drift.

He knows what he's seeing, but he doesn't understand. She hadn't been the monster when it pulled him from the car . . . but she *had* been the monster when it tore apart the shed? Now she looks like herself . . . but is she dangerous or safe? He's spent the last hour praying he would find her—or rather, he's been praying she would come and save him. Now he can't decide if he should run to her or flee.

She isn't what he thought. Was she *ever* what he thought?

Before either one of them can speak or make a move, Brian loses sight of her. Snow spins around him, thickening and blinding, and his mind reels wildly and crazily away. He's dizzy, and afraid, and floating in the dark . . . and then he's fading. Disappearing. Hopelessly alone.

Chapter 14

Holly feels dazed when she doesn't see police lights. She'd been standing at the trailer door, staring at the red and blue flickers in the distance, when the *thing* rushed toward her. Now she's kneeling on the ground. Did she faint and fall down? The trailer's disappeared and everything is different—all except the snow blowing in her face.

There's a house farther off, low and blocky, indistinct. A ranch-style house. Where did *that* come from? She's woozy and disoriented, turning all around, and sees a metal toolshed that's mangled and collapsed.

Her brain is saying, *Look*, from a couple seconds earlier. Her eyes spotted something that her mind hadn't processed. Now it's front and center. All-important. Red alert.

Holly wipes her face to clear away the snow. Someone's sitting on the ground, dead ahead, pretty close. He's holding something big—another person?—on his lap.

Brian, Holly thinks. *It's him. It's really him.*

She gasps on a breath, about to yell his name, when the snow swarms around him in a horrifying way. The body he's been holding tumbles to the ground. Brian's virtually invisible but Holly sees him levitate, his body like a limp, dark puppet in the air. He's upright, his arms and legs are slightly spread-eagle, and the snow packs around him with the density of spray foam. Layer after layer, gathering and growing.

It's got him.

No, it is *him.*

Brian is the thing.

He's hidden in the mass of animated snow, suspended with his limbs padded and enlarged. Standing on the ground now. Massive and impossible.

It's motionless. It stares at her. She can't discern a face but she's positive it's Brian. She also knows he hasn't been the monster every time. She feels it in her gut, and then she knows something else, the same way she knows the darkest stuff inside herself.

It isn't just him. It's both of us.

Her chest feels hollow, and her stomach loops and lurches.

If Brian hurt Vance and left him there to die, is the body on the ground now dead because of her?

We're killers. Both of us are killers.

She feels the monster watching her. Relentlessly. Intensely. It's tall, dense, and burly with a shaggy fur of snow, and it constantly reforms without really changing, so it always seems to move without truly moving. It's menacing and primal. Holly's seen what it can do.

But it's Brian inside. Only sweet, soft Brian.

She's about to say his name when the monster runs toward her. Except it doesn't really run. It avalanches at her, like a thing that ought to fall apart but only seems to grow. Holly stands up with seconds to react. Her muscles are electric and her skin feels hot. She braces with her boot heels jammed in the snow. Eyes wide, fists up, rigid as a rock.

The monster barrels past her, spinning her a full three-sixty with its force, but she somehow keeps herself up.

Then it's gone. Brian's gone. Vanished in the dark.

There's not a footprint or any deep disturbance in the snow, but Holly doesn't doubt herself. It happened. It was real. Maybe it's insane but everything's insane now. All impossibilities are totally in play.

She suddenly remembers the other person's body, orients herself, and runs to where it was. There's an unconscious man lying on his side, not quite fetal but delicate and childlike. She rolls him onto his back, afraid that she'll discover some horrifying wound, but he only has a lump in the center of his forehead. She notices the clothesline pole right beside him and assumes the poor guy knocked himself out.

"Hey," she says. "Hey."

She baby-slaps his cheek. Pat, pat, pat. He's slowly coming to, fluttering his eyelids. He mumbles something . . . groggy, thick. Words made of clay. Holly leans close to shield him from the wind.

There's an unfamiliar smell, meaty and metallic, that reminds her of Brian. It's the old man's blood squishing in her coat. She fights down a gag and the ground turns beneath her. This is all too much. Too horrific. Too familiar.

Her mind sharpens up at the sound of someone calling, "Who's that? Who are you? What are you doing?"

A man with a flashlight is waddling toward her. He's tall and round, at least a hundred pounds overweight, with a pale, bald head jammed between his shoulders. He looks like a classic cartoon snowman. She gets a better look when he comes up close. He's about fifty with a big, broad face, puffing out breath and visibly distressed.

"Who are you? Hey, what's wrong with him? What happened? What's the matter?"

"He knocked himself out," Holly says. "He hit the pole."

"What?"

"He hit the clothesline pole but I think he's waking up."

The man barely listens. He seems impervious to the weather, wearing nothing but flannel pajama bottoms and a button-down sweater. His head and hands are bare. Holly wouldn't be surprised if he had slippers on his feet. And yet he stands up straight, blasted by the wind, as if he's strolling through his yard on a breezy summer day.

"Where's the other one?" he says. He shines his flashlight around. "There were two of them. They tried to get inside. Where'd he go? They tore the siding off my wall and someone's got to pay! There's something on your coat. Whose blood is that? Hey!"

She's getting angry at his questions. Too many questions.

"Move your light," she says.

"What?"

"Your light's in my face!"

She swats his flashlight away but he doesn't seem to care. Instead, he turns his head in the direction of the beam, following the long, moving cone around the property.

"My shed! Oh, my God!" he says. "What happened to my shed?"

He wanders off to survey the wreckage up close, talking

to himself, sounding more and more distraught. The man in Holly's arms has mostly woken up, but his eyes look screwy and he's mumbling incoherently.

"Olive . . . olive . . . alai . . . Oliver, a-*liver*."

Holly quakes from the cold and overstimulation. The storm, the smell of blood, the men, her crackling head. Then the big guy's back and lighting up her face again.

"What happened to my shed? Hey, is he awake? Make sure he doesn't run. I already called the cops," he says with fritzy energy. "My siding's brand new! Six thousand dollars just last summer! They wrecked my shed, too, and someone's got to pay."

"Shut up!" Holly yells. "Shut up, shut up, shut up!"

The man swings the light and ambles to the left, seemingly oblivious and maddeningly dense. All his stupid ramblings sizzle in her head. The flashlight's afterglow messes up her vision.

Another voice calls from up around the house.

"Gary! Gaaaare!"

"Who's that? Is that the other one?" the big guy says.

He illuminates the falling snow in wide, swooping arcs until he settles on a figure walking straight toward them. It's another tall man. He marches through the drifts with confidence and strength.

"Were you the other one?" the big guy asks. "What do you want, what are you doing here?"

"I'm looking for my husband," the new man says.

"What's that again?"

"I said I'm looking for my husband!"

The men are close together now, strangers in the storm, panting out vapor that expands in the light.

"Oh my God, I can't believe this," the big guy says. "Someone wrecked my siding. There's a man back there. There's a girl there, too, and someone broke my shed!"

"What man? *Where?*"

"Over there, with the girl," the big guy says. "Where's the girl? Where'd she go?"

He shines his flashlight around but Holly's taken off.

The beam doesn't find her when she runs toward the house. She faintly hears the new man cry the name "Gary" after presumably discovering his husband on the ground.

Out of sight, around the corner, Holly keeps running. She needs to get away. She doesn't know *why* because her thoughts are topsy-turvy. Just that nobody can help her here. Nobody is safe.

She barrels through the drifts and makes it to the road, where the snow is much shallower than back behind the house. Her head's ablaze. She runs until her insides hurt, looking everywhere for Brian, like she's running for her life.

Chapter 15

Kendra has barely driven away from Vance's trailer when the dispatcher relays the details of two emergency calls.

The first was from a tourist named Oliver who lost his husband in the storm.

The second was from a local Kendra knows well, an insurance agent with the unlikely name of Dan Danson. Everyone in Pinebuck calls him Double D.

When Double D was a child living in Oklahoma, a tornado obliterated half of his family home—the half containing his room and everything he loved. As soon as he was grown, he left Oklahoma in the dust and moved a thousand miles northeast, all the way to Pinebuck, to guarantee he'd never see another tornado. He tells this story to every new client as a firsthand warning to *get yourself insured.* He's Kendra's own agent, and his genuine fear of risks makes him so convincing, he's even swayed typically unworried Cookie to beef up her coverage.

Tonight, Double D has called to report that two strangers came to his door, ripped the siding off his house, and destroyed his utility shed.

Imagine all the clients he'll tell about this, Kendra thinks.

His place is located a quarter mile off the main drag, in the same neighborhood where a power outage has also been reported. Kendra hits the gas, trusting her tire chains but struggling in her head for some kind of traction. Another missing person. More mysterious strangers. Property damage and a blackout. All before the smell of Vance's blood has left her nose.

She arrives at Double D's five minutes later, leaves her truck idling in the street, and wades into a madhouse of injury and confusion. On Kendra's insistence—and despite Double D's reluctance to open his home to chaos—they get Gary onto his feet, help him into the house, and sit him on the couch while they wait for the ambulance. Now they're all inside, with the light of battery-powered lanterns, stunned by the elements and everything they've talked about.

Double D is nonstop motion, waving a flashlight around, dropping towels everywhere that snow has melted off boots, and chattering and fretting about the floors, the siding, and the shed.

Gary rests in the living room with a shocking knot in the middle of his forehead. Oliver sits beside him, holding his hand and encouraging him to keep his eyes open.

Kendra feels as if *she* hit the clothesline pole.

She's still piecing it all together. Most of the fundamentals—the parts that make sense—settle into a timeline: Gary and Oliver lost each other, Gary found Brian—presumably the "Brian" who'd called 911 from Vance's place—and Double D's house and shed suffered damage. There'd also been a woman no one could identify. But then Kendra focuses on all the other details. Specifically, the parts that don't make sense.

For starters, Gary and Oliver insist they saw a monster. She's suggested that their eyes were playing tricks in the storm—that a power line fell, everything was darker, and suddenly the snow made imaginary shapes. But they swear they saw a monster and she can't change their minds. She understands it coming from Gary, who's so concussed he probably thinks Big Bird is standing in the room. And she can almost understand it coming from Oliver, who has the look of someone very high who's trying to be sober.

But what explains the damage to the house's outer wall? Twenty feet of siding ripped off the frame, along with some of the sheathing and a mess of insulation. And then the shed, peeled apart like a takeout box. Kendra's seen plenty of peculiar storm damage over the years—a long line of trees knocked over like dominoes, snow that's rolled itself together into big, fluffy bales—but she simply can't believe the wind did this.

What if Vance's fears were right? What if there's a bear? But no kind of bear can freeze a person's arm off.

Double D strides up to Kendra and says, "You need to radio Tanner."

"The ambulance can handle snow," she says.

"No, for the siding! For the outside wall! That was six thousand dollars. Top-tier vinyl! Tanner installed it in July and now it's ripped apart. I need him here tonight. Everything's exposed! You need to call his truck. I tried his phone, he didn't answer."

"Tanner's plowing," Kendra says. "It's a blizzard."

"Use your radio! He's got to seal the wall, it's getting worse every second!"

"It's gonna be all right, D. I know you have insurance."

"That's not the way it works!" he says, sounding like a kid whose favorite toy is getting mangled. "You wouldn't crash your car *because* you have insurance. You can't just shrug and let things fall apart. The snow's getting in. There'll be water damage. Mold. We've got to fix this now! We've got to focus on *prevention*!"

He wanders into another room, talking to himself, and then the ambulance arrives and parks out front. Kendra waits until the stretcher is right outside before opening the door. The EMTs enter with a bracing rush of air. Kendra knows them well—the kind of likeable, shock-proof medics you want for an emergency. She ought to be relieved that the cavalry's arrived, but their presence has the opposite effect on Kendra, reminding her of every other time they've been together. Other storms, other injuries. A lot of other nights that didn't go well.

She directs them into the living room, where Oliver stands aside with the helpless, taut expression she's seen on countless worried loved ones. He reassures Gary that he's going to be okay. Once they're home, he says, he'll pamper him and treat him like a prince. When Gary doesn't answer or even open his eyes, Kendra worries his concussion might be getting worse. But when the medics talk to Gary, he looks at them and answers. It's only when his husband speaks that Gary won't respond.

Kendra gets it. There they'd been, a solid couple with a longtime bond, when something came along and split them down the middle. You can't unsee your partner leaving you behind. She wonders if their history is strong enough to weather this. They'll talk it through. They'll try to be the couple they believed they were. But Oliver will always be the one who fucking bailed.

Kendra steps outside, shuts the door behind her, and walks around to the side of the house. She tucks her chin against the wind. The coat's cold zipper chafes her throat. To her right is Double D's annihilated wall. Entire strips of siding, many of them bent or cracked, have settled haphazardly along the foundation. Fiberglass insulation sags off the house like a weird, twisted mass of fuzzy pink snow.

What if Double D's clients saw him now? Kendra thinks. He fled Tornado Alley, fortified his house, and eased his mind with insurance . . . only to panic in a blizzard with his property in shambles. Security is never much more than an illusion, like a pristine mountainside right before an avalanche.

Just last spring, she had her own false safety with a girlfriend she started to believe she would marry. After dating for three seasons, she and Taz moved in together and kept a happy rhythm all winter. Steady jobs. Cozy nights. The comfort of routine. They had a year of shared experiences, challenges, and wins, all of which felt like ironclad insurance they could draw upon instantly if something went awry.

Then Taz decided she was sick of harsh winters. *I can't spend another year in Pinebuck*, she said. But Kendra had her house and job. Pinebuck was home, and she was feeling too old to suddenly uproot for no better reason than a life without snow. And so they talked, and they argued, and they finally acknowledged they wanted different things.

The breakup was quick and strangely undramatic. Taz simply needed change, while Kendra stayed the same.

Kendra still wonders if she should have gone with her to Albuquerque. But who could say another sharp rift wouldn't happen? She'd be no better off than poor Double D, who pretended tornadoes were the only storms to fear. How can anybody ever feel totally secure when the world blows to shit with no kind of warning?

For all she knows, something might attack her right now. But she simply moves forward. What else is there to do?

Kendra makes it back to the clothesline pole, stands where Gary fell, and sees a lone set of tracks leading to the other side of the house. She follows it. The snow is falling heavier than before but once she rounds the corner, there's a buffer from the wind and the footprints are less disturbed and easily discernable.

The tracks go all the way to the street out front. She hopes whoever left them kept running in the road so she can hop into her truck and follow with her headlights.

Another set of lights is steadily approaching. Kendra hears a low, deep scrape. It's Tanner in his plow, coming up the road and throwing off a big wave of snow with the blade. Kendra waves her arms but she's too far back. Tanner speeds by, never seeing her at all.

Double D bangs out the front door and yells, "Stop! Wait! *Hey!*"

He makes his way to Kendra's side and even follows her into the road when she struggles over the snowbank. They stand there, mute, until the snowplow's lights fade around a bend. Double D's upset that his handyman has vanished. Kendra's irked that the plow has scraped away the prints.

"Oh my God, I can't believe this," Double D says. "You've got to call him back!"

Kendra walks toward her truck.

"You ought to get inside," she says. "Tell the EMTs not to release Gary and Oliver from the clinic until I send a deputy over for a statement."

"You're leaving? But you can't! What are you doing, where are you going?"

"I'm going to find who wrecked your wall."

"Okay," he says. "Good. Okay, okay, okay."

He blunders over the bank, mumbling to himself the whole way back to his house. Kendra climbs into her truck, shakes the powder off her hat, and leans her face against the heat vent. She's been chewing the same wad of nicotine gum for thirty minutes and it's dead, dull, and hard. She cracks the window, spits the gum, and rubs her cold jaw. There's already a fresh inch of snow on the windshield. She's hidden from the world and wishes she could stay that way. Instead, she turns the wipers on and slowly drives forward, using her frame-mounted spotlight to look for footprints and people in the vast, dark spaces bordering the road.

She gets on the radio with Deputy Fickett.

"I found Vance's shotgun fifty paces from the trailer," Fickett tells her. "Dumb luck. It was buried and I tripped on it. There were two sets of tracks near the light-up tree. Both sets seem to have come *out* of the woods. I didn't find tracks of anybody leaving."

"Is the medical examiner there yet?" Kendra asks.

"Any minute."

"Is Davis there?"

"Yep. I'm driving to Route 4 now to find the spun-out car."

She fills him in on everything that happened at Double D's.

"We're looking for a man named Brian and a woman in a bloody coat," Kendra says. "Have Davis call the hotels and B&Bs. One of them is missing a guest named Brian. And have the ME call me direct as soon as he examines Vance. I want to know what took his arm off so I can rule out a theory."

"What theory?"

"Snow monster," Kendra says.

Fickett laughs. Kendra doesn't. She doesn't believe there's a monster, but she's learned the hard way to cover all her bases and eliminate guesses, especially the crazy ones, before they gain traction in other people's heads. They end the call and Kendra keeps driving down the road, but she doesn't see footprints or anything peculiar.

"Fuck," she says.

She hits the brakes and skids to a halt.

She steps outside, unlocks the truck bed's security drawer, and grabs a ziplock bag she stashed with her gear. Back inside the cab, she opens the bag and takes out an emergency pack of Camels. She fires one up. Takes a drag. Breathes smoke.

If she can't have security, she'll take familiarity, relying on her habits and herself to get her through. Because like everyone tonight, from Double D to Gary, she can't assume anyone will help. She's on her own.

Chapter 16

ONE YEAR EARLIER
Three Days Before the Bad Date

Parallel parking wasn't a life-or-death emergency, but damn it, Holly thought, it felt that way.

She'd driven home from work and found an opening in front of their apartment. Otherwise, the whole street was packed tight with cars. This was it—the only spot—and she'd been struggling for minutes.

Her car wasn't big. There was ample room to fit. But she'd always sucked at parking, even in ideal conditions, and tonight the situation was particularly bad. She was tired. She was hungry. The slippery winter drive had left her high-strung. Night had fallen with a squall of thick, wet snow, and she had difficulty seeing out the fogged-up windows.

She knew what she was *supposed* to do. Line up her steering wheel with that of the front parked car. Reverse into the empty spot at forty-five degrees. Halfway in, elegantly straighten to alignment with the curb so her bumper curves smoothly past the front car's tail. Slowly glide backward to the second parked car. Stop. Make adjustments. Simple as a diagram.

In her job as a developer, she made things fit. She knew

when an image needed to move twenty-five pixels to the left. She nestled blocks of text precisely into place. But she couldn't fit a car inside a car-sized spot. Something went wrong every time she tried. Like a rocket being launched a fraction off-course, her trajectory increasingly deformed toward catastrophe. She'd almost scrape bumpers. There'd be zero room to straighten out. She'd fit inside the spot, parallel and neat, but find herself several feet distant from the curb.

With each failed attempt, her thoughts needled in until her brain was like a pincushion, quivering and stuffed. Why did every failure make her think of other failures? She hadn't always been this way. What had changed? She couldn't point to any one moment in her life, like a heart-breaking failure or sudden disillusion. Instead, she felt the drag of countless little moments that had quietly become her ordinary life.

In college and her early twenties, she'd always seemed to gain momentum from her wins. She'd been talented and bright. Happy and creative. She'd painted, drawn, and screen-printed—building on successes—for bands and local shops and most of all herself. She'd parlayed her strengths into a decent-paying job and did the art she really loved on weekends and nights.

Then her art slipped away, imperceptibly at first, the way a body might slip into chronic unhealth. She always felt sapped. Just a little. Just enough. Her imaginative sparks often sputtered out, like holiday lights that fritzed after Christmas. Like a full night's sleep that only left her groggy. Like simply coming home, limp from the day, and struggling to park the goddamn car. Once she finally got inside, there'd be dinner, time with Brian, maybe weed to calm her nerves . . . and then she'd think about her job until she fell asleep, and in the morning, she'd have lost another whole day.

Now her mind was on that instead of on the car, which resulted in her lurching back and scraping her bumper on the curb.

She inched forward into the road again and idled in the dark. Cars beeped behind her. Irritated. Blocked. Forced to drive around her in the oncoming lane. Her defroster wasn't working, so she rolled down the windows. She needed the passenger side clear to see the empty spot and the driver side open to wipe the snowy mirror. Headlights came and went, blinding her with glares. A car splashed slush directly through her window, splattering her cheek and neck.

She made a fresh attempt, hasty and aggressive, and edged too tight against the parked car's bumper. Halfway in and halfway out, she was jutting into traffic now. A long line of cars whizzed and swerved around her.

It shouldn't have mattered that she couldn't parallel park. She was excellent at driving. Confident and nimble. She was good at lots of other things that should have added up. Instead, she always found herself defined by her losses.

Suddenly, her mind flashed to a memory of Brian. They'd been camping and he'd spent thirty minutes on the fire. He kept making careful heaps of kindling, twigs, and leaves, but every time they flickered, they collapsed or fizzled out. Eventually, he quit and Holly took a shot. In no time flat, she got the sticks blazing. Holly thought of that a lot—not the fact of her success, but the fact that Brian's failure hadn't bothered him at all.

Yesterday, he'd screwed up and drilled through a pipe, and then he'd felt *better* after everything was done. That was Brian every day. Defined by his wins.

A truck roared by. She swore it clipped her mirror.

"Maniac!" she yelled, jittery and small.

She couldn't just sit there, idling and frozen. She had to keep trying. She had to fucking park. But when the traffic died down enough to try again, she couldn't get her foot to move off the brake. She was shivering. Her breath felt shallow in her lungs.

She called Brian's phone and asked if he was home.

"Yeah," he said. "What's up?"

She said, "I can't park."

"Where are you?"

"Right out front."

"Hold on," he said. "I'm looking out the window now."

She paused a long time, trying not to cry. She'd told him more than once not to help her so much. He didn't need to hang bright pictures on the walls or buy her new sketchbooks she ought to buy herself. But here she was now, hanging on his voice.

"There's plenty of room," he said. "You're good to go."

"I'm not," Holly said.

"What happened? What's the matter?"

She hated that question.

"I've been screwing this up for the last ten minutes."

"You've got this," he said. "Give it one more shot."

She should have said, *I will*, or, *I can try*.

She said, "I can't."

Chapter 17

"*Hi, you've reached Brian. Please leave a message and I'll call you back. Thanks.*"

"It's us," Holly says. "It's happening to both of us. Of course you didn't answer. We've switched. Tag, you're it.

"I feel like I'm having a psychotic break and a heart attack and a meltdown in the middle of a blizzard. I'm trying to get my head straight. I'm clear. I think I'm clear.

"One: there's a monster. Two: we're the monster.

"It's you, and then it's me, and after me it goes to you again. I saw it happen near the shed—you must have seen it, too—but more than anything I feel it. It's us. It's really us.

"But it doesn't seem to happen from the inside out. We aren't bursting through our clothes like the Incredible Hulk. We haven't lost our phones. The snow picks us up and packs all around us like an animated suit. Like we're *inside* a monster.

"And then I feel warmer after being inside. Instead of freezing me to death, it protects me somehow. Maybe that's what's happening. Maybe it's protecting us.

"But I keep blanking out whenever it comes over me. It's almost like the night . . . fuck, I don't remember. I still can't entirely remember that night. But it's similar. It all feels connected somehow. Like we're so messed up, we're causing all this. It happens when we're scared. It happens when we're threatened.

"We've got to lay low until we figure something out. We're dangerous. We need to steer clear of other people. Especially the cops . . . they're looking for us now.

"Call me back and leave a message. Tell me what you're thinking. What you know. Where you *are*. We've got to find each other, Bri. If we're together when we change again, maybe we can snap ourselves out of it somehow. Maybe we can stop it."

Holly takes off her coat, flips it inside out, and puts it back on. The coat isn't reversible, but she manages to zip it up backwards so the liner faces out and the old man's congealing blood is hidden inside. A lot of falling snow has sneaked beneath her collar, and her skin feels chilled underneath her sweater. She shakes the powder from her hair and flips up her hood, and then she starts walking to keep herself warm.

No idea where to go. No strategy or goal. But she can't just freeze and surrender to the storm, so she presses on and tries to make sense of what she knows. Everything's insane and everything's a scramble, but there's one thing her mind keeps coming back to.

Brian's not a killer. He doesn't have it in him. But we already know, without a doubt, I have it in me.

She plants her feet in the snow and makes herself hard. *Unyielding*, Brian called her. She is. She was. She had to be.

So much about them had reversed last winter. Before the Bad Date, she'd been weaker. He'd been stronger. After that night, they seemed like different people, and for the first time in their relationship, Holly took control.

She stayed at Brian's bedside in the hospital; took him home when he was stable; wrangled the insurance and prescriptions; and managed the chores, bills, meals, and everything else alone. She brought her newfound efficiency from home to the office, surprising her colleagues and superiors, who'd expected her to come back shaken and distracted.

Brian returned to his own job, physically recovered but otherwise brittle. She saw him off every morning with positive encouragement, feeling like a mother at a school bus stop. He struggled at work, was passed over for a promotion, and took sick days without being sick. Holly tried supporting him however she was able. She let him rest on weekends, got him into therapy, and soothed him back to sleep whenever he had nightmares.

When she finally got promoted to project manager, her salary jumped above Brian's. She did her job superbly and everybody noticed. At home, she reawakened her dormant creativity, and by the end of the summer, she'd rented a tiny studio to focus on her personal art several times a week.

Brian cheered her on, but she could tell he always missed her when she left him on his own. Holly, on the other hand, craved time alone.

In the studio, she sketched and painted for herself. All she wanted was a few small hours of reprieve, when she could loosen up and play and let herself breathe. She worked on pictures she could comfortably control. But recently, the art itself was asking her for things. Messiness.

Intensity. Violent lines and colors. She didn't *want* to make art revisiting her trauma, but her own safe art was calling her a liar. None of it was honest. None of it was true.

But what was she supposed to do? Surrender to the nightmare she'd actively and tirelessly worked to dispel? How would that help Brian? How would that help her?

Tonight, she can't dispel it. But she can't surrender, either. So she hardens up as usual and focuses her thoughts, efficiently assessing where to go and what to do.

First things first, she thinks. *Orient yourself.*

After running from the site of the annihilated shed, she'd made her way to a cross street, rolled over the bank, and then walked backward, sweeping snow into her prints so they wouldn't be obvious to anybody searching. Now she's in the residential area of Pinebuck, wading through the deeper snow along the edge of the bordering forest. The road is on her left, dim but faintly visible.

She needs to find Brian, whatever shape he's in. But Brian, as the monster, hadn't left prints. Where would he have gone? Does the monster have a pattern? From the field . . . to the forest . . . to the trailer . . . to the neighborhood. Always moving closer to the center of the village. Is the monster doing that or is it only just them? Are they trying to escape or trying to attack? Either way, Holly guesses that he's gone toward Main Street—a twenty-minute walk, according to her phone.

She decides to go the same way, hoping she has time before she's dangerous again. At least she knows the *feeling* that proceeds her transformations. It's a lot like the urges she's been suffering with art, as if a strong, dark hand is clawing for control. But if she runs away from people before the monster claims her, no one else in Pinebuck needs to get hurt.

The drifts along the woods are difficult to navigate. She stops and looks around for any trace of life, but between the storm and the power outage, there isn't much to see. A smattering of houses is dark or faintly candlelit, and with no sign of vehicles or people outside, Holly makes her way back onto the road. This part of the neighborhood hasn't been plowed tonight, but walking here is dramatically better than wading through a season's worth of snow near the trees. She's exposed, but it's a risk she's willing to accept.

One minute later, the risk goes bad.

Lights appear in the distance, intermittently visible through waves of falling snow. They're moving left to right, getting stronger as they come. The snow briefly parts. She gets a momentary glimpse and sees that it's a truck, driving slowly with a searchlight. Probably a cop.

The truck draws closer to the road Holly's standing on. There appears to be a T-junction fifty yards away. The cop could turn left and drive the other way or turn right and head straight toward her. Even in the dark, she can see her own prints. A searchlight would make her trail impossible to miss.

She has maybe ninety seconds before the truck turns.

Then, from *behind* her, she hears a growing rumble and turns to see a vehicle with orange flashing lights. It's a snowplow, coming up fast in her direction, with a big curl of powder flying off the blade.

Holly doesn't hate police, but she doesn't trust them, either. The night of the Bad Date, they questioned her—and doubted her—longer than they should have. Hour after hour, she was bottled in a room, while Brian lay concussed in the hospital without her. Tonight, if an overzealous cop takes her in, she'll be bottled up again and ready to explode.

The plow, on the other hand, is easier to escape. The door would be unlocked. She wouldn't be a prisoner. So she stands at the roadside and flags down the driver.

The snowplow slows and crunches to a halt. The thing's gigantic—essentially a dump truck full of salt, with a ten-foot blade and tires as tall as Holly's waist. She strides toward it, so blinded by the headlights that when she finally gets alongside, the afterglow makes the driver difficult to see.

He rolls the window down and says, "You all right?"

"I need a lift," Holly says.

"Come around the other side."

Holly gets to the passenger door seconds before the police truck reaches the intersection fifty yards away. She steps onto the running board and climbs into the plow. The cab is enormous, with a wide gap between Holly and the driver. In the middle, near the dash, is a levered console of snowplow controls. The driver watches her, apparently sizing her up, while Holly keeps her eyes focused out the windshield.

The cop turns left . . . *away* from the plow.

"Thanks," she finally says, looking at the driver.

He's a compact man, barely bigger than herself. Midthirties. Short hair. Corduroys and flannel. His face looks pliable and rigid all at once, like a wire frame covered with a skin of warm clay.

"This is a bad night to be out," he says.

"Tell me about it."

"What's your name?"

"Jane."

"I'm Tanner. Good to meet you. Where are you staying?"

"I'm going to sound ridiculous," Holly says, "but my boyfriend planned the whole trip and I can't remember the name of the place. It's a little B&B with a blue sign."

"Where's your boyfriend now?"

"Honestly, the whole thing's embarrassing. I went out for a hot chocolate, got lost coming back, and now he's meeting me on Main Street so we can walk back to the B&B together."

"Tell you what," Tanner says. "We'll pick him up, too."

"That's great of you to offer. We'll be fine, though. Really."

"Please. I insist. I'll drive you both home."

He puts the snowplow in gear and starts forward with a scrape. The power of the engine quakes through her body but her joints feel locked. She's queasy from the smell of blood warming in her coat.

"We had a newlywed couple here in November," Tanner says. "They wandered into a storm and never came back."

When he keeps going on about the dangers of the weather, Holly catches herself resenting the guy—someone kind, maybe lonely, offering to help—the way she does with an awful lot of people these days. Coworkers. Friends. Brian most of all. Talking too much, asking too many questions, never knowing when it's time to shut the hell up.

They're almost at the intersection when Holly spots the police truck again. The searchlight is off. The brake lights are on. It idles in the road, not far ahead, having stopped there and waited for the plow to come along. The cop turns the red and blue light bar on, and the siren *bloop-bloops*, summoning the plow.

Holly crackles like ice dropped into water. Tanner seems to radiate his own sudden tension, scrutinizing Holly out the corner of his eye as if he knows she's been lying and manipulating him. The plow goes slower but keeps scraping forward.

"I need to hide," Holly says. "I got in a scuffle at a bar."

"A scuffle?"

"I gave a guy a bloody nose. It wasn't my fault. I panicked and I ran and then I got lost."

The red and blue lights are coloring their faces.

"Can you help me out?" Holly says. "I'm already leaving tomorrow morning, and I'd rather not get arrested for punching a handsy skier."

Tanner nods as if he understands the way it might have gone. A little booze, a little boldness. Somebody was asking for it.

"Get down in front of your seat," he says.

Holly slides and crouches.

"She might have already seen you. If she didn't, stay low and don't make a sound. This truck's a lot bigger than hers. We'll be way above her eyeline."

"I'm sorry," Holly says. "I didn't mean to get you into this."

"You sure it wasn't worse? Just a bloody nose?"

"Positive," she says.

Tanner pulls alongside the police truck, puts the drive into park, and rolls down his window. Flakes blow around the cab. The flashing lights remind Holly of last winter, but it's darker on the floor where the light can't reach. It's warmer there, too. The heat vent blows directly on her cheek, and the smell of thawing blood rises all around her.

Rather than holler through the passenger window, the sheriff gets out, walks over, and stands beneath the plow's driver-side window. Holly hears her voice very close, very clear. Nothing but the door and Tanner in between them.

"I saw you in my rearview," the sheriff says.

"Everything all right?" Tanner asks. "I passed the ambulance at Double D's."

"We've had some incidents tonight. I'm looking for a couple of tourists. A woman and a man. Maybe not together. The woman might have blood on her coat."

"She's hurt?" Tanner asks.

When the sheriff doesn't answer, Holly can't tell if she's giving Tanner a *police business, can't say more* kind of pause or the kind that indicates a measure of suspicion. For all Holly knows from her position on the floor, Tanner's tipping off the sheriff with a big wink-wink.

A powerful gust comes through the window, sending snow across the cab and onto Holly's head. Puff after puff, as if it's aimed directly at her. Almost like she's summoning the weather to conceal her.

"When you passed Double D's," the sheriff finally says, "did you notice any footprints in the road? Maybe someone walking or ducking out of sight?"

Tanner turns from the sheriff and gazes out the windshield. He has the tight, lowered brow of someone thinking hard. Holly watches him intensely and can almost hear him thinking: Why would someone in a bar fight wander out here?

"The only people I've seen were closer to Main," Tanner says. "It's a ghost town here, especially with the power out."

"Well, let me know if you see anybody where it doesn't make sense."

"I will," he says. "We don't want another situation like the Skylars."

Another long pause. Is she gone? Is it safe? Holly's joints feel tense enough to creak out loud. And then it seems as if the sheriff walked away and turned back, because her voice sounds a little farther off. Almost shouting.

"You haven't seen anything *else* tonight, have you?"

"Like what?" Tanner asks.

"Something weird you maybe saw and convinced yourself you didn't? Anything that might sound crazy to admit?"

"I don't know what you mean."

"Never mind. Forget it. Oh, but shit," the sheriff says. "Sorry to put this on you, but call Double D. His wall got trashed and he's having a conniption. You better let him know you'll swing by tomorrow."

"Got it," Tanner says. "Be careful out there."

He rolls up his window, the cab abruptly hushes, and the last swirling flurries settle on the floor. Holly doesn't move until the flashing lights fade. Tanner revs the engine and the truck starts moving, but before Holly's even climbed back into her seat, she feels something wrong in the direction of the plow.

"Why are you backing up?"

"We shouldn't follow her," he says. "I'm going to take a cross street and then we'll find your boyfriend."

"She isn't going to stop us again. Just drop me off at Main."

But Tanner's undeterred and keeps backing up. He passes the intersection in reverse, lowers the plow, and makes a left turn onto the cross street. There's nothing she can do aside from jumping out. Which she might yet do if the feeling comes back . . . the feeling of her body summoning the storm, as if she's ready to become something terrible again.

"So where's your boyfriend, really?"

Holly doesn't answer.

"I'm happy to drop you off," he says. "But if you're in worse trouble than you told me, maybe what you need is someone who can help."

Holly stares at the headlight tunnel in the road—starburst flakes, darkness on either side, like an endless white kaleidoscope of absolutely nothing. Her vision and her thoughts narrow in together, but she's partially aware that Tanner's studying her face.

His eyes are off the road. He's waiting for an answer.

"Stop," Holly says.

"What?"

"Stop the truck!"

Tanner looks ahead and jams on the brakes, but there's an awful lot of weight to stop, and even with the frictional resistance of the plow, the truck seems to skid farther than it should. Holly braces on the dash. Tanner leans against the steering wheel. The scraping vibration of the blade rumbles down. The truck finally stops.

There's a body in the road.

Holly's out of the truck before Tanner.

She slips on the running board but hangs onto the door, which swings her away from the truck until she loses her grip, lands hard on one boot, and topples sideways into the road. Then she's right back up and running to the body.

Did Brian do this?

Don't be dead, don't be dead.

There's a woman on her back, so close to the truck that her legs are partly buried in the plowed snow. Another few feet and they'd have smashed her with the blade. She's wearing a pink coat, fluffy mittens, and a hat that leaves her curly hair tufting out the bottom. Her arms form a T, as if she planned to make a snow angel. She's positioned with her head farther from the truck, so the headlights shine along the length of her body, and it takes Holly a few seconds to realize the woman's eyes are open.

She looks about forty but her expression—bright, faintly smiling—has a quality of childlike enchantment. She starts to move her arms because she is, in fact, making a snow angel, seemingly oblivious to Holly and the plow.

Tanner hustles up and says, "Mrs. Denver," sounding partially relieved and partially dismayed.

He squats and helps the woman into a sitting position. She looks at Tanner's face, laughing when the flakes curlicue between them.

"You shouldn't be in the road," he says. "Come on, let's get you up."

He helps her to her feet and brushes snow off her coat.

"What the hell?" Holly says.

"She had an accident a few years back," Tanner says. He taps his noggin as if to say: *brain injury.* "She has episodes now. Like a happy little kid."

He holds Mrs. Denver in place and checks their surroundings, peering through the snow at the nearest houses, most of which glow with ordinary light. The power's still on in this part of the neighborhood.

"I think that's hers," Tanner says, pointing at a Colonial house with a TV flickering in the front window. "Wait in the truck one minute. I've got to take her home."

Mrs. Denver tugs away and walks up to Holly. Her sweet, warm breath smells of marshmallow cocoa. She has an animated face and fresh, rosy skin, as if her mind's regression rejuvenated everything. No worry lines or wrinkles. Not an inkling of fear.

"How'd you get hurt?" Mrs. Denver asks Holly.

Is some of Vance's blood still showing on her coat? Holly checks, but Mrs. Denver isn't looking at her coat. She stares at Holly's face with innocent intensity, exactly like a whip-smart five-year-old would do if she were asking—really asking—if Santa Claus is real.

"I'm fine," Holly says.

Mrs. Denver shakes her head. "Something's wrong with you. I see it!"

Holly flinches from the words as if they've literally cut her. Everyone she's met tonight has looked at her suspiciously, but only Mrs. Denver—guileless and sweet—has sliced to the core of everything she hides. Now she sees herself vividly, through Mrs. Denver's eyes, as someone badly damaged under a disguise.

Snow spins around them in a miniature cyclone, and suddenly the three of them are standing in the eye. Mrs. Denver twirls away and gazes at the snow, as if the angel she was making in the road had been a marker, and a real live angel might appear at any moment.

Not an angel, Holly thinks.

A feeling builds, terribly familiar in her body. Before it happened once, she wouldn't have believed she was capable of uncontrolled violence and rage. Now she knows different. Something's seriously wrong with her.

She wants the storm to pick her up. Obliterate her. Blot her out.

Devour her entirely and carry her away.

Chapter 18

Mrs. Denver walks away and climbs over the snowbank, out of Tanner's reach before he can control her.

He doesn't want to leave his plow but can't just let her go, and so he chases her over the bank onto the dark, snowy lawn. A blast of stinging crystals hits him in the face. He glances back to see if the woman—he doubts her name is really Jane—is back inside the truck where he wanted her to stay. The passenger door is open and the cab looks empty.

Tanner spots her down the road, almost out of sight. She runs along the blacktop he plowed minutes earlier, fast and surefooted. Silent in the dark. The storm seems to follow and engulf her. Then she's gone.

"Wait!" he yells. "Stop!"

He shields his eyes against the wind, straining for a glimpse.

She'll take the plowed road to the junction, Tanner thinks. *Then left toward Main, where the plow hasn't been. Slower. Leaving prints. Maybe I can catch her.*

But Mrs. Denver's off her lawn now, twirling in the snow and growing hazy as she wanders onto someone else's property. From there, she might go anywhere.

None of this is *right*. Looking back and forth between the women who've abandoned him, Tanner feels trapped by a bad, familiar tension . . . like a pair of strong wires, pulled in two directions, each with a hook in the middle of his head.

From inside the house directly to his right, he hears a male voice hollering a name. The name is barely audible but sounds like "Sally."

Chuck Denver, Tanner thinks. *He's looking for his wife.*

Tanner acts fast. He lets the mystery woman go, catches up with Mrs. Denver, and leads her by the hand to her own front porch.

He's about to ring the bell when the door flies open. Chuck Denver rushes out and almost slams into Tanner. The men jolt back, startled and defensive. Chuck is wearing boots and an unzipped coat. He has the five-alarm look of a husband who's discovered that his wife has disappeared in the middle of a blizzard.

Mrs. Denver stands aside and chuckles to herself, as if it's all good fun now that everyone is here. Chuck's expression goes from fear to something like fury. He pulls her into the house and Tanner enters, too, as if an unseen force has sucked him inside. Once they're in the foyer, Chuck shuts the door. He holds his wife at arm's length and looks her up and down, like somebody assessing a life-sized doll.

"What are you doing? Why'd you do that? You can't go outside without telling me!" he says.

Mrs. Denver stares at him with soft, watery eyes. She quivers like a girl being scolded by a parent after doing something fun without considering the risk. Chuck's relief takes over and he pulls her into a hug. Mrs. Denver hugs back with her face against his chest.

"I found her in the road," Tanner says. "I almost hit her."

"I was showering," Chuck says. "I left her on the couch and when I came back out . . . I couldn't have been gone more than ten minutes."

Tanner smiles and it's weird—he *knows* that it's weird—but his face has a mind of its own sometimes. Mrs. Denver breaks the awkwardness by mumbling an apology. Chuck lifts her chin and reassures her with his eyes. Tanner watches them together. They're a vision he aspires to. The permanence. The fit. How Chuck can look at her and everything about her just glows.

"She's having a bad week," Chuck says. "I leave her alone, it's usually fine. But then she does things without really thinking things through."

"You could always tie her up."

Chuck stares and doesn't answer. His eyeballs are ice cubes.

"Like only by her ankle," Tanner says. "To keep her safe."

His boots feel frozen to the hardwood floor. Something creaks in the house, as if the frame is under pressure.

"Thanks for bringing her back," Chuck finally says.

Tanner hears the *leave now* crispness in his voice. He nods and turns away and opens up the door.

"Take care of her," Mrs. Denver says. "She should have come inside."

"Who?" Chuck asks.

"She's hurt. We ought to help her."

She says it with a bright and optimistic urgency, like things will be okay as long as they *believe*.

"What's she saying?" Chuck asks. "Someone needs help?"

Tanner pauses at the door and the wind whips around him while he stares at the snowplow's cold, empty cab. He doesn't like admitting that he lost the other woman. He also doesn't like the air of judgment from Chuck, who couldn't keep his own wife securely in the home.

"If someone needed me," he says, "I wouldn't let them go."

Chapter 19

Brian wakes to a car alarm.

He's lying on the crushed hood of a Honda Civic. The windshield is spiderwebbed under his back and he immediately starts sliding off the car. He lands sideways—first a foot, then a hand—and tumbles onto the road without banging himself up too badly. But the Civic's alarm blares beside his head, and between the noise, the blinking lights, the tumble, and the storm, Brian feels blitzed.

He shuts his eyes and covers his ears to give himself a breather. Then he looks and counts one, two, three damaged cars. They're parked in a row on the side of the road, looking as if a boulder hit the side of number one, bounced onto the roof of number two, and crashed onto the windshield and hood of number three.

That was me, Brian thinks.

But he isn't quite ready to digest that yet because his mind's still frantically assessing his surroundings. He's on an orderly street—aside from the broken cars—with tidy houses and a modicum of light. The power's on here. He senses that he's closer to the heart of the village . . . maybe a side street where people chose to park off the main drag. In the distance, there's a traffic light. Green. Yellow. Red.

But nobody is driving here and Brian feels alone. He stands and looks around, praying that he won't find a body in the road or any worse wreckage than a few trashed cars.

Because it's me, he thinks again. *It's me and then it's Holly.*

The fact is so bizarre, reality distorts itself. Commonplace things feel strangely out of place. The car alarm. Electric light. Ordinary gravity. They're too intensely real for a weird winter dream when he barely even feels connected to his body.

"No, no, no," he hears someone say.

Two women have approached the rearmost car, a mid-sized sedan with a concave door. Brian sees the window is totally exploded and the front left wheel is at a bad, crooked angle.

"Are you playing right now?!" one woman says. "I told you I shouldn't park on the road all night!"

Her companion spots Brian. She cocks her head as if to say, *I know this isn't* my *fault.*

"I saw it," Brian shouts. "It was a truck. Hit-and-run. It sideswiped the cars and almost ran me down."

Both women are looking at him now, possibly assuming he's the owner of the Civic. Then they all see a man hurrying toward them. He comes from the direction of a large country house—probably a winter inn—that stands beyond a barrier of ornamental trees. The man clicks off the Civic's alarm with his keys, hurdles the snowbank, and rushes up to Brian.

He looks like a twentysomething who used to play high school sports, and he's hurried outside only partway dressed in a flat brim hat, an aqua coat, and Timberland boots. He isn't wearing pants. He might be wearing shorts, but his pale, hairy legs are bare below his coat. He radiates cologne with a hint of chlorine.

He's a bro. He's a jock. Brian thinks *Brock*.

"Yoooo," Brock moans.

Brian watches him examine the damage to his car. His body language indicates fragility and shock, combined with an exaggerated man-up bluster. Someone broke his baby. Someone's gonna pay.

"What the hell. What the *hell*." He looks from Brian to the car, to the women, to the car again. "Yo, that's my whip!"

One of the women says, "It isn't just you. Look at mine!"

"What the fuck happened?"

"He was here. Ask *him*."

"It was a truck," Brian says again. "A big white truck. It didn't have its lights on. I almost got hit."

"A truck?" Brock says, looking up and down the street.

The more talkative woman approaches, and Brian sees her clearly. She's about the same age as Brock, with a round, pretty face in a fur-lined hood. Her eyes look sharp enough to cut through glass. She examines Brian and Brock, then the road, then the Civic. Her companion hangs back and hugs herself tight.

"You're saying a truck hit the side of one car and the roof of another," the woman says to Brian, "then pancaked his windshield, hopped off, and drove away. That's some Mario Kart shit."

"Yeah," Brock says. "That's impossible. No way."

"And there's no fresh tire tracks?" the woman says. "No white paint on any of the cars? I don't know what happened, but there wasn't any truck."

Brock steps up and grabs Brian's coat.

"You're lying. It was you."

"That's crazy," Brian says. "Look at that . . . look! You think I did it with my hands?"

"You had a rock. A fucking bat." He tells the woman, "Check around. Whatever he used, it's got to be here. It must be in the snow."

She drops her chin and lifts her brows, looking at Brock as if to say, *No, you aren't barking orders*. Then she turns toward Brian with the same disbelief.

"This skinny-ass man didn't use a bat," she says.

"A sledgehammer, then! Whatever, go find it!"

"You need to stop yelling at me."

"Chill. I'm on your side."

The woman turns to her companion and says, "He did not just tell me to chill."

"I can't look for a sledgehammer and hold him at the same time!" Brock says.

In spite of this, he pushes Brian away and kicks around the snow, searching all around to find a buried hammer.

Brian feels dizzy, as intimidated by the woman's edge as he is by Brock's bluntness. They didn't believe *truck*, it's too late to say *bear*, and he can't say nothing when they already suspect him. They'll all believe *monster* if he changes right now, and he suspects—after the slippery drive, the shotgun, and the shed—it happens when he's scared. When he's threatened. When he's small.

All it might take is Brock getting rough.

At the moment, Brock's preoccupied with kicking through the snow. Brian backs up very slowly in the road.

"I'm sorry, hold up," the woman says to Brock. "Where's your damn pants?"

"I was in the hot tub," he says.

"Off the patio? Tonight?"

"It's a *hot* tub. I heard the crash and the alarms and ran right out."

"You got your hat and coat and didn't get pants?"

"Does it matter?! Help me look! He had to use something and it's here! We gotta find it!"

The woman folds her arms and watches as he kicks a wild, snowy mess all around his car.

Her companion says, "Hey."

She has to say it twice.

"*What?*" Brock says.

"Your boy's running off."

Chapter 20

Kendra needs luck but won't admit it to herself.

She resents the way luck is sometimes essential when of course it's unreliable and dangerous to trust. Better to pretend she's really in control, even when she's floundering, and can't control a thing, and might make mistakes only luckiness can fix.

She lights a cigarette and drives. Nicotine's reliable. Her truck is, too. The metal-studded tires have a trustworthy grip, and whether she's patrolling on ice, pursuing a suspect, or driving to avoid the loneliness of home, her F-150 never lets her down. So she smokes and checks another stretch of unplowed road, relying on her habits and her truck for steady traction.

Kendra and most of her deputies have been searching all around Pinebuck, but with no clear description of the woman and man they're looking for, they'll need a new catastrophe, or someone acting weird, or yes, goddammit, a real stroke of luck.

At least they'll have names soon. The station is calling every hotel and B&B in the village to see if one of them has an unclaimed reservation for a couple. And any time now, Deputy Fickett will locate the spun-out car and run the plates . . . assuming the car is still there and registered correctly.

But all the information in the world, Kendra knows, won't make the couple magically appear. Back in late November, she had way more info—and far more support—for another urgent search that ultimately failed.

Fourteen hours before they went missing, Mitch and Becky Skylar were in a booth in Cookie's diner. Kendra had been near them, eating breakfast at the counter, and only casually assessed the newlyweds at first.

They were in their early twenties and radiated honeymoon. Mitch was broad-shouldered with a baritone laugh. He had long, sandy hair and an easygoing posture. His puffy coat, hanging on a peg, was the color of a glow stick. If Kendra had been forced to guess, she might have guessed correctly that Mitch was a highly competitive snowboarder who wasn't talented enough for real competitions.

Becky had a pixie cut and bold, penciled eyebrows. She was on the healthy side of curvy, like Kendra herself had been two decades earlier. Becky smiled more than she laughed, but her smile looked generous and heartfelt and warm. She hunched toward her husband, as if everything between them was a good, delicious secret. Kendra later learned that Becky was the breadwinner, a privileged girl who worked harder than her peers and was well on her way to serious money in a PR firm.

She might not have remembered the Skylars except for two details.

The first was Becky's foot, which had an orthopedic boot with a waterproof cover. A fresh pair of crutches was halfway under the table, halfway on the bench.

Unbeknownst to Kendra, Becky had been treated at the village clinic one day earlier after fracturing her ankle on Pinebuck Mountain.

The second memorable detail was something Mitch said.

It happened in one of those moments when a very noisy room briefly falls silent and a handful of words are startlingly clear. Kendra had her head down. She heard Mitch say, "Aww, me also crash auto car," and saw him stretch his eyes wider with his fingers.

Referring, Kendra would later surmise, to the Korean American snowboarder with whom Becky had collided on the mountain. But there in the diner, all Kendra knew was that a man was doing racist caricatures in public. And the woman he was with finally started laughing. And the two of them were so delighted with each other, they didn't notice Kendra glaring from the counter.

She'd seen this kind of thing with countless other tourists and usually absorbed it like everyday pollution. And yet it didn't leave her system. Nothing ever did. It wasn't Kendra's job to police people's humor, and she wasn't so fragile as to wilt from a joke, but sometimes a little dose, puny on its own, was suddenly enough to make her feel sick.

How much of her—her memories, emotions, and beliefs—was poisoned after years of other people's stink? Throughout her life, she'd taken shit for so many things. Being gay. Being fat. Being Black. Being single. So *yeah*, a sporty couple who was none of those things, making third-grade jokes in her hometown diner, might have been a dose too many that morning. She might have let the stink linger in her nose.

Hours later after nightfall, patrolling in her truck during the year's first storm, Kendra saw Mitch and Becky Skylar again. They were heading north along Jasper Lane, midway between Main Street and Batalin's B&B, which was one of the village's more outlying establishments. Credit card statements would later reveal that the Skylars had eaten woodfired pizza at Smoke and Oak and then proceeded to drink six pints of beer and three shots of whiskey between 7:30 and 10 P.M. at the Black Diamond.

When Kendra drove past them, they were obviously struggling. Drunk, cold, wobbly. In an unfamiliar place. In a blizzard in the dark. There were only three or four inches of snow on the ground at that point, but Becky had the broken ankle. Mitch walked beside her with one arm hovering at the small of her back, ready to catch her if she slipped but, because of her crutches, unable to truly support her.

They looked at Kendra when she passed. Kendra kept driving.

"Welcome to Pinebuck, sweethearts," she said to herself.

And that was the last she thought about the Skylars until the next day, sixteen hours later, when Kendra learned she was literally the last person to have seen them. A fact she instinctively kept to herself.

The Skylars' friends and relatives, far away in Boston, hadn't noticed Mitch and Becky falling off the radar for the night—it was their honeymoon, after all—but Mel Batalin noticed their absence at the B&B. Had they crept out early in the morning, unseen, or had they never made it back the previous night during the blizzard? Batalin played it safe and alerted Deputy Fickett at 10 A.M. Fickett kept his eyes peeled but didn't look hard because the Skylars' disappearance wasn't yet pressing. Tourists were a slippery bunch, often pulling all-nighters, falling into different beds, or merely driving home without settling their bills.

But then Mitch's mother called. First the B&B, second the police. She knew she sounded foolish, like a clingy mother meddling with her son's new marriage, but it wasn't like Mitch and Becky to ignore texts for so many hours. All she wanted was to know the two of them were safe.

When Fickett told Kendra, Kendra felt ill.

Right from the beginning, nothing seemed right. People lost their way in storms, but the Skylars' walk from the bar to their lodging had been less than half a mile, on a well-lit road, with houses all around. All they'd had to do was keep going straight. If they'd decided to turn back, they'd have turned up on Main Street. Their car was still at the B&B. They hadn't called an Uber. And no matter how drunk the two of them had been, how far could they have wandered with Becky on *crutches*?

Foul play was never ruled out, but there wasn't a motive, let alone a suspect. One plausible theory was that the young husband had killed his new wife—it certainly wasn't unheard of—but how could Mitch have fled from the village undetected? And even if he had, where was Becky's body?

Kendra and her department seemed to have everything they needed for the search. They had the Skylars' car and personal items from the B&B. They had eyewitness accounts from the previous day and night. They had a verified timeline and an estimated point of disappearance. They had search-party volunteers, tracking dogs, and helicopters. They had Verizon trying to locate the missing couple's phones.

What they didn't have was luck, and luck was what they needed when all their best efforts simply weren't enough.

Mitch Skylar's mother made it clear: *Not enough.*

Caroline Skylar had arrived in Pinebuck, all the way from Boston, less than seven hours after Kendra first heard of Mitch and Becky's disappearance. By the time the couple's other relatives and friends appeared the following day, Caroline had become a whirlwind of questions, criticisms, and pressure on the village to do much *more.* After days of fruitless searching, she called her own press conference and singled Kendra out.

"It is egregious that two newlyweds, one of whom suffered a debilitating injury a single day earlier, can disappear without a trace in a village this small," Caroline read from a statement. "Since coming to Pinebuck, we have received minimal information or reassurance from the sheriff, who has, from the beginning of our terrible ordeal, offered little in the way of competence or hope. In my opinion, she has a lot to answer for."

Kendra had to eat it.

Did others in the village think the same way? The Black woman sheriff—approaching reelection—who lost a pair of sweet, white, newlywed tourists. What else were people saying on or off camera?

Kendra worked hard to put the comments from her mind. But while a desperate mother's words ought to be forgiven, whenever she thought of Caroline, she thought the word *bitch.*

Given the public facts, Kendra knew the bitch was wrong.

Privately, however, she knew the bitch was right.

Mitch and Becky Skylar shouldn't have disappeared. All they'd needed was a ride that Kendra should have offered. She's never told anyone, and that includes Cookie, how the couple had annoyed her that morning in the diner. How yeah, Mitch and Becky had been assholes, but no, they had not deserved to vanish in the storm.

Tonight, she has another chance. She has to get it right. Find the *new* missing couple, keep the goddamned peace, and be the version of herself she doesn't have to keep secret.

For now, she keeps driving in the dark, blank snow. After fifteen minutes of absolutely nothing, she gets a report of damaged cars and a possible altercation outside the It's a Wonderful Inn. Three guests had heard a crash on the street and run outside to check the source; the owner called the station. A fourth person, unidentified, reportedly fled the scene in the direction of Main Street.

Kendra hits the gas, praying for some luck.

Chapter 21

ONE YEAR EARLIER
Two Days Before the Bad Date

Brian and Holly walked through a mostly empty shopping mall. Eighty percent of the businesses had failed or moved away. The ones that remained were obviously doomed. There was a health-food shop with nobody inside. A jeweler selling discount engagement rings. A store full of keepsakes, incense, and dreamcatchers.

Holly kept wondering aloud what had happened. Did the mall die gradually or suddenly collapse? Brian kept describing all the fun they would have if they were totally alone and literally owned the place.

They saw an area that used to be a sporting goods store. The security gate was up, the lights were all on, and see-through corrals were stationed near the entrance. A rescue dog group had rented the space for an adoption event, and each of the corrals was full of homeless puppies.

Brian automatically began drifting over.

Holly caught his arm and said, "Don't. We'll regret it."

"Too late," he said. "I've already made eye contact. See the tawny one there, staring right at us?"

Holly kept his arm but let Brian pull her. They walked

like sleepy children, silent and defenseless, to a ten-pound ball of desperate, eager fuzz. The puppy was a boy, not yet fixed, and pawed the metal fence when they squatted down to greet him. His tail flicked and fluttered. He was a pale yellow mutt with white and black highlights, and he smelled like a midwinter holiday nap. Brian hooked his index finger through the bars. The puppy mouthed and slobbered it.

"Look at the gray ones over there," Holly said.

"You're just diverting from the fact that this one's perfect."

"I am."

"Feel his fur."

Holly shook her head.

"Come on," he said. "He feels like a towel that's been fluffed in the dryer."

"This'll only get sadder when we have to walk away."

"Unless we bring him home."

"Bri," Holly said.

It wasn't the first time the two of them had faced a big decision and discovered they were moving slightly out of sync. Early on, Holly had waited for a good, long time before determining she trusted him enough to have sex. *I love you* happened later. Brian said it first. And when their individual leases ended last summer, Holly automatically assumed they'd each renew, while Brian scoped apartments that were big enough for both of them.

Whenever they diverged, they talked things through until they patiently, eventually, and comfortably aligned. But when it came to getting a dog, they were seriously split. Brian had broached the subject on numerous occasions, and Holly had deflected or dismissed the conversation.

"You know how people say you don't pick a dog?" Brian asked. "How in cases like this, the dog picks you?"

"You know how people say marry in haste, repent at leisure?"

"Okay. So it's a really big move. Let's break it down."

Holly closed her eyes, took a breath, and played along.

"He'd need a checkup and shots," she said. "He'd need to get fixed."

"That's all one thing once we get a good vet."

"That's a *fortune*."

"We're doing fine with money. Plus, I'm getting my promotion in another two months."

"You don't know that."

He did, though. Neither of them doubted it.

"We work every day," she said. "Unless we pay for doggy care—another big expense—he'll be stuck home alone five days a week."

"It's better than staying in a kennel in a rundown mall, or being bounced around foster homes, or worse if no one takes him."

The puppy scampered off and pounced on his mates until they all rolled together in a lightweight pile. Brian watched Holly following the action. She didn't make kissy sounds or call the puppy back. He returned on his own, cannonballed the fence, and wagged until Holly couldn't not reach out. She rubbed his downy ears with her fingers through the bars.

"What if we split?" she finally said.

Brian stared at her. "We won't."

"Hypothetically. We're talking about a dog's entire life. That's ten or fifteen years of unforeseen events."

"I don't see us breaking up."

"Hence the *unforeseen*. Think about him, with his big wet eyes and his heartbreaking, perfect little nonstop tail. Pretend we take him home and suddenly break up."

"Joint custody," he said. "A week with you, a week with me."

"That'd be terrible," she said. "He'd never feel secure."

They huddled at the bars with their fingers on the puppy. Holly petted his head. Brian rubbed his belly. The puppy settled down and snuggled at the fence as if believing they would stay exactly as they were.

"Maybe someday," she said. "But not tonight. We should go."

"What if someone else adopts him?"

"Happy ending for the pup."

"I don't know," Brian said. "They won't be awesome like us. He'll know he got stuck with *ordinary* people."

They stood and watched the puppy staring up for several seconds. Then he ran around the pen, wrestled with his mates, and didn't notice when they turned and started walking off.

Beyond the bright light of the adoption clinic's space, the long main corridor was relatively dim. They passed an empty store with mirrors on the wall, reflecting back and forth at nothing in the dark. It was late. No one else was anywhere in sight. They had a creeping sense that none of this would last another year.

Chapter 22

Brian reaches Main Street.

Brock is thirty seconds behind him and shortening the gap.

Brian pauses at the edge of the illuminated street. There aren't a lot of people walking around, but the bars and restaurants are open, and there are streetlights, neon signs, and rows of glowing bulbs strung above the road. It's all so normal and incongruously festive. The smell of fried food. Voices in the distance. The muffled thump of music from a nearby pub. Even the temperature and wind are noticeably gentler.

Brian feels as if he's sprinted into a calm, protective bubble, but all he's really done is left himself exposed. He's visible to anyone, especially to Brock, without the darkness or the whiteout or anywhere to hide.

He turns left and keeps running. Everything depends on what he does now, in the quick half-minute out of Brock's line of sight. If he ducks into a bar and mingles with the crowd, he might find cover . . . but he also might draw attention. There are walkways between some of the buildings, but he has to assume Brock will check them all, and if they're gated at the farther end, he'll get himself trapped.

He jogs past a gift shop. A bakery. A pizza joint. When several people step out of a nearby building, Brian darts between a pair of parked cars. The people don't notice him and walk the other way. He walks around a bumper to continue up the road and slips on the snow packed against a wheel, sprawling on his stomach with his arms and legs extended. Cold, dirty slush splashes in his mouth.

Slapping wet footsteps are coming up the walk. Brian's low and in the road, hidden by the cars, but he'll be totally exposed if Brock hits the street. Not to mention someone else might notice Brian cowering and stare just long enough to draw Brock's attention.

A Toyota Tundra is parked nearby. Brian crawls through the snow to drag himself under. It's a very tight fit, ten inches tops. He scrapes his front against the asphalt, head cocked sideways, and rips the back of his coat along something on the undercarriage. But he manages to cram himself in and then he freezes, listening intently to the sound of Brock's footsteps.

The sound comes and goes, halting and irregular, presumably as Brock checks the walkway and windows or stops because he knows that Brian must be close.

The Tundra is nineteen feet long and Brian's under the middle. Along the sidewalk side, a snowbank conceals him, and the roadside is packed with plowed-up snow. The only real gaps are at the truck's front and rear, where Brock would have to lower to his stomach for a look.

Brian's problem now is that he can't see *out*. Brock's footsteps are impossible to locate with any real precision, and once the sound recedes, he could be anywhere from gone to dangerously close. Brian waits with the snowmelt seeping through his clothes. His cheek and ear sting from the rough, cold road, and the smell of old gas irritates his sinuses. Pathetic and alone, on his belly in the dark, he can't imagine Holly being this weak.

He counts the passing seconds for two full minutes, and then he struggles out backward and crouches at the rear of the truck. A few more people are walking on the sidewalks now, taking advantage of the temporary snowfall lull, and he pretends to lace a boot while he peeks around the bumper.

No sign of Brock . . . *Wait.* There he is.

He's a whole block away, keeping to the sidewalk and heading in the opposite direction. His naked legs are pale underneath his coat, but he walks like a man impervious to cold. Energized. Bold. Full of pissed-off steam. He checks the window of every establishment he passes. He vanishes between two buildings, long enough to search the passage end to end, and then he comes back out and checks another window. Eventually, he might suspect he's gone too far, and if he doubles back, Brian will need a better place to hide.

He can't move until Brock is off the sidewalk again. Once the coast is clear, he'll dash between buildings, into one of the shadowy gaps that Brock has already searched.

While he's crouching at the truck, waiting for his chance, Brian notices identical fliers taped to every light pole. They all say MISSING but he can't discern more. He glances to his left and there, beyond the sidewalk, a copy of the flier is displayed inside a window. There's a hotline number and a photo in the middle. The photograph is hazy through the winter-fogged glass, but it seems to show a woman and a man, close together.

For an idiotic second, Brian thinks it's him and Holly. But that's ridiculous. Impossible. Of course it isn't them. Still, the boldfaced MISSING resonates hard. They deserve their own flier after everything tonight, like any other suspect or victim in the news, involved in something hideous or sinister or tragic. The photos always commonplace. Safe. Surreally happy. *Here they were before the nightmare squeezed in around them.*

Brian looks for Brock again.

Shit. Brock is gone. He's either walked inside a bar or stepped between buildings. How long until he pops back out and turns around?

Now or never, Brian thinks. *Go, go, go.*

He clambers over the bank, gets his footing on the sidewalk, and turns to see Brock reemerging in the distance. Brian freezes like a kid pretending to be an inanimate object. Incredibly, it works. Brock glances left and right, somehow doesn't spot him, and keeps on walking in the opposite direction. Brian hurries to the nearest gap between buildings, a narrow passage with a long row of oversized garbage bins.

Crouching in the snow behind the rearmost bin, he unlocks his phone, dims the screen, and plays a new message from Holly. He's so relieved to hear her voice, his insides spin and he has to hit pause until his dizziness subsides.

Last thing he knew, Holly was in front of him as he transformed near the smashed aluminum shed. Now he has proof he didn't hurt her. She survived.

He gets a handle on his spin and starts the voicemail over.

She sounds so close, he feels a rush of heat as if she really were beside him, speaking in his ear.

"*It happens when we're scared,*" she says. "*It happens when we're threatened.*"

He never used to panic when confronted with a threat. Not until the night she had to save his life. Fear was an emotion he refused to entertain . . . until it spread like oil under everything he felt. Now it bubbles nonstop, right below the surface, and any little crack or pressure brings it up.

He almost can't remember how he lived another way. Had he known a set of skills or optimistic tricks, or had he simply been naïve after years of good luck? How could he have ever seen a puppy at a mall and declared, with perfect confidence, they ought to take it home? As if commitment were a wish that always came true. As if the future couldn't possibly obliterate their plans.

For months, he's been anxiously expecting her to leave. And what's he really done to encourage her to stay? Promises. Apologies. Pretending he's okay. A winter getaway he'd hoped would magically restore them.

They both know it's normal that he's struggling with his trauma. Holly knows he's trying—it's not as if she *blames* him—but Zoloft and therapy and time haven't worked. Eventually, she's bound to see him as a puppy that she needs to walk away from instead of taking home.

They're too far apart and always drifting further. He doesn't understand how she keeps getting stronger, and she doesn't understand why he keeps getting weaker.

Every time the monster's come, right before the change, he's felt a kind of emptiness underneath his fear. Like a deep, black hole with a deeper hole inside it—a hollow at the core of everything he is. It's hopelessness. It's knowing he's increasingly alone.

Now he's trembling. Almost crying. Slushy wet behind a garbage bin.

He calls Holly back. Of course she doesn't answer.

"Holl. I think you're right," he says. "Everything's connected to our memories and fears. For me, it all started with the storm around the car. Then a stranger with a gun. Then the shed . . . I don't know. Maybe it was not feeling safe around *you*.

"You must have had your own set of triggers when you changed. The snowy car. The blood. Maybe the police?

"It's totally insane that any of this is true. I'd say we're both crazy but other people saw it. There's damage. Someone's dead. The monster's fucking real.

"We've got to stay alive and try not to change. Maybe this'll end when the blizzard winds down. Maybe we can ride this out if we're together. I'm on Main Street now, but somebody's been chasing me. I'm going to find a better place and call you when I'm there. I'll try to stay put. I'll tell you where to find me."

He pauses with his eyes shut, imagining she's with him.

"If we don't make it through, I'm sorry for the year. You must be sick to death of dragging me along. If we *do* make it through, I'll understand if you decide . . ."

He can't say the words.

"I'll call you back. I love you."

Brian ends the call and sees the snow is barely falling,

at least within the relative enclosure of the walkway. He checks his phone's radar. The storm is in a lull but there's another fierce band heading for the village. Now's the time to go and find a more remote location so he doesn't run the risk of hurting someone else. He googles a tourist map of Pinebuck—illustrated, cute—and locates a nearby park with a gazebo. It's perfect, Brian thinks: a structure with a roof at a landmark spot that's probably deserted.

He puts his phone away and creeps toward the walkway entrance. The street looks beautiful and bright beyond the gloom. He keeps his back against the wall, opposite the garbage bins. The sidewalks are busier with people here and there, but there's nothing like a bustle. Nothing like a crowd.

He peeks around the corner. Right to left. Left to right. He checks the road, up and down, and looks across the street. He waits a full minute, scanning everything in sight. Brock has disappeared. The benefit of running from a guy without pants is that he probably tapped out when he got too cold.

Suddenly the MISSING sign catches Brian's eye again. Another lost couple, right here in Pinebuck. What if this is more than a coincidence, he thinks, and the couple had been victims of the same ordeal?

Brian steps out and walks to the nearest light pole. He peels the sign off and heads to the corner of the block, where he'll turn and make his way toward the park with the gazebo.

He reads while he walks.

Mitch and Becky Skylar. Hotline number. Reward for information. Physical descriptions, last seen wearing. Missing since the storm on November 28.

The paper feels fresh—not seven weeks old—which means the village or the family has continued posting fliers. The couple's still missing. They haven't found the bodies. If the Skylars had their own monstrous transformations, they didn't make it back when the storm finally ended.

What if riding out the blizzard doesn't work? Brian thinks. *What if this is it . . . the final separation Holly and I have been steadily approaching all year? Never quite connecting. Rarely eye to eye. More and more apart until we vanish from each other.*

He crumples the sheet and chucks it down. The snow has totally stopped. Brian wonders if the lull is having an effect . . . maybe Holly's changed back from the monster to herself. He's about to call her again when he hears someone running.

He turns around. *POW!*

Brock knocks him over with a thump to the chest. Brian goes down, fortunately twisting off-center when he falls so his head lands safely in a thick mound of snow. Still, he's stunned, his hip struck the sidewalk hard, and before he gets his wits about him, Brock is kneeling on his stomach. He's right in Brian's face. Yelling things. Swearing. He grips Brian's coat and holds him on the ground. There might be other people watching from a distance—he hears voices of concern and muffled exclamations—but it's hard to get a sense of anything but Brock. His anger and his weight. The pressure and the ache.

Brian sinks deeper into the mound beneath his head until the snow falls inward, covering his face. He tries to shake it off but more tumbles down. Brock holds Brian like a bully after school, burying a smaller, weaker child in the snow. Brian swats and flails and tries to worm away, but Brock bears down and tangles up his arms.

Darkness roars open underneath his fear.

Change, Brian thinks. *Let it come. Make it happen.*

He flexes every muscle and his body goes rigid. Brock feels lighter, like he's softening or shrinking. When he grabs Brian's hair to finally pull him up, Brian feels tension in his scalp. In his *scar*. In the jagged length of skin—slightly raised, slightly numb—where a brick hit his head and left him dazed and bloody during another bad attack on another winter night.

He rises off the ground as if he's in a different body.

It's happening. I'm changing. Stronger, stronger, stronger.

Only Brock's still on him. Nothing's changing. Nothing's happening. The monster isn't coming, and he's totally alone. His rage funnels inward, his fight seeps away, and Brian goes blank and powerless and limp.

He wishes Brock would choke him out.

End it. Get it over with.

And then he hears the bright, bold siren of police.

Chapter 23

In the forest, at the end of a crooked line of wreckage, bizarrely cracked trees have fallen in a ring.

Half a dozen pines are broken at the trunks. Some are fully snapped and toppled in the snow. Others are only partly cracked and tilt at wicked angles with pale, splintered wood bristling at their wounds. All of them have fractured limbs and scraped-off bark. The damage has an epicenter, like a blast site where sudden force radiated outward, but the powder on the ground is clean and undisturbed, as if the snow itself had raged in a frenzy of destruction and abruptly settled down in the blizzard's current lull.

At the border of the ring, a gargantuan pine is fully uprooted. The trunk is almost horizontal, hovering a few feet off the ground with its farthest end snagged on another tree's limbs. The exposed roots form a huge, muddy tangle with a cavity below.

A strange mass of ice slumps against the trunk. It appears to be a sculpture of a humanoid creature with an oversized torso contracted in a hunch. The left knee is up, the right knee is down. One massive arm braces on the trunk, as if it broke the big pine right before it froze. The other arm drapes with its knuckles on the ground.

The head hangs low. It doesn't have a face.

The overall effect is that of giant, monstrous snowman—like a chainsaw carving at a midwinter fair. Except it isn't warm or festive. Only grim. Only cold.

Holly's body is encased deep inside the ice. She's trapped in total dark and absolute quiet, with a tight, solid pressure holding her in place.

Her first clear thought is that she can't breathe. Her mouth won't open and her nose feels plugged. She tries to move her limbs and jolt herself free, but she has no way of knowing what she's trying to escape. She's blind, deaf, disoriented. Paralyzed with cold. Is she buried? Is she dreaming? What the hell is happening? She feels all her muscles straining and contracting, but she can't move at all. Not a finger. Not an eyelid.

Her brain shoots fireworks of warning and alarm. Every thought, every cell shouts *breathe, breathe, breathe!* Suffocation hurts. It's agony and fear. It's total fucking panic. She feels herself asphyxiating, minute after minute, way beyond the point when she should have passed out. But instead of losing consciousness, she's more and more alert.

A new kind of terror billows up inside her. Is she trapped in a coma? Is she already dead? What if she's unnaturally preserved this way—paralyzed, alone, in endless suffocation—and her mind keeps panicking and suffering forever?

Her brain screams *No!*

And *Help me!*

And *Brian!*

Chapter 24

Brian's in the back seat of the police truck.

The sheriff and Brock sit up front beyond a security divider with a meshed metal screen.

Brock's real name is Joey, but *Brock* is already lodged in Brian's head. He can't remember how the sheriff identified herself. He only partially remembers being picked off the sidewalk, guided to the truck, and locked in the back.

He still feels strangely disconnected from himself, as if his body is concurrently in different times and places. Walking up the street. Getting tackled to the ground. Rolling in the snow and sitting in the truck. All of it is real and none of it is real.

Brock is explaining his version of events—the damaged cars, the chase, why he isn't wearing pants—and the sheriff lets him talk with little interruption. She must be pretty sharp, having quickly and correctly determined who's who: she found Brock acting like the obvious aggressor but quickly ascertained Brian was to blame. That's why he's in the back while Brock's up front.

She was looking for me, Brian thinks, *for all the other reasons.*

He watches her through the security mesh without

directly staring. Afraid to meet her eye. Afraid of her assessment. Brock takes a long, loud, animated time explaining what's essentially a very short story. He repeats himself a lot, backtracks to details that don't really matter, and colors every moment, from hearing the crash while he was chilling in the hot tub to holding a resistant Brian on the ground. He stresses, more than once, that he's here on vacation, as if his status as a guest carries more weight.

The sheriff seems cool enough to let him carry on, as if she understands the value of an unfiltered witness, but she also seems fatigued by Brock's histrionics. Brian thinks of how to act when it's his turn to talk.

Explain yourself but keep it short. Stay calm and be polite. Show her you're the real victim in the middle of a mess.

Brock wraps up and waits for her reaction. The sheriff twists around and fixes on Brian before he has a chance to figure out his story. She doesn't even question him. She waits for him to talk.

"I was going to meet my girlfriend," Brian finally says. "I just happened to be passing when the cars got damaged. He thought I was responsible and that's why he chased me. It's all a big mistake. I don't want to press charges."

"Press charges?" Brock says. "Man, are you for real? My car gets trashed and you're literally the only person in sight. Ask the girls," he tells the sheriff. "It was their cars, too!"

The sheriff looks at Brock with an indrawn sigh.

"I need to talk to Brian. Without interruption."

She waits for Brock to register her words and settle down. It takes him several seconds longer than it should. The sheriff turns back to Brian and says, "Start at the beginning. An emergency dispatcher took your 911 call earlier tonight about a spinout."

The call, Brian thinks. *That's how she knows my name. And Holly saw cops coming to Vance's trailer, so they must have found the body. Fuck. This is bad.*

"My girlfriend and I skidded off the road," he says. "We didn't get hurt but the car got stuck."

"You didn't stay at the car and call for help there?"

"We didn't have a signal. It must have been the storm. But we were close to the village, so I walked—"

"What's your girlfriend's name?"

His mind skips and stutters but he finally says, "Holly."

Her look seems to indicate she knows he almost lied.

"So Holly stayed with the car," the sheriff says, "and you walked to Vance Rickman's. You called 911 from his property. The dispatcher heard gunshots."

"The old guy, yeah. He was shooting into the woods. He thought he saw a bear."

The sheriff's eyes flash with recognition. Vance went on and on about the bear that killed his friend, and everyone in Pinebuck probably knows the story.

Use it, Brian thinks. *Maybe she'll believe it.*

"He was all keyed-up, insisting that he saw one. I didn't know bears were out this time of year. But half an hour ago, I saw—"

"What happened with you and Vance?"

"Nothing," Brian says. "He wouldn't help, and he was scaring me with the gun, so I finally just left and walked toward the village."

"That's the last you saw him?"

"Yeah," Brian says. "I walked a while and ran into a man

named Gary. He and his husband had lost each other in the storm, and here's what I was saying—we *saw* something out there. This thing, a bear, whatever it was . . . it chased us and we ran."

"*Stop*," Brock says. "You're such a bad liar."

The sheriff shuts her eyes, faces him, and waits.

"What?" Brock says.

"Please. Don't. Talk."

Brock goes *fffft* with exasperated lips. A fine mist of spittle floats in her direction. She glares at him and waits until he shrugs like *fine*, and then they both twist around toward the backseat again.

"All I'm trying to do is find my girlfriend," Brian says as guiltlessly as possible. "Has anyone picked her up? Can you tell me if she's safe?"

"A deputy's looking for your car," the sheriff says. "I should hear from him soon. Now tell me what happened with you and Gary."

"We hid inside a storage shed and something tore it open. I don't know what it was. I barely saw a thing. Gary went one way and I went the other. I didn't know what to do, so I ran toward Main Street. I know it sounds crazy, but there's really something out there. It's dangerous. It's big." He pauses for effect, as if he doesn't know more. "Is Gary okay? Has anybody seen him?"

"He's being treated at the clinic."

"You can ask him what happened. He'll say the same thing."

The sheriff doesn't acknowledge this—of *course* she'll ask Gary—and snaps right back to the unfinished timeline.

"After the shed, you were on Chestnut Avenue, near

the It's a Wonderful Inn, when three vehicles were damaged. Did you tell the owners you witnessed a hit-and-run involving a truck?"

"I lied," Brian says. "They were angry. I was flustered. I should have told the truth, but I didn't think they'd believe there was some kind of creature—"

"This is bullshit," Brock says. "A giant bear is chasing you around and doesn't catch you? I caught you no problem. It wasn't that hard. You can't really think we'll fall for this crap."

"Last warning not to talk," the sheriff tells Brock. "If you want to wait outside, go on and freeze your legs."

Brock tenses up but doesn't leave the truck. He looks like a man who's used to punching walls, regretting that his hand hurts, then swearing at the brick. He glares through the mesh of the security divider.

The sheriff says to Brian, "I think you know more than you're telling me."

What does she *know?* he wonders. *Has she come across Holly? Other damage? Other bodies?*

"I haven't done anything wrong. I got in a crash, I went for help, I got attacked. More than once," Brian says, "including right here. You can't believe I wrecked a metal shed and three cars with my bare hands."

The sheriff doesn't answer.

"You've got to let me go so I can try to find my girlfriend. I can't skip town. My car's stuck in a field. I promise we'll come to the station as soon as I find her. We'll make a full statement and answer every question. Please," he says with desperate need. "She's out there alone."

The sheriff looks at him a while—considering?

believing?—but finally turns away and puts the truck in drive.

"I'll find your girlfriend," she says.

"What about me?"

"You're staying at the station for the night. Out of trouble. You're coming, too," she tells Brock. "I need a full statement."

"Unbelievable," Brock says. "What about my car? I'm supposed to leave it on the street in that condition?"

She keeps her flashing lights on, checks the road in both directions, and pulls a U-turn while a handful of bystanders watch.

"Fine," Brock says. "But I'm pressing charges against this motherfucker."

"You can do that tomorrow if we have enough reason."

"If we have enough *reason*? What's the other option . . . put a polar bear in cuffs?"

Brian can't imagine being so brash. It's almost like Brock doesn't see her as a cop.

"You were fighting in the street," the sheriff tells Brock. "Depending on the facts, I could charge you, too."

That shuts him up.

Brian gazes at the ordinary scene beyond the glass. Glowing bars and restaurants. Fresh, frosty air. Wonderland people in a wonderland world, oblivious to anyone or anything in shadow. Brian's felt a similar division all year. Inside and outside. Him and all the rest. Even when he's in the world, freely making choices, he feels as if he's witnessing an unfamiliar self whose behavior and emotions aren't entirely his own.

For a minute back there, before he read the MISSING

sign, he felt as if he might take control of what was happening. Stay away from triggers. Reunite with Holly. All they had to do was make it through the blizzard. His theory seemed correct when Brock roughed him up and Brian *didn't* transform because the storm was in a lull.

But now he's powerless again. He's bottled in the truck, and he senses in his bones that the lull is almost over. Very fine snow flutters from the sky. The wind is picking up, blowing crystals at the windshield and buffeting the festive lights strung above the road. Last he checked the weather app, the blizzard's next onslaught was bearing down hard.

"You've got to let me out," he says.

The sheriff keeps driving.

"Everywhere I go tonight, something goes wrong. Call it bad luck. Call it anything you want. But everyone around me keeps getting hurt."

Her eyebrows lift in the rearview mirror.

Brock laughs and says, "You're threatening a cop? Fucking priceless."

"No," Brian says. "I'm not . . . I didn't mean . . ."

But what he truly means is ludicrously, hopelessly insane. Fat wet flakes hit the windows and melt. They're thicker near the lights now, tumbling in the wind, and whether it's for real or only in his head, Main Street is ominously different somehow. Like a photo marked *before* of the site of a disaster.

The shed—torn apart from the outside—was bad enough. What'll happen if he changes *inside* the truck? He pictures the divider violently expanding with their bodies up front, crushed against the dash. Heads bursting open on the windshield glass. Back when Brock attacked him,

Brian tried to be the monster . . . but that was in the open. He doesn't want to *kill* him. And the sheriff's only acting how a cop ought to act.

He has five or ten minutes, maybe less, to get away.

What would Holly do? he wonders. *What would I have done a year ago, back when I was gutsier and solved every problem?*

"I lied," Brian says. "I talked to my girlfriend on the phone right before you found me. Everything happened like I said, but when we talked it all through, we knew I looked guilty. First the shed and then the cars . . . people kept accusing me of things I didn't do. We were going to lay low where nobody would see us. Just make it through the night and drive home tomorrow."

For once, Brock manages to keep himself quiet, but he looks ecstatic that Brian's finally copped to being such a weasel.

"Where is she now?" the sheriff asks.

"If I tell you," Brian says, "will you promise to go easy on her? Please. She's had an awful night. I'm the one who lied."

"I'll give her marshmallow cocoa and a big, warm quilt. But if you don't tell me now—"

"She's at the park with the gazebo."

"Don't you have a room?"

"I didn't want to risk it."

"Why?" the sheriff says.

"Because I'm paranoid now. I've been chased and attacked and threatened and accused. Everyone in Pinebuck seems to have it out for me. All I want to do is get back to Holly."

The sheriff doesn't react. Did he overplay the victim card?

Eventually she says, "There isn't a gazebo. But I know the park you mean."

She kills her rooftop lights and turns left at the next intersection, driving onto a dim and less populated side street. Brock groans about the detour, clearly irked that his night in the hot tub has turned into a police ride-along, but he's wised up enough not to openly complain. Shops and lodgings give way to tidy, private homes, and when the sheriff turns again, they're on a long, curving road with more trees and fewer houses. The view is dark on either side, but the wind seems to grow more violent in the woods, and the snow falls angrier and thicker in the headlights.

Another minute passes and the landscape opens. The road runs parallel to an unplowed parking lot. Beyond the lot, there's a field and a pair of little hills where, even from a distance, the snow appears grooved. Brian guesses it's a sledding spot, but just as he had hoped, there's no one else around at this time of night, and the nearby woods are dense enough to vanish in.

A squat, rectangular building stands at the opposite side of the parking lot, closer to the field. It's probably a public restroom facility. There's also a pavilion with a long row of picnic tables. A heavy snowbank blocks the entrance to the lot.

The sheriff rolls up and parks along the bank. Then she looks past Brock, out the passenger-side window, at the restroom building and the shadowy pavilion. "I better not get out there and only find snow."

"I'll go with you," Brian says. "If Holly sees you coming and doesn't know I'm here . . ."

The sheriff turns off the engine, takes the keys, and activates the emergency blinkers. Tick, tick, tick in the dark, quiet truck. She opens her door and steps outside, letting in a whoosh of cold, flurried air. The smell of snow—slightly reminiscent of a nosebleed—activates terrible alarms in Brian's head.

"Stay put," she tells the two of them.

"Why would *I* leave?" Brock says.

She shuts the door, walks past the headlights, and has a long, awkward struggle climbing over the bank. Once she clears that, she starts across the parking lot in knee-high drifts, steadily but slowly heading for the restroom building.

One person gone, one person left. Brian doesn't feel particularly triggered, but he can't just *hope* he's not about to change.

"You should go out there and help her," he says to Brock.

"Shut the fuck up."

"If my girlfriend sees a cop and doesn't see me, she's liable to run. The sheriff's out of shape and probably won't catch her. Then we'll have to drive around, checking every street. You'll be forced to ride along all night long. But if my girlfriend runs and you're out there, too, you *know* you can catch her. It'll end right here."

Brock stares out in the direction of the sheriff, who's definitely laboring to wade through the snow.

"She said to stay put," he says. "You only want her pissed at me instead of you."

Wind rocks the truck with a big rush of powder. When

it settles, Brian's heart rate is noticeably higher and his skin feels weird, like it isn't really his. Snow falls chaotically in thick, shifting curtains as the sheriff disappears around the corner of the restrooms. Brian feels symptoms of the change coming on. His body has the hot-cold shivers of a fever, and everything around him has a dark static charge.

He doesn't know if it's for real or if he's worried it's for real. What if fear of being triggered is another kind of trigger? All he knows for sure is that he has to get away. He needs to take a chance he doesn't want to take.

"I used a metal bar."

"What?" Brock says.

"Like a crowbar but thicker. I used it on your car."

Brock looks at Brian with a dull, slack expression. He seems too surprised for his anger to have sparked, like the first few seconds after being slapped.

"You didn't find it in the snow because I dropped it down a sewer," Brian says. "I've done it before, on other vacations. I find the dumbest-looking car and mess it up. Just for laughs. I never get in trouble and I won't tonight, either. No one saw me do it. Plus, the sheriff doesn't like you. I'll be out tomorrow morning, and there's nothing you can do."

Brock leans closer. Now he looks angry. He bares his lower teeth, breathes through his mouth, and hooks his fingers in the mesh of the security divider.

"I'll tell her what you said."

"I'll deny it," Brian says, trying hard to sound as fearless as he used to be.

Brock appears to think. Very calm, very sharp. Like his uncontrolled anger finally has focus.

"How about this?" Brock says. "I don't know how he did it, Sheriff, but he unlocked the door and tried running off. I caught him just in time. He fought so hard, I had to fight back. Broke his nose. Broke his arm. He's a little fucked up but he didn't get away."

Brian struggles to conceal a bad wave of dizziness. He's tingly and his eyes feel jittery and raw, as if the air inside the truck is full of powdered glass. Brock's frozen in the spot between imagining and doing, but a few more cracks ought to get him moving.

"You won't do anything," Brian says. "You're one of those guys who sucker punches someone in a bar and hopes the bouncer steps in before *you* get hit."

"I've been hit plenty."

Brian laughs at him. "I'll bet you have. You had me on the ground and didn't do shit. You waited for the sheriff, just like now. You're such a cliché. The attitude. The clothes. It's all a big costume and everybody knows it. Those women in the road tonight . . . I saw the way they looked at you. A scared little boy with his little toy car."

"You're the one who ran."

"I can't run now."

Brock turns away and looks out the window. The restroom lights barely penetrate the snow, the pavilion's disappeared, and the parking lot is nothing but a long span of white. If they can't see the sheriff, she can't see the truck.

Brock steps out and opens Brian's door.

Chapter 25

One mile away, where Holly's trapped and panicked in the monstrous shell of ice, the forest wakes up.

The sound of creaking, clattering trees is quiet in the distance but rapidly approaches like a thresher in the dark. Strong and unseen. Violent. Energetic. Wind blows a gyrating onslaught of flakes. The blizzard's starting up again, as furious as ever. Twigs and snowy clumps tumble to the ground, and everything strains and shivers in the much colder air.

The ice shivers, too. Hairline fractures spread across the surface. Snow swarms the shell, the cracks grow deeper, and a harsh, brittle noise vibrates the air as if a huge piece of glass is crunching under pressure.

Holly's limbs begin to loosen and she feels herself shift. She still can't breathe or understand her plight, but she knows whatever's holding her is softening or crumbling. The numbness of her skin quickly turns cold, as if her nerves have been exposed to a thousand bright pins. Her body slumps with gravity. She starts seeing textures. Her head is a cacophony of cracks, pops, and fractures.

Suddenly, she's falling in a crash of broken ice. She tumbles over chunks, feeling bumps and jagged edges on her hands, ribs, and hips, while an avalanche of blocks pounds on her back. Then she's lying on the ground, face down amid a heap of rough, frozen rubble.

Holly lifts her face with a big, shocked gasp. She's never felt a fuller, more explosive rush of air. Her first exhalation is a half-choked cry, as if it's agony to find herself newly resurrected. She coughs and quakes and breathes again, gasp after gasp, and everything around her bursts incredibly to life. More falling ice clatters down around her. Holly jolts hard as if she's actually electrified. She flails and jerks away, awkward in the wreckage, and crams herself tight against the uprooted tree. She's wide-eyed and feral. Her hair blows wild in the cold, snowy gusts.

For a while, she's incapable of anything but breathing. Eventually, her heartbeat finds a calmer rhythm, but she doesn't feel any less volatile and coiled.

Snow forms momentary vortices and whorls, either sucking flakes in or whisking them away, until a strong burst of wind clears the air enough to see. The giant heap of ice actively disintegrates. Bigger chunks crumble, the crumbles turn to powder, and it all keeps scattering and fluttering away. But Holly's seen enough to understand that every fragment had been part of something bigger—something terrible and whole.

The body of the monster must have turned solid, preserving her inside like a zombified corpse.

What? she thinks. *What?*

"What? What? WHAT?"

She yells the word a dozen times, shouting at the storm, until it finally stops seeming like an ordinary word and sounds illogical and alien and meaningless and crazed.

Snow falls thicker. Her surroundings start to vanish in the whiteout dark. She stands and holds the toppled tree's roots for support. Her face is raw, she's dangerously cold to her core, and she aches from the battering she suffered in the fall.

But she has to get moving. Find a road. Find Brian.

Because the blizzard isn't over yet. None of this is over, and now she knows another bad way it might end.

Chapter 26

Kendra's sick of snow.

Sick of seeing it and feeling it. Driving in it. Walking in it. She plans for snow, reacts to snow, and dreams about snow. Every day, she thinks and talks and hears about snow. Maybe Taz was right and Kendra should have followed her to Albuquerque, where the snowfall is light enough to handle with a broom.

Now she's trudging through the parking lot, blinded by the blizzard, trying hard to focus on the job. Not the snow.

One man dead. One man concussed.

One damaged home. Three trashed cars.

One obnoxious tourist, Joey Kolker, who on any other night she'd have spanked into place, but who on this particular night managed to catch . . .

Another tourist, Brian Dunn, who's timid and polite but trouble, trouble, trouble. The story of his night might have seemed explainable if not for Vance's arm and the superhuman wreckage.

Brian blamed a *bear*. Gary and Oliver blamed a *yeti*. They wouldn't be the first people tricked by a storm. Disoriented, scared, their senses overwhelmed—suddenly a moving tree looks otherworldly, or a commonplace animal looks like a monster. Maybe it's a deranged moose, Kendra thinks. Antlers might explain Double D's wall, the devastated shed, and the bashed-in cars. But a moose didn't freeze Vance Rickman's arm. Separate explanations, then. A moose and something else. She has a hard time seeing Brian as a murderer, let alone a murderer dismembering his victim. Could it *all* be the weather? Crazy wind. Blown debris. A freak blast of cold that froze an arm solid?

She's missing key pieces of the whole weird picture, and the number-one piece right now is Brian's girlfriend, who's hiding in the goddamn never-ending snow. Kendra knows it's reckless leaving Brian and Joey alone—she can barely see her truck at the entrance to the lot—but on the off-chance Holly's really hiding in the restroom, she has to follow through and try to end things now.

Kendra huffs and coughs from the effort and the cold. The cigarettes tonight haven't done her any favors. The caffeine and sugar she consumed are burning off. Her feet feel swollen inside her boots, and tromping through the snow has left her rubbery and sweaty. When she walks around the corner of the restroom facility, a straight shot of wind freezer-burns her face.

She checks the women's room first. The door isn't locked. It should have been secured for the nighttime hours, but she's grateful for the heat and the respite from the elements. Nobody's inside. She opens every stall and doesn't find prints or water on the floor. She hurries back out and walks along the building, but the snow around the men's room door is undisturbed. She checks it anyway. Nothing. Dry tiles. Empty stalls.

It seems ridiculous that Holly would hide at the pavilion,

an open-air structure near a warm, safe building . . . but the last time Kendra did less instead of more, Mitch and Becky Skylar vanished with a poof. She makes her way over and it's farther than it looks, especially in the snow, where every deep step takes an extra second. She can't see her truck parked along the road. Just the dim, red pulse of the blinkers at the back, and the fat, smudgy glow from the lights up front. It makes her feel alone. Untethered in the storm.

How'd I get here? she thinks. *Where'd I go wrong?*

Because it isn't just tonight. It's been week after week, feeling buried under weight she never saw coming. Only last year, she had a girlfriend who loved her. A cozy little home. Mostly friendly locals. A manageable job in a manageable village where she helped people, fixed things, and held herself together. Now she lives by herself in her hollow little house. The village and her job feel increasingly chaotic. She's noticed certain locals giving her the eye. She has way fewer answers and a lot more doubt.

She's been trying to believe that it's all bad luck, but lately, Kendra's thinking that it's all just her. Not that she's responsible for everyone's behavior, but she hasn't done enough to mitigate the havoc. She's sure as hell tried, and yet there comes a certain point—people dying, for example—when all her efforts can't sugarcoat so much failure. In November, Caroline Skylar accused her of incompetence. Who would disagree, watching her tonight?

Somewhere along the way, Kendra's life shifted, and she went from being one thing to being something else. Back to smoking. Overeating. Wallowing in snow because again, same as last time, she isn't in control. She's exhausted all the time. Incompetent in *life*. Maybe she, and not the winter, made Taz leave. Same as how she, and no one else, let the Skylars disappear.

The trouble with accepting fault is having to redeem herself . . . exactly when she feels too faulty to improve. All she seems to do is watch herself trudge. And at times like these, when she's fighting through exhaustion, she struggles to imagine how tomorrow will be better or how anything she's lost or gotten wrong can be restored. Shouldering the blame won't make her nimbler. She'll only have *more* weight freezing her in place.

She reaches the pavilion and steps onto the platform. A dozen snowy picnic tables stretch out before her. The supports aren't wide enough for anyone to hide behind, and the only prints she comes across are several hours old. Holly hasn't come yet. That or Brian lied. Either way, she's left the men alone for more than five minutes, and it feels as if she's wandered much farther, much longer.

She gives up the search and starts walking back.

Things could be a lot worse. She has Brian. She has Joey, who can place him with the cars. She has Gary as a witness to the mess at Double D's. Vance's death will be explained by the medical examiner. By now, Deputy Fickett's probably found the spun-out car and run the plates, and soon enough, they'll know where Brian and Holly booked a reservation. There's a very good chance Holly's waiting there now.

Kendra hears a violent noise, like a crunch or a crash.

It comes from the direction of her own hazy truck. Too metallic for a falling branch or anything in nature. Too prolonged to be a car wreck, and anyway she hasn't seen another set of lights. She struggles forward with her heartbeat dangerously revved.

When she's close enough to see her truck, everything is wrong.

At first, she thinks something must have landed on the roof, but the cab is blown *out* instead of crumpled in. The passenger doors are open with the windows exploded. The roof looks deformed and slightly convex, like a partially expanded Jiffy Pop top. The light bar's askew. The windshield is spiderwebbed and nearly off the frame. Inside the truck, the security divider is blasted out of place and pins the front seats tight against the dash. The whole backseat is cratered and distorted.

Forget about bear. Forget about moose. Only a bomb could have generated this kind of force. Except she never saw a flash. It hadn't *sounded* like a bomb. There hadn't been a shockwave, either, Kendra thinks, and she doesn't see shrapnel.

She doesn't see *them.*

Kendra spins around. Looking far, looking near. All she sees is snow, on the ground and in the air, even when she walks a full loop around the truck.

No, no, no. How can they be gone?

She finally spots Joey's hat fallen in the road. Kendra walks over, picks it up, and shakes it off. He left a messy trail, as if he crawled instead of walked. She follows to a spot where he appears to have turned and climbed over the bank.

She climbs over, too, and almost falls on top of him.

Joey's in a ball, hugging both knees with his head jammed low. He looks impossibly compact, as if he's literally shrunk, and his uncovered legs are Styrofoam white. He's trembling so hard, his hair seems to bristle. Kendra kneels beside him, partly sheltered by the bank, and hears a high-pitched whine coming from his throat. He isn't obviously injured but he seems to be in shock.

"Joey," Kendra says.

He doesn't jolt back or acknowledge her at all.

She moves his arm as if she's opening a bird's folded wing, and Joey lifts his head enough to show his face. He's expressionless and stunned, eyes open to the snow, with a thick flow of mucous from his nose to his chin. He's blubbering and whining. Like he doesn't even see her. Like a child so scared, he'll never quite recover.

JOEY'S THOUGHTS COME in flashes. Hectic. Overlapping. He can't make sense of everything that happened. He'd been waiting for the sheriff to investigate the restrooms. Brian egged him on until he stepped out of the truck, opened the back door, and reached inside. He wanted to shake Brian up more than really hurt him. Slap him once or twice. Punch him in the nuts. But then the snow blasted in and whipped all around them, whiting out Brian and the whole backseat . . . and after that, Joey's memory scatters into chaos.

It's possible that Brian kicked him out of the truck. He doesn't remember falling, but he does remember lying there, looking upward at the wind-whipped snow from the ground. Something felt wrong. Unnatural and bad. Almost like pressure threatening to blow.

He can't remember getting up or scrambling away. His memories and thoughts are less like a movie and more like a rapid-fire series of explosions. Getting blown off his feet by a force like a shockwave. The crash of breaking glass. An awful screech of metal. Terrifying snaps and cracks. Steel bursting open. And throughout it all, snow—more and more snow—raging like an icy tornado in the dark.

Before he fled, he saw something awful in the storm. It was horribly obscure and hard to understand, and it reminded him of something he had seen years ago.

One night when he was seventeen, he'd argued with his parents and made a big show of storming out of the house. He'd gotten into his car, sped backward down the drive, and felt a bump beneath the tires. Almost like a *pop*. He'd stopped the car and waited, feeling feverish and weak, before he finally stepped out to see what he had hit. The family's old cat had run beneath his wheels. He'd loved that cat. They'd gotten her the year Joey started kindergarten. Luna, they had named her, but they all called her Loony. The car had killed her instantly. He'd found her on her stomach, partly flattened, partly twisted. She'd been sprawled and misshapen, like a hideous distortion, and her soft white fur had looked terrible and cold. A gush of blood and organs had erupted from her mouth.

Whatever Joey saw tonight reminded him of that. Something wrong and awful with a body, and a head, and a shape that seemed to sprawl in horrible directions.

It's all his mind can see now, in endless different ways, as if he'll never look at anything again without remembering.

Chapter 27

ONE YEAR EARLIER
One Day Before the Bad Date

"I smoked too much," Holly said. "I feel like I'm sinking in an underwater pod and all the warm sun is fifty leagues up."

"Pretend you're a jellyfish," Brian said. "The kind that can glow like a neon bubble."

"You smoked too much, too."

"I did. I'm all floaty."

They were lying on their backs, naked after sex, with their sides pressed together underneath the blanket. The lights were out. The radiator creaked in the corner. They were cozy hip to hip, but just beyond the window blinds, and all around the bed, the night seemed to threaten them with cold dark hands.

"How great will summer be?" he asked.

"I can't imagine."

"Let's try."

"Mmmm," she said. "Okay."

"The windows are open. It's breezy and it smells like rain. What's the word for that?"

"Petrichor."

"I always want to say pterodactyl," Brian said.

"So it's breezy and the sky is full of pterodactyls. When I cross the room to see them, I don't mind being barefoot. The floor feels softer when it's warm," she said. "Like caramel."

"The rain comes and goes, and then the sidewalks steam."

"We walk through the steam, wearing lightweight clothes, and our skin feels buttery and tingly in the sun."

"Let's get ice cream."

"Yes. They have a new flavor."

"It tastes like all the best memories of childhood. Campfire marshmallow. Movie-night popcorn."

"And something unexpected and mysterious. Like the flavor of a moonlit cloud above a swimming pool."

"We bike around parks where everything is green."

"Except the flowers. And the rainbow sparkles in the grass. And the bright gold coins we shake from the trees."

"Right," Brian said. "To pay for all our day trips and overnight adventures."

"Everything's better in the summer. Sex is better, too."

"Sex is good now."

"But it feels more playful when it's warm," Holly said. "Winter makes it feel like wilderness survival. Like we have to cling together or the elements will kill us."

Brian rolled toward her, propped his head against his hand, and touched her belly with his open palm, right below her navel. Holly turned to look at him and reached for his hip. Their arms made a warm, elastic crosshatch between them.

"Let's go to the ocean for a week this summer," Brian said. "Someplace private with a secret little beach."

"The ocean takes forever heating up," Holly said. "It's iffy in July."

"August, then."

"August."

"We'd better pick a place right away before they're gone. A lot of people book those trips a year ahead."

"That's crazy," Holly said. "Who can plan that far? It's like the dentist when they ask about next year's visit. I'm always like sure? I'll be free on Tuesday morning in another twelve months?"

Brian laughed and said, "We'll chance it. Unless you have a tooth cleaning scheduled that week."

She moved her arm off Brian, pulled the blanket to her throat, and pinned it with her chin. Brian watched her face while she gazed at the ceiling, which appeared dark gray in spite of being white.

"Can we afford it?" Holly asked.

"That's what credit cards are for."

"Who would watch the puppy?"

"We're getting it?!"

"*Would* meaning *if.* There's a lot of woulds and ifs."

Regardless of the blanket sealed at Holly's chin, the warmth kept escaping and a chill crept in, especially where Brian's raised head made a gap. They were dewy after sex. Now the dew felt cold. Their positions were uncomfortable but neither of them moved.

"That was really strong weed," she said. "I can't really think about stuff right now."

"You were good with pterodactyls and make-believe ice cream, but now you're too high to think about a trip?"

"Can we talk about it later?"

"Can we talk about it now?"

They both held their breath in the manner of a staredown. Holly looked petrified. Brian spoke first.

"I never understand when you shut things down."

"You're mad."

"I'm not mad," he said. "I feel like something's wrong."

"Fine," Holly said. "I'll tell you what's wrong. We're planning a vacation in the middle of the summer, and we might not even be together in the summer."

He sat and tugged a portion of the blanket up with him. His head was off his palm. His hand was off her belly. They weren't far apart, but the room was so dark, their faces looked shadowy and grainy to each other.

"You said that at the mall last night. Where's this coming from?"

Holly didn't answer.

"Do you want to break up?"

"No," she said. "God."

"Are you sure?"

"Yes."

"Really?"

"Yeah. I'm being dumb," she said. "I always see monsters when I look way ahead."

A truck passed the building on the road outside, big enough to vibrate everything around them. The atmosphere was different after it was gone. Cottony and thick. Stiller than before.

"I shouldn't have pushed about the puppy," Brian said. "That's a long-term thing. A serious commitment. But a quick summer trip, only six months away . . . You didn't worry like this about a one-year lease."

"I did. We talked for weeks."

"Do you regret moving in?"

"No."

"What am I missing?"

"Don't you ever worry like this?" Holly asked.

"Yeah, I mean . . . of course. But then I switch it off because it doesn't really help. I worry but I try not to *act* that way."

"I can't switch it off and act another way. I wish I could. I want to. I'd love to see a puppy in a mall and bring it home or tell the fucking dentist I'll be there next year. We're different."

"So we're different."

"Not a healthy, yin-and-yang kind of different. Another six months, you'll be jumping out the window. Even right now, you must be thinking, Christ—here's a carefree talk about the ocean in the summer, and suddenly my girlfriend is drowning our relationship. Honestly," she said. "You don't *like* this, do you?"

She sat and hugged her knees underneath the blanket, with her shoulders and her spine open to the air. Brian sat beside her, equally uncovered.

"You're having a rotten month," he said. "Eventually, I'll have one, too, and we'll be even. Not to mention I'm a lot to handle already, always charging into everything in sight without a helmet."

The radiator hissed in the corner of the room, making sounds that a well-kept unit wouldn't make.

"Hey," Brian said. "Look at me. I love you."

"I love you, too. I'm sorry."

"Don't be sorry."

He pulled her close, cradling her head with his elbow, and felt Holly's breath moving on his chest. She curled in tight, draped her leg across his body, and rearranged the blanket so it covered them completely. They clung together, not quite comfortable or warm.

"We're okay," Brian said. "We're together right now."

"Are we?" Holly said.

"Aren't we?"

"I don't know."

Chapter 28

Holly stands beside an oak, sheltered from the wind, at the edge of the woods in sight of an empty road.

She tries to piece together everything that happened. She remembers running away from Tanner and Mrs. Denver, worried she would hurt them if she stayed near the plow. After that, she must have turned back into the monster, at which point her mind stopped recording memories. Presumably, she entered the woods at this exact spot, because the trail of damaged trees has led her to the road. The monster stormed in, and now she's staggered out again.

Holly checks her phone and plays Brian's latest message. She's relieved to hear his voice, know that he's alive, and listen to his own half-baked theories.

Holly opens her weather app and scrutinizes the radar, pondering a gap in the animated loop. It's a slender little void, shaped like a sickle, with heavy bands of snow before it and behind it. The gap had been a lull in the blizzard over Pinebuck, right around the time Brian left his message.

Right around the time she was frozen in the ice.

Holly feels the air leaking from her chest. She slumps

against the oak, slides down the bark, and settles on her heels as if her body's been deflated.

They can't ride it out. They won't survive the blizzard. When the storm briefly stopped, the monster froze around her, and she senses if the storm hadn't roared back to life, there'd have been no animating force to release her. Whoever is the monster when the blizzard truly ends will be hopelessly encased to suffocate and panic. They'll be conscious when it happens. They'll be horribly preserved. She or Brian will be frozen in a lost block of ice, suffering or dying very slowly. All alone.

Brian said he's sorry for the year. She is, too. She's sorry for his weakness—how he flinches, and defers to her, and always seems brittle. She misses having someone she can lean on more. She hates that she's constantly required to be strong. Can-do Holly. Hardcore Holly. She feels as if she holds herself together so hard, all the little pieces might suddenly explode.

"*If we do make it through, I'll understand if you decide . . .*"

He didn't finish, but he didn't have say it out loud. Holly knows what he was thinking, and the thought makes her cry. She's been trying to outrun what happened last winter, but it's always at her heels and at the edges of her sight, threatening to swallow her completely from behind. For all her headlong speed and efforts to evade it, here she is again, as desperate as the night she saved his life.

That might have been the last time she truly ran toward him. Ever since, she's been barreling ahead without rest, hoping he would figure out a way to keep pace. Because she can't slow down. She has to move ahead. She doesn't want to leave him, but he's right: she's sick of dragging him. She's terrified of looking back and being just like him. Shrunken, or afraid, or frozen with inertia. Is that the only way they can really be together?

She doesn't cry long. She's like a shaken-up bottle with a quick, messy fizz before the cap's back on and the pressure's back in. They can grapple with the future and the past later on . . . but only if they somehow make it through tonight.

She calls him back and leaves a message.

"Riding out the storm isn't going to work," she says. "Whoever's still the monster freezes that way. It happened in the lull. I was wide awake and suffocating. Brian, it was awful. It was godfuckingawful. So listen, here's the plan . . ."

She pauses. *What's the plan?*

"You said you were on Main Street. I'll head in that direction. No matter how this ends, we shouldn't be alone. If we can't stop the memories and flashbacks and triggers, maybe we can help each other weaken their effect. I love you, Bri. I'll find you. We'll make it through together."

She ends the call and checks her phone map. East along the road, follow the bend, take a right. She'll be standing on Main Street in less than ten minutes.

Brian's probably the monster now, leaving more wreckage. Maybe she can track him so they're standing face-to-face again. At least they'd be together one last time.

Chapter 29

"Hey," Cookie says, crackly over the phone.

"You're still in the diner?" Kendra asks.

"How'd you guess that when you called me on my cell?"

"You have your diner voice on."

"I always have a diner voice," Cookie says. "The grill was overdue for a full-on clean. Once I did that, I got cleaning fever. Something in a storm revs me right up."

Kendra's envious of Cookie with her clear-cut work. Find a mess, clean it up, know a job well done. For the past five minutes, she's been sitting alone in a borrowed police truck, staring at the snow that swarms against the windshield. It reminds her of the static on old TVs. She used to watch it as a kid whenever she was stressed because the fuzz had a way of focusing her mind. Tonight, the wild snow has a similar appearance, but it only makes her thoughts scatter into noise.

"Rough night?" Cookie says.

"Can you tell?"

"Well, you're smoking."

"You hear me blowing smoke?"

"I hear you holding it in."

It's true. She has a cigarette pinched between her fingers.

Kendra breathes out, except there isn't any plume. What happened to the smoke? Did it all stay inside her?

She gives Cookie the lowdown on the whole crazy night, from Vance's dead body and Double D's house to her newly wrecked truck and Brian's disappearance.

After Kendra found Joey sobbing in the snow, she radioed for help. Deputies Fickett and Davis drove out to meet her in two separate vehicles. The men were predictably dumbfounded by the state of her truck, and the overall chaos obscured the fact—at least for now—that Kendra had let a suspect in custody escape. She commandeered Fickett's vehicle and instructed the deputies to share the third truck back, drop Joey at the emergency clinic, and carry on the search for Holly and Brian.

"Hell of a night," Cookie says. "What did Joey have to say?"

"He was too scared to talk."

Deputy Fickett, on the other hand, had talked quite a bit. Before the deputies drove away, Fickett told Kendra he'd located Holly and Brian's car on Route 4 and looked up the plates. He got their full names and registered address, but they didn't have criminal records or anything of note. Not a moving violation or a parking ticket. Nothing.

"But then he looked online," Kendra tells Cookie. "Brian Dunn and Holly Byrne were involved in a violent incident last winter. One of those piece-of-shit Facebook accounts—local crime uncensored, that sort of thing—published their names and some of the details. Fickett called the town's PD and got the full story. Apparently, Brian and Holly were attacked by a stranger in a parking lot. They fought back and killed the guy. No explanation of why the man attacked in the first place. No drugs or alcohol in his system. No history of mental illness. No connection to Brian and Holly. It's like he just snapped and picked a random target. The parking lot's security cam caught the whole thing, so Brian and Holly weren't charged. Defense from imminent harm. And now they're here. A pair of magnets for unexplained violence."

Kendra's holding another cigarette she can't remember lighting. She stubs it in the jelly of a half-eaten Danish. The pastry bag survived the damage to her truck. Out of everything tonight, it's the only thing she's rescued.

"You still think I worry too much?" Kendra asks.

"Is that why you called? You want my permission?"

"I can't get ahead of this. I can't begin explaining it."

"Nobody explained why the man attacked Brian. Nobody explained why I lost a breast to cancer. You'll kill yourself thinking too hard about why."

"I'm stuck on *how the hell* and *what the fuck*," Kendra says. "Of course I'm gonna sweat whatever comes next when nothing is predictable and nothing makes sense. Aren't you ever scared you'll lose your other breast?"

"Being scared beforehand didn't save the first one. But I get it," Cookie says. "Worry all you want. Just try not to give yourself a heart attack about it."

"An aneurysm feels more likely," Kendra says. "Now I'm back to chasing Brian, and I can't find Becky."

"Holly," Cookie says.

"Holly. Right. Jesus."

"Maybe you'll get lucky and find the Skylars, too."

"Ha," Kendra says. "You're saying I should look on the

bright side because I might stumble on a pair of frozen bodies."

"I'm saying you could stumble on an answer to a problem. Whatever comes next isn't always bad."

"Is my pessimism as annoying as your optimism?"

"Yes," Cookie says. "But I'm the one who's right."

"Thanks for talking to me, Cook. On a night this bad, I'm grateful you're my friend."

"On a night this bad, I'm grateful you're the sheriff."

They each say goodbye, and Kendra ends the call. Her mind has sharpened up, partly from the nicotine, but mostly from the clarity of talking things through. For hours, she's been moving in a haze of self-pity. Now she's heard herself complain and her attitude disgusts her, like the Danish with the cigarette stabbed in the jelly.

Kendra feels anger—at herself and at the blizzard—and it's anger she can work with. Anger she can use.

She rolls her window down, chucks the pastry in the snow, and drives away, hardened with a sharp new edge.

She hasn't gone far when the dispatcher relays details of a 911 call.

Sally Denver saw an unknown woman near her house. The woman needed help, she said, and vanished in the storm. Kendra hits the lights and speeds toward the Denvers' house. Sally's had delusions ever since her accident—brain damage, awful thing, she's never been the same—but Kendra just *knows*.

Sally saw Holly.

Chapter 30

Picking up the Skylars had been so easy.

Her with the ankle cast, eager for a lift. Him with the young man's confidence, unafraid of strangers. Snowfall obscuring everything around them. It had been less than one minute from the offer of a ride to Mitch and Becky Skylar getting in the truck.

Hell of a night. Glad to help. Let the lady have the seat . . . you can squeeze in between us. If you want, I'll let you fiddle with the plow once we're rolling. What're your names? Where you staying? Are you here with friends or family? I'm Tanner. Good to meet you.

Everything unfolded just as he'd imagined. Exactly as he'd planned it in his head a thousand times.

Tanner had once read that Michael Phelps visualized each moment of an Olympic swim—every night before he slept, every morning when he woke—so he never had to think when he really hit the water. What did Phelps like more: dreaming it or doing it? Maybe in the end, it all felt the same, so the swim was like a dream and the dream turned real.

Honeymoon. Congrats. Just the two of you alone. Shit, this stupid blade. Apologies for swearing. The plow isn't answering controls like it should. It ought to be . . . forget it. I've got to stop the truck and reset the console. Sorry for the holdup. Only take a minute. Do me a favor? Help me out and watch the angle of the blade. Keep your eyes on it close and tell me what it does.

They turned away from him and watched the blade, as diligent as children. Becky near the passenger door. Mitch next to Tanner. He pressed the stun gun to Mitch's neck for five Mississippis. He had to press hard when Mitch jerked away, spasming and grunting and astonished by the pain. It wasn't like the movies—it didn't knock him out—but it slumped him to the floor for a few crucial seconds.

Becky looked confused before she looked afraid. He punched her in the face hard enough to daze her. Blood gushed instantly from both of Becky's nostrils. Then he grabbed Mitch's hair and pulled out the knife. Mitch didn't fight. His eyes showed fear. So did Becky's when she saw the blade under Mitch's chin.

She did as she was told, dribbling blood and crying. Took the heavy-duty zip ties out of the glove box. Secured her husband's wrists behind his back. Then his ankles. Tied her own ankles, turned toward the door, held her wrists out behind her, let herself be bound.

Once the two of them were zipped, Tanner held up the knife, showing all seven inches of the well-honed blade. He told them not to move or one of them would die. He didn't say which. It was better if they wondered. They didn't move or talk. Both of them were trembling. He assured them that he didn't want to hurt them any worse. He told them it was all about money, nothing more, except he didn't say *how* it was all about money. Kept them guessing. Kept them hopeful they'd be fine if they behaved.

He swayed them with his words. He changed them with his eyes. They looked at him the way Mrs. Denver looked at Chuck. Small. Apologetic. Under his control. As if he'd conjured them from memory or shaped them from a dream.

Prior to the Skylars, all he did was dream. Dreaming was enough until it led to real planning, and planning was enough until it led to preparation. Preparation led to test drives all last winter. When he came upon the Skylars, the scene was so ideal, he'd have sworn the whole blizzard had arrived just for him.

Now he relishes the memory. The night it turned real. He's played back the details innumerable times, but it's been forty-eight days since he had them in the truck. Forty-eight days of wanting it again. Imagine Michael Phelps going months out of water. He'd probably want to kill himself. He'd probably go insane.

Tanner needs another tourist. He has another storm. But he's been driving around for hours and his time is running out. It makes him jittery and sick from his balls to his brain.

And he *had* one. He got her in the cab, nice and easy, but he lost her when he stopped to help Mrs. Denver. She was perfect, and her boyfriend was out there, too . . . and she was hiding from the sheriff. Obviously desperate. Why would she have taken off? What was his mistake? He'd radiated small-town helpfulness and charm, and yet instead of glowing back at him and following his lead, she'd fled as if believing he was something else entirely.

He hasn't found an isolated tourist ever since. He's had to plow the streets in the populated areas, but now he's back to looping through the darker, outer roads. All he needs is someone drunk. Someone lost. Someone cold.

He scrapes through the snow, minute after minute, saying, "Look, look, look," and, "See, see, see."

Chapter 31

Holly's dangerously cold.

Until now, her transformations left her warm and reinvigorated, as if her body had miraculously blazed back to life. But getting frozen in a block of ice was altogether different. She was cold when she escaped, and she's only gotten colder. Her bones hurt. Her toes, ears, and fingertips are numb. She's damp inside her clothes and raw where she's exposed. She's full of wild, nervous energy but doesn't feel strong, like a racecar revving with the wrong kind of gas.

Main Street is startlingly bright after the darker road that brought her here. Endless flakes of snow flutter and tumble in the light, concealing most of the parked cars and facades but giving the space a vast, almost daylit glow. She senses lots of people in the buildings all around her. It makes her feel locked outside. On her own.

She needs to find Brian, and she doesn't have long. Never mind triggers, memories, and fears . . . the physical stress alone might turn her into a monster. Holly shivers hard and clamps down harder. She walks toward a bar, craving whiskey and warmth, but when she pauses at the window and looks inside, there are too many bodies and way too many eyes. It's an alternate reality of normal, buzzy people—a whole other world just beyond the glass.

She makes herself walk, takes out her phone, and texts Brian the name of the bar. She's been texting her location intermittently as she goes. Intersection of Greenlawn and Chestnut. Corner of Chestnut and Main. Winterware Gifts. The Peppercorn Pub. They're breadcrumbs for Brian if he changes into himself again and has a chance of finding her, whatever shape she's in. All she knows of *his* location is a generalized "Main Street." She might as well be searching in a mile-wide snow globe.

Sideways snow whips up the block. Holly keeps trudging—what else is there to do?—until a long, sharp gust scissors through her coat. She's right beside a chocolate shop. It's closed until tomorrow. She ducks inside the front door's archway for shelter. Her stomach churns and puckers at a passing whiff of restaurant food. She's thirsty, too. Her body feels fragile and depleted. She sits on the step and eats a handful of snow. It hits a filling in her tooth like a quick metal chisel.

Hypothermia is possible. Frostbite, too.

Get up, she thinks.

Why?

Get up before you can't.

COOKIE STANDS AT the front window of the diner and watches the blizzard. Always changing, never changing. Mesmerizing motion. Now and then, the snow parts and she can see across the street, and during one of those gaps, she sees a woman walking.

Nothing strange, Cookie thinks . . . but her antennae

start to quiver when the woman takes shelter under the chocolatier's arch. Everyone in Pinebuck either lives here or has a room for the night, and there are plenty of open bars where she could warm herself up. Unless, of course, she's trying to avoid other people.

The woman sits and eats snow. Maybe drunk, Cookie thinks. Maybe she's been fighting with a boyfriend or girlfriend. Or maybe it's the woman Kendra needs to find. The odds aren't ridiculous in such a small village. A woman on her own, hiding out, eating snow—Holly Byrne or not, Cookie can't let her go.

She hustles back behind the counter, tears open a packet, pours powder into a paper cup, and adds hot water. Stirs it. Snaps a lid on. Thirty seconds later, she's opening the diner door.

Cookie's lived in Pinebuck for so long, she's more or less impervious to windblown snow and doesn't even clench at the hard-driven cold. She props the door with one hand and holds the cup with the other.

"Hello!" she yells.

The snow makes the woman briefly disappear, but several seconds later, she's visible again. She's standing now, still inside the chocolatier's arch, with her neck craned forward to see who's calling.

"Help me out?" Cookie says.

The woman doesn't answer. She glances side to side as if to say, *Me?*

Cookie lifts the cup and says, "Free hot cocoa! I'm closing up and don't believe in throwing things out."

"That's okay," the woman says.

"I'll add a splash of bourbon if you take it off my hands.

Just promise me you'll write a good review of Cookie's Diner."

The woman hesitates. She isn't a deer in headlights—just an ordinary deer, with unknown thoughts, staring at a person offering a treat. Instead of answering again, she starts to walk away.

Cookie grinds snow into the treads of her shoe and squeaks her sole loudly on the slick diner floor. She throws down the cup and makes herself fall. She means to make a show of it but slips too far, and when she really hits the floor, it genuinely hurts. She keeps the diner door partly open with her foot, and reaches with her hand to clatter a chair onto its side.

Cookie hams it up with an overlong wail.

Twenty seconds later, the woman reappears.

HOLLY HEARS THE squeak, the clatter, and the wail. When she turns around, the diner woman isn't at the door. Instead, Holly sees her foot lying on the threshold. The door's propped open and the foot isn't moving. The woman must have slipped, and she must have fallen hard for Holly to have heard it through the steady rush of wind. She might have really hurt herself.

Shit, Holly thinks.

She jogs across the street, looks inside the diner, and finds the woman on her side in a mess of splattered cocoa. A chair is knocked down, as if she grabbed it when she slipped.

"Are you all right?" Holly asks.

"Oh!" the woman says. She rolls onto her back and reaches out. "Help me up?"

Holly takes her hand and lifts her to her feet. The door falls shut and suddenly it's quiet. The snowflakes that followed Holly inside briefly hover, then begin to settle softly on the tables and the floor. The woman keeps a grip on Holly's arm for support. A sweet smell of chocolate wafts up between them.

"Thanks," the woman says. "Talk about embarrassing!"

"Did you hit your head?"

"Maybe. I don't think so. The pain just stunned me and I didn't want to move."

"Can you walk?"

"Ohhh, my hip. I don't trust myself yet. Will you walk me to the counter?"

Holly guides her over. The woman limps slowly down the length of the diner, holding Holly's arm until they finally reach the end. She takes a deep breath, stands on her own, and hobbles behind the counter like she's opening for business.

"Thanks again," the woman says, laughing at herself.

"You're sure you're all right?"

"I'll be bruised until July, but I'll probably survive."

Holly nods. "I need to go."

"Nuh-uh-uh. Now you *have* to take cocoa with a little splash of bourbon. Unless I'm keeping you from huddling on the street in a blizzard."

I look suspicious, Holly thinks . . . but she doesn't want to leave. A drink. A little kindness. Shelter from the cold. She feels herself relaxing and surrendering a little. She also knows she'll look more suspicious if she bolts. The woman puts a bourbon hot cocoa on the counter. Holly sits and takes a sip. The sugar hits her tongue, the liquor warms her throat, and she settles on the stool as if she's been there for hours.

"I'm Cookie," says the woman.

"I'm Jane," Holly says.

"I haven't seen you here before. You ought to come back for breakfast. We'll be open bright and early."

Holly nods politely and shivers with her cup. She feels as if she's thawing fast enough to crumble. Cookie asks her where she's staying, and she has to tell the truth, because she can't recall the names of other real places.

"Have you been here long?"

"Just tonight," Holly says.

"Here with family?"

"With my boyfriend."

"What are you doing out alone? Sorry," Cookie says with an upfront smile. "I'd say I'm being chatty, but I'm really being nosy. You don't have to answer."

Which means, Holly knows, she'd better answer quick. She takes an overlong gulp to the bottom of the cup, and the drink is too hot all the way down. Holly gestures to the bourbon on the shelf behind the counter.

"How much for another splash?"

Cookie waves her off, grabs the bottle, and tips it over the cup. Three or four fingers. Quite the extra splash.

"Thanks," Holly says. "My boyfriend's back in our room. He didn't feel like wandering the village in a storm."

"But you did?"

Holly takes a sip and pauses for effect. "Can I ask you a crazy question without you thinking I'm crazy?"

Cookie laughs and says, "Shoot."

"I was reading online when I was planning for the trip

and came across some really strange stuff about the village," Holly lies. "Are there any local legends or mysteries in Pinebuck? New Jersey has the Jersey Devil. Minnesota has the wendigo . . ."

"You're asking if the village has its own special monster?"

"You said you wouldn't call me crazy."

"I only said *shoot.*" Cookie watches her intently for a bit too long. "I've gotten much weirder questions from much weirder people. Doesn't bother me at all. What bothers me," she says, "is being treated like a dope."

Holly leans back with an expression like, "What?"

"You're out at night alone, eating snow in a doorway, and I'm supposed to believe you're looking for the abominable snowman. I don't mean to pry, but you aren't being honest. You look like a woman who got herself in trouble."

Holly doesn't answer. She sees the better play. Having lied very boldly, she can lie very plainly, and the plainer lie will sound like a reasonable fact. As long as Cookie thinks she really pried it out.

"Maybe you got involved with somebody you shouldn't have? Happens all the time in a place full of strangers."

"No," Holly says. "Nothing like that."

"Something else, then?"

"No—"

"*Damn it,*" Cookie says.

Holly's startled off her game. She's been staring at the bourbon in the bottom of her cup, and when she looks up to understand the outburst of anger, she sees that Cookie's gaze is focused outside. But there's so much snow blowing past the window, Holly can't see whatever set her off.

"Duck down and get beside me," Cookie says. "Do it quick."

She says it with enough alarm that Holly drops off her stool, makes her way around, and squats next to Cookie on the hidden side of the counter.

"The deputy's across the street," Cookie says. "They're patrolling nonstop, up and down Main."

Holly knows she overreacted when she crawled behind the counter. Cookie guessed she'd want to hide, and Holly proved her right. But as long as Cookie's ignorant of why she had to hide, there's still a chance to fool her with a reasonable story.

"Why am I hiding?" Holly says without getting up.

"That's what I've been asking you. And you still haven't answered."

Cookie bows her head and speaks toward the countertop, presumably to hide her moving lips from the deputy.

"Be straight with me," she says. "I'll know it if you lie. Have you done something bad? Not a little thing. *Bad.* I don't care if you sold a dime bag or shoplifted mittens, but if I'm going to help you out, I've got to know the truth."

The pressure in the air feels dangerously wrong, as if the room might implode with an inrush of snow. Holly feels the bourbon rising from her stomach—not quite vomit but close enough to taste. Her head goes swimmy and her eyesight warps.

"See how my coat is inside out?"

"I noticed," Cookie says.

Holly extends her wrists to show the blood around the cuffs.

"A guy harassed me in a bar. I kind of broke his nose. He was drunk and fell on top of me and bled all over my coat. I didn't mean to hit him that hard, but he deserved it."

Cookie squints at her and says, "The drunk ones often do. So then he blubbered to the cops?"

"I left before they came and flipped my coat to hide the blood."

"And your boyfriend?"

"We had an argument tonight. I left him in our room and went to drink it off."

"A scuffle in a bar," Cookie says. "I can live with that. You're telling me the truth?"

"I'm telling you the truth. Is the deputy still out there?"

Holly can't see the window from underneath the counter, so she watches Cookie's eyes searching outside. Ten long seconds. Nothing. No reaction.

Finally Cookie mumbles, "There he is again. He's waving."

Cookie waves back, but it's more of a salute, as if to say: *I see you. On your way now. Go.*

"Maybe we'll get lucky . . ." Cookie says. "Nope, he's coming."

Holly gets a heat rush all through her body. Her legs feel spring-loaded. The space behind the counter isn't deep enough for hiding if the cop walks in and pulls up a seat.

"Is there a back way out?"

"Blocked," Cookie says.

"Women's room?"

"There's only one bathroom here. But the cooler ought to work. He won't look there."

Cookie steps around her, walks to the far end of the

counter, and opens up the walk-in cooler on the right. The door is heavy duty with an old, dull skin of pockmarked metal. Cookie waves her over, walks into the cooler, and reemerges with a big plastic bucket in her arms. Holly crawls past her and continues into the cooler. The space is tall and narrow with stacked crates, boxes full of produce, and shelves packed with bottles and oversized cans. The floor is concrete. The ceiling has a pull string fixture with a lightbulb. Holly sees her breath. It's just above freezing.

Cookie thumps the bucket down and turns toward the cooler, acting like she's simply getting prepped for the morning.

"I'll get rid of him," she says. "Five minutes tops."

Cookie shuts the door with an energetic slam.

She wasn't limping, Holly thinks. *Even with a big, heavy bucket in her hand.*

But it's too late now to make a different choice. She has to stay inside in case there really is a deputy. Holly cups her ear against the cold metal door, hoping for a hint of muffled conversation, but all she really hears is the motor of the cooler. She walks through the whole interaction in her head, and it's impossible to know who played whom.

You're paranoid, she thinks. *Give it five minutes.*

Holly gives it ten.

She's jittery and cold and angry at herself, and she decides to crack the door and take a peek outside. There ought to be a button to release the outer latch. Instead, there's just a hole where the button used to be, and the hole's plugged tight with a flush piece of metal. She pushes on the door. Is it locked or only stuck?

She pushes on it harder. It's definitely locked.

Either Cookie's with a cop and can't let her out, or Cookie isn't with a cop and *hasn't* let her out. No matter what, pounding on the door won't help. But she needs to find Brian; she's running out of time, and her thoughts start fritzing with the onset of panic. She's powerless. The cooler makes her badly claustrophobic. She remembers being frozen like a wide-awake cadaver, wanting more than anything to break herself free.

Holly checks her phone. The signal strength is down to one little bar. She does a Google search and waits half a minute for results, and then she taps on the number and the call goes through.

WHEN COOKIE TALKED to Kendra thirty minutes earlier, she wouldn't have ruled out the possibility of spotting Holly Byrne. But she never would have guessed she'd trap her in the cooler. Assuming she's correct and has the right person.

She calls Kendra's cell instead of dialing the station. The call goes to voicemail.

"Get over here quick," Cookie says. "I think I have your girl."

She stands near the window and waits for Kendra's truck. Her thoughts wander far beyond the storm outside the diner to the broader, darker blizzard all around the village.

She thinks about Vance. Cookie always liked him, peculiar as he was, with his big metal sculptures and obsessive fixations. Always building something new and planning for the future. Often snagging on the past and scared of what was coming. When he woke up this morning, he couldn't have predicted he'd be dead inside his trailer with his arm ripped off.

She was chilled when Kendra told her, and she's chilled right now. For all her talk of shrugging off imaginary threats, Cookie's not immune to trouble in the flesh. How could ordinary tourists freeze an arm, wreck a shed, and obliterate a truck from the inside out?

She doesn't believe in monsters but they keep coming up. The woman in the cooler mentioned local legends, and Kendra said that several different tourists saw a creature. Cookie wonders if a lot of different people are involved. Maybe it's a hoax. The *creation* of a legend. A handful of jokers conjure up a monster, tell their stories online, and wait for Hollywood to call. Only now they've lost control, people have gotten hurt, and the little game of make-believe has gotten awfully real.

The diner phone rings.

Cookie walks behind the counter, picks it up, and says, "Kendra?"

"No," a voice says. "It's me inside the cooler. Is it safe to come out? Or was there never any cop?"

The connection's bad, and fragments of her words garble out, but Holly's clear enough to understand. Cookie takes a breath.

"I apologize for lying. The sheriff wants to talk to you."

"It was just a little bar fight. I'm sure the guy's fine."

"It's Holly, right? Listen. There's been trouble here tonight that needs sorting out. The sheriff found your boyfriend. She's coming here now. I know it's cold in there. I promise you'll be out very soon."

"You can't *do* this," Holly says, sounding volatile and

fierce. "This is crazy. It's illegal. You realize I could sue? I could even press charges."

"I'm sorry," Cookie says. "Bundle up and hang tight for just a little longer. We can hash this out together with the sheriff."

Cookie hangs up and walks to the end of the counter. Holly pounds on the door, but the broken latch holds. She's yelling now, loud enough to hear outside the cooler. Mostly stuff like "Let me out!" and "You don't know what you're doing!" Answering her shouts will only make it worse, so Cookie returns to the front of the diner, hoping Kendra's truck will finally appear.

Holly falls silent. No more banging. No more yelling.

The stillness brings an unfamiliar tension to the room, like an overstressed cable threatening to snap. Cookie gazes outside until her eyes lose focus. Her thoughts seem to vibrate hard enough to hum. She tells herself it's nothing, but the pressure keeps changing and the blizzard looks fierce. Something's very, very wrong.

The hum inside her head rises to a roar, merging with the rush of the storm's growing wind. It presses on the window, and presses on her skull, until it feels as if the diner and her brain will implode. Cookie backs away, staring at the whiteout. The front door groans. The panes creak and crackle.

A window explodes and the storm bursts in, filling up the room with snow and shattered glass. Like a bloom. Like a cloud that's beginning to condense but can't quite hold a distinguishable shape. Cookie staggers backward and knocks over a stool. She reaches the end of the counter, squinting at the snow as it masses, and intensifies, and seems to move toward her. It's formless but it's *more* than ordinary snow.

She doesn't think *Monster*, but she does think *Hide*.

Cookie fights the wind to open the cooler door. The force shoves her in with a blast of wild snow, shattering the lightbulb and throwing her down between the buckets and the crates. The door slams shut and locks her in the cooler. Everything is quiet and absolutely dark.

Cookie sits back against the cold metal door. The air seems to clear. Her breath begins to settle. Incoherent thoughts start turning into words, but her voice feels weirdly disconnected from her body.

"The storm," she says to Holly. "That was . . . I don't know. We're safe. Kendra's coming." She laughs to herself. "Relax. We're gonna just relax. I'll call her. I should call again. She'll come and get us out."

She extends one leg to take her phone from her pocket. Her foot touches something unfamiliar in the dark. Not a bucket or a boot. Almost like a mass of hardpacked snow—solid at the core but softer on the surface. She pulls her foot away and turns on her phone, illuminating her hands and the glitter in the air.

And then she looks up and can't believe what's bearing down on her.

Chapter 32

When Chuck Denver opens the door, he looks like anyone getting a late-night house call from a cop. He's surprised and confused. Bristly as a porcupine.

"Sheriff . . . what the hell?"

"Hi, Chuck," Kendra says. "We got a call from Sally. What's happening tonight?"

"You got a call . . . shit. She called you? Did she really?"

"I'd better come inside."

"Seriously?" he says. "I mean, of course. Come in, I'm sorry."

Kendra steps inside, Chuck shuts the door, and suddenly the atmosphere is hot and weirdly quiet. He leads her into the living room. Sally's on the couch, watching Chuck and Kendra with a juvenile air of nervousness or guilt.

"Hi, Sally," Kendra says with a smile. "I'm here about your call. Want to tell me what you saw and who you talked to tonight?"

Sally frowns at her lap, seeming hesitant to answer. Chuck sits beside her, holds her hand, and takes the lead.

"You called when I was making popcorn?"

"Are you mad?" Sally asks.

"No," Chuck says. "I only wish you'd told me."

Eventually, she loosens up and chatters out her story. Her memory is sharp and oddly vague in equal measure. She gives a detailed description of the woman she claims to have seen, but she can't say exactly how the woman needed help.

When Sally's done talking, Kendra thanks her for the call and says, "You did the right thing."

Chuck provides his own version of the story and finishes with Tanner bringing Sally home.

"What did Tanner say about the woman outside?"

"He didn't see a woman. I thought she made it up." Chuck pauses with a grimace that catches Kendra's eye. "Weird guy," he finally says. "I don't mean to sound ungrateful."

"But?" Kendra prompts.

Chuck leads her to the foyer, out of Sally's earshot.

"Tanner said I ought to tie her up. He wasn't joking. You know the way he smiles? I don't know . . . he pissed me off. Forget it. I've been wound really tight all week."

Kendra can't imagine how Chuck doesn't crack. He looks exhausted from the strain of looking after Sally. From her wandering and mood swings and unpredictability. From parenting a woman who's supposed to be his partner.

He says, "I'm sorry for the false alarm."

"Actually," Kendra says, "the woman Sally talked about matches the description of somebody I'm looking for."

Chuck looks thrown. "She didn't make it up? I've been thinking . . . never mind."

"What?" Kendra asks.

"I guess I thought maybe she was talking about herself. Like part of her, you know—the Sally that she used to be—might have woken up and seen herself in trouble."

False hope, Kendra thinks. *That's how he doesn't crack. He honestly believes Sally might recover.* She expects to see him crumple at the loss of his delusion. Instead, he seems to naturally accept the cold facts, as if acceptance is another way the man won't crack.

Kendra says she'll keep him posted just to ease his mind, and then her thoughts snap back to everything they've told her.

"What time was Tanner here?" she asks.

His answer makes her squint and concentrate hard.

If the Denvers' accounts are accurate, Holly was here only minutes after Kendra spoke with Tanner in the road and asked him to report anything suspicious . . . specifically a tourist with blood on her coat. Which means he must have picked her up *immediately* after or Holly had been with him in the plow the whole time.

Either way, Kendra thinks, Tanner kept her in the dark.

Chapter 33

Two adorable children shriek at Brian's face.

He's right outside their house, way too close to their bedroom window. A girl and a boy, probably siblings, somewhere in the ballpark of five years old. The boy shrieks first and the girl joins in. They must have heard Brian making noise as the monster, looked outside, and seen him in the snow—a boogeyman watching from a few feet away.

Their bedroom is dim, with only a night-light glowing, but a hall beyond their door is suddenly illuminated, lighting Brian's face outside the window. The kids jump back and scramble to the hall, and Brian runs away before the parents show up.

He doesn't stop for five minutes, long enough to hope that no one's followed his trail. His surroundings are obscured by the densely blown flakes, and even what he sees has a vague, wintry sameness. Drifts. White expanses. Snow-capped houses. He shelters in the lee of a tarp-covered boat—peculiar near a mountain home—and feels as lost as if he really were floating in the sea.

Last he remembers, he was kicking Brock's chest. He'd braced himself firmly on the seat, waited for Brock to lean inside, and shoved with his boot as forcefully as possible. Brock had looked surprised, having probably expected Brian to be passive, and then he'd fallen out of the truck and landed on the ground.

Brian hopes Brock was able to escape. He hopes the sheriff did, too.

He tried not to hurt them but he still feels guilty. The monster isn't *him*—it's more like a symptom—but it's difficult to tell himself apart from the damage. At a certain point, anyone who can't control their illness has to wonder if they're terrible for everyone around them.

He wishes he could vanish. Shut his eyes. Disappear. Feel the whiteout again, tumble through oblivion, and simply blank out instead of waking up. But he has to keep trying, and he has to find Holly, so he takes out his phone and plays her latest message.

Holly says riding out the storm won't work. When the blizzard had a lull, she was frozen in the monster. *It was awful,* Holly tells him. *Godfuckingawful.* He's struck by the fear and desperation in her voice—almost reassured that they're feeling this together, but rattled by the cracks appearing in her armor.

Brian thinks back, remembering the lull when Brock finally tackled him and pinned him to the ground. It should have made him change like any other trigger, but he hadn't transformed when the snow stopped falling. The ending of the storm really *will* be the end. One of them will live while the other one dies. Or freezes, Holly says. Lost and out of reach.

When her voicemail is over, Brian reads her texts. Winterware Gifts. Peppercorn Pub. She's been telling him exactly where she's gone along the way. Her final text is only one word.

Chocolatier.

He checks the radar and sees they're in a final, strong band before the storm winds down. The forecast estimates less than thirty minutes. Heavy snow, lighter snow, flurries . . . then it's over. He taps on a map, orients himself, and quickly makes his way to a semiplowed road. From there, he starts to run—burning lungs, burning legs—and doesn't slow down for over ten minutes. By the time he reaches Main Street, he's running on adrenaline and very little else. His head feels as fuzzy and chaotic as the blizzard.

Chocolatier—right or left? Brian goes left, following an instinct he doesn't have the energy or clarity to question. Of course she won't be there, but maybe there's a clue. Anything to point him in the next best direction. He's trying so hard to organize his thoughts, he walks right past the chocolatier's shop and doesn't pause until he notices the block feels darker. A streetlight is out on the opposite side of the road. Below it, through the snow and beyond the parked cars, there appears to be a diner. It's difficult to see but something looks wrong.

Brian walks across the street. There are no pedestrians or drivers anywhere in sight. Even if there were at this time of night, all they'd care about is hurrying to someplace warm. All the bars and eateries are farther down the street. Nothing's open nearby. He's totally alone.

The diner isn't lit. One of the plate glass windows is shattered inward. The door is open with its upper hinge snapped off the frame. Brian steps in, tentative and tense because Holly, as the monster, might be waiting inside. Everything congeals in his body like lead.

He crunches over glass and powder on the floor, moving back along the counter to a walk-in cooler. The snow is piled heavily in drifts against the door. He stands in front of it, with a dark passageway to the left and the counter to his right. When he holds up his phone, the screen is startlingly bright. The cooler door is locked, but the hinges look deformed, and the screws around the latch have almost come loose.

Holly's inside. He senses her. He *knows*. He doesn't understand why she hasn't burst out, because however strong the cooler door really might be, it doesn't seem strong enough to hold the monster in. Is it possible she changed and was able to control herself, trusting he would find her if she only stayed put?

"Holly?" Brian says.

He knocks on the door. There's a big thump back. The force rattles the latch and vibrates the frame. Something topples in the cooler and a growl starts to rise, ominous and rumbling. Brian backs up and fumbles with his phone. He drops it and the screen fractures on the floor. Its light goes out, the growl settles down, and the dark, cold quiet muffles in around him.

Brian steps forward. He kneels in the drift and lays his palms on the door with his face so close, his eyes can't focus.

Here we are again, he thinks. *It's always like this.*

Impossible to face each other. Difficult to speak. If it wasn't a metal door, it would be something else. Brian presses his forehead on the ice-cold metal. He wishes he could touch her. Holly's face. Holly's hand. He imagines he can smell her—not her perfume or soap, but Holly's own scent, coming from her skin and suffusing her clothes. He wishes he could hold her in a warm, safe place and honestly believe she's happy to be with him.

"I'm sorry," Brian says. "I've tried so hard to pull myself together, but I'm all fucked up. I just can't do it. There's something, I don't know . . . something wrong with me, I think. I love you, and I'm pretty sure you love me, too, but I feel so weak. I never have *fight.* I know you want to leave me. I should have let you go. You shouldn't have to try to save me all the time."

I hate myself, he thinks.

He grabs the cooler's latch.

I'm the problem, and the problem ought to disappear.

All he has to do is open the door. The monster might attack and kill him on the spot. Maybe if he's dead, everything will stop. Or maybe *he'll* become the monster one last time, and when the storm finally fades—soon, very soon—he'll be frozen, out of reach, in a lost block of ice. Either way, he thinks she'll be better off without him.

Brian stands up, resolutely numb, and kicks away the snow piled at the door. He grabs the frozen latch and braces for the pull. He isn't even scared. He's ready and relieved. One big tug and everything will end, and he won't have to live like a victim anymore.

LAST HOLLY KNEW, Cookie ran into the cooler. The door slammed shut and everything was blank.

Now she feels snow whirling off her body, blown as if her pores are generating wind and a thick, cold weight is flying off her skin. Her thoughts sharpen up faster than before. She knows she's in the cooler.

Where's Cookie? Did I hurt her?

She can barely see a thing in the wild, snowy dark. The cooler door is open and the diner's unlit, but there's just enough light coming from the street for Holly to perceive a few vague shapes. Toppled cans near the threshold. A corner of the countertop. Snow rushing fast onto something right in front of her.

It's Brian on his knees, slowly standing up. She can't see his face but she's positive it's him. He found her, and he's here, and now she's losing him again. She tried so hard to make it all stop, but no matter what she does, where she goes, or how she thinks, the monster keeps rampaging out of her control. She's denied it. She's avoided it. She's focused on dispelling it. Nothing makes the goddamned thing go away.

Instead of feeling rage, Holly feels soft. She's sick of always fighting and resisting and defending. She wishes they'd been given one clear minute—her and Brian, face-to-face—before the storm came between them.

She throws herself forward, hugs Brian tight, and holds him while the snow whirlwinds around them. She's terrified and trembling in the storm's cold roar. Whatever happens now, she won't let him go, and she holds Brian close and surrenders to the storm. Maybe they'll survive. Maybe they'll be frozen. Their heads squeeze together in the onslaught of snow, and right before the whiteout smothers them again, she feels Brian's breath mingling with her own.

Chapter 34

ONE YEAR EARLIER
The Bad Date

A year ago, Holly and Brian focus on the present. They finish up their workdays and arrive at their apartment within twenty minutes of each other. They kiss hello, take turns showering, and put on snazzier clothes.

They get in Brian's car. Each of them relaxes into customary roles. He's comfortable behind the wheel. She's happy as a passenger. Brian parks in a lot two blocks away from their favorite restaurant, a cozy place with mediocre food but plenty of sentimental value. They turn off their phones, drink G&Ts, and eat too many appetizers. Their conversation expands into loose, buzzy tangents, going anywhere and everywhere, with no real goal except to talk and unwind and let their thoughts swirl together. Brian doesn't talk about puppies or vacations. Holly doesn't hint that their relationship's in trouble.

Snow starts falling, but Brian doesn't worry. He's never been afraid of bad-weather driving. When they finish eating and drinking, Holly uses the restroom while Brian walks to the parking lot so he can dust off the car, drive back, and pick her up. She appreciates his chivalry but then she thinks twice, deciding she should follow him and catch him at the car.

Brian walks the two blocks and enters the parking lot alone, unaware that Holly is jogging in the snow, only one minute behind him. He grabs a brush from the backseat and sweeps off the windshield. The parking lot is quiet and very well-lit. No one else is pulling in or cleaning off their car.

A man enters the northwest corner of the lot. He's skinny, white, and thirtyish. His short, dark hair is oddly matted from the snow. He wears sneakers, sweatpants, and an open denim jacket, his chest bare underneath. He doesn't seem affected by the cold. He's carrying a brick. The brick is burnt clay with fresh, crisp edges.

Brian's happy and oblivious. He clears off the car, opens the back, and drops the brush onto the floor. The man walks toward him, silent in the snow, leaving moonwalk prints in a long, straight line, as if he hasn't once wavered since emerging from the dark.

Brian shuts the door and sees the man behind him, drippy and distorted in the window reflection. He spins around, immediately sensing he's in danger. They're twenty feet apart. The man's face is neither blank nor particularly crazed. It's a spotlight, startling but hard to look away from. Brian can't process everything he sees. Messy hair, naked chest . . . Is he carrying a *brick*?

The man keeps coming, slow enough that Brian could react somehow. He could jump inside the car, lock the door, and drive away. He could raise his hands to fight. He could run. He could shout. Only days ago, threatened by a stranger in the liquor store, confidence had grown like voltage in his body. Now his brain short-circuits, and his limbs won't move, until there's nothing left to do but suffer the attack.

At the very last moment, Brian turns and cowers, slipping in the snow he brushed off the car. The man swings the brick. It hits the back of Brian's head, right below the crown, and opens up a cut that immediately bleeds. He slumps against the car, sliding down the door until he's kneeling on the ground. It's pure dumb luck when Brian falls sideways and dodges—by an inch—a second heavy blow.

The brick hits the car instead of Brian's head, and the impact knocks it from the man's clenched hand. Instead of picking it up again, he shoves Brian down and holds him on the ground. He doesn't say a word. He claws Brian's face, scratching at his cheeks and prying at his mouth, and then he spits in Brian's eyes like he's hissing out venom.

Brian squirms beneath him but he can't get free. He's dazed and his arms feel rubbery and weak. The man starts reaching one-handed for the brick, pawing through the snow near the car's front wheel.

Right before he finds it, Holly drags him off Brian. They fall down together in a tangle in the snow. The man turns even more feral than before. He thrashes on the ground and knocks Holly away, and then he springs up, pounces on her chest, and wrestles with her arms to pin her down tight. Holly kicks and strains. She tries to butt him with her head.

Brian lies bleeding, watching Holly fight.

The man's denim jacket slips off his shoulders, and his bare upper torso is hideously pale. His sleeves bind him up.

Holly manages to flip him. Now the man is on his back with Holly on top. He's electrically enraged and squeezing at her throat.

Holly shoves his face. His head bumps the blacktop, hard enough to stun him. She grabs him by the hair and bangs down harder. Over and again, thump after thump. His head hits the ground until his neck looks elastic, his eyes go funny, and his body falls limp. Eventually his skull sounds like a sponge. Holly doesn't stop. It's possible she can't. She picks up his head and smacks it down repeatedly, way past the point of needing to subdue him. His blood pools wider in the underlying crystals, like raspberry syrup darkening a snow cone. It's slippery on her hands. Hot and steamy in her nose.

She finally slows down and lets his head go, because there's nothing left to take away and little left to hold.

The man doesn't move.

Brian sees the whole thing, semiconscious near the car, while his own wounded head keeps bleeding in the snow. Holly crawls toward him, settles at his side, and leans above him with the flurries falling past her hair. The shadow of her head darkens Brian's face. She keeps pressure on his wound and calls 911. He fades in and out, increasingly confused.

"I'm here," she says. "I'm right here. I'm with you now. I'm here."

HOLLY AND BRIAN were inseparable for weeks after that. The hospital, the cops, the worried friends and relatives—they had to stick together to survive the whole circus and to slowly and emphatically reclaim a normal life.

Eventually they did, but *normal* felt peculiar.

A patch of Brian's hair had been shaved to stitch the wound, and he was constantly compelled to rub the growing stubble. The spot became a cowlick, maybe from the scar, and maybe from his habit of touching it compulsively.

He had nightmares that often left him anxious all day, and when he didn't have nightmares or didn't feel afraid, he could suddenly be startled by his carefree mood, as if he'd caught himself obliviously strolling near a cliff.

Happiness was dangerous. He had to keep his guard up. He watched for threats and problems and began to see them everywhere. But much of what he did to minimize trouble had the opposite effect and made things worse.

He dodged conflicts at work, even when an argument was justified and safe, and found himself steamrolled by self-assured colleagues.

He risked more accidents with overcareful driving—hesitating at intersections, merging too timidly, and slowing down abruptly when a light turned yellow.

He shied away from strangers. First the iffy ones. Then everyone.

He avoided their favorite restaurant, along with the parking lot two blocks away, until the whole surrounding neighborhood became a black hole.

He exercised to lift his mood but pushed too hard with runs and heavy lifts, which left him worn out and weaker than before.

He started therapy, which made him think he had to be on Zoloft, and Zoloft made him question if he had to be in therapy. He probably needed both but didn't trust either.

He saw them as a pair of overlapping Band-Aids and worried something terrible was festering beneath them.

Solitude unnerved him, so he clung to Holly. Then he felt more adrift whenever she was gone.

Holly also shifted to a new, peculiar normal. She often forgot to eat during the early weeks of Brian's recovery, but when her hunger roared back, her appetite changed. She reached for vegetables and fruits and protein powder, telling herself she wanted to be healthier and leaner. Her revulsion at the sight of any meat was unacknowledged.

She dismissed her own nightmares as obvious and trite. What was there to say about a strong, recurring dream in which she smashed her own head into thick, bloody mush? How would chewing on *that* help her through a morning?

She developed strict habits and focused on to-do lists. With smarts and flexibility, her world could be controlled. And with every good routine, she accrued benefits until she almost stopped noticing when anything was wrong.

She advocated for herself at work, at times without need but always with success, and rarely wondered if her wins clipped her colleagues' wings.

She mastered parallel parking, taught herself basic plumbing, and kept an updated list of other skills to explore.

She was more outgoing and confident with strangers, especially the ones with egos to confront.

Now and then, after painting in her studio, she ate alone at the restaurant that used to be their favorite, determined to reclaim her affection for the place.

She exercised to boost her mood, training too hard with

high-intensity intervals, and pushed through her injuries with Tylenol and wraps.

She considered going into therapy, if only as a method of proactive self-defense . . . but so much in her life had its own good momentum. Better fitness. Growing skills. A promotion at her job. Would she genuinely benefit from dredging up trauma?

She already had Brian to remind her what had happened, and she found herself increasingly inclined to be away from him.

Together, they were tense. Together, they were lost.

Brian tried to hide his difficult emotions, aware that he was constantly afflicting her with need. More and more, he felt like her sniveling little brother, who wasn't quite safe without her supervision.

Holly tried to bottle *all* of her emotions, instinctively afraid they would suddenly explode. She felt like a killer in a friendly neighbor's skin.

When they talked about their days or talked about the future, they said the right things and wore their best faces as perfectly as robots who happened to be dating.

When they got around to sex, it was always a production. Often scheduled by Holly, or else it simply wouldn't happen. Often cut short by Brian's failure to perform. What little sex they did have was hardly worth the effort. They went through the motions and positions on cue, as if to imitate a porno both of them had seen and neither of them liked because of too much plot.

Everything was like that. Dinnertime. Daytrips. Even conversations had the feel of being scripted for disappointing roles they didn't want to play.

In the fall, they were edgy at the onset of cold. They felt the shorter days squeezing in around them. They saw each other differently in ways they wouldn't name and felt themselves paling and disfiguring in pain.

Winter bore down. The new year came.

And then they planned a trip to Pinebuck to see if they could change.

Chapter 35

Kendra fails to raise Tanner on the police truck's radio. She considers the possibility that Tanner is in danger . . . but her gut says no. He's somehow involved.

She drives around the darkened roads, chain-smoking and struggling to think in any clear direction. The snow stops falling and the night feels done. Except it isn't done. Nothing's been resolved or figured out, and if she doesn't act fast, everything tonight will be a shitstorm permanently frozen into place.

She checks her phone for the latest forecast and finds a voicemail from Cookie. Her phone must have rung. She simply hadn't heard it.

Kendra hits play. Four seconds, short and sweet.

"*Get over here quick. I think I have your girl.*"

Suddenly, the night explodes back to life. Kendra races to the diner, hoping Cookie's right and there's a chance, fucking finally, to turn things around.

She rolls onto Main Street. The village feels strangely and unnaturally subdued, as if the blizzard left everything and everyone concussed. She reaches the diner and parks in the shadow of a blown-out streetlight, knowing something's wrong before she even leaves the truck.

She steps outside and pauses at the curb, drawing her Glock and shining her flashlight on the dark diner with its shattered window, its twisted door. She holds them with her hands crossed at the wrists, so the barrel and the light aim together in the gloom.

"Cookie?" Kendra shouts.

No one answers. Nothing moves.

"Police! I'm coming in!"

She steps through the door and sweeps her light around the room. Toppled furniture and snow are strewn across the floor, and her boots crunch glass when she walks farther in. The booths look clear. She leans over the counter, scanning right to left, and finds only snow and additional debris.

"Police," she says again. "Show yourself. I'm armed."

She says the words primarily to break the heavy calm, because she isn't really scared of someone jumping out. Her fear has a deadness instead of an alertness. Her *senses* are alert . . . but only to discover something motionless. An aftermath. A horror past the flashlight beam.

No, she thinks repeatedly. *No, no, no.*

Her mind won't logically accept the scene around her. Where the evidence is pointing. Why her dread keeps growing. How her life might change if she discovers something awful and she's forced to acknowledge it instead of saying no.

She walks along the counter to the hallway in the back. Her light illuminates the corridor, revealing nothing between her and the restroom at the opposite end. The walk-in cooler is open nearby, but she isn't yet close enough to peek inside.

"Cook?" Kendra says. "It's me. Are you here?"

Her heart feels dangerously amped, beating too hard and slightly off-rhythm. The lack of sound or movement fills her with anxiety. She feels as if her lungs are full of cold tar. Her flashlight reflects off the open cooler door, showing dents and brutal scrapes on the inner metal surface. A mass of blown snow lays drifted near the entrance.

She makes herself move and shines her light through the door.

Furred with thick snow, the cooler's like a strange cave hollowed out of ice. All around the floor, the ceiling, and the walls, the snow is splashed and marred with ultravivid red.

A body's worth of blood. Pooled in hardened puddles. Stiffened into icicles. Welded to the walls in vicious spurts and splatters. As if a blood bomb violently exploded and immediately froze everywhere it burst.

Kendra's head swirls. The sight discombobulates her. Half a minute passes while her flashlight trembles and the scene's grisly details sharpen into focus. The metal shelves are mangled. Some are empty, some are crushed. Littered all about are dented cans, ruptured bags, and everything a well-stocked diner might refrigerate, from condiments and cheese to vegetables and eggs.

There's a lot of cold meat. Beef patties, bacon strips, sausages, and ham. Strewn amid the snow are bigger hunks of meat that she would associate more with a butcher than a diner. They're different shapes and sizes, only partially exposed. They all look fresh but frozen to the bone. Some of them are bare. Some have scraps of clothes.

Nestled in the back is a decapitated head. One of Cookie's eyes is open in the snow.

Kendra falls to her knees and vomits on the floor. The Danishes, the coffee—everything inside her. She jams her flashlight into a drift, grips the handle of her gun, and crawls from the cooler in a numb, woozy daze. She finds herself staring at a bottle on the floor. It's Cookie's favorite bourbon, lying on its side. Kendra pulls the cork and takes a big glug. Bourbon dribbles off her chin and burns down her throat.

She stands and throws the bottle at the diner's far wall. Broken glass scatters on a booth. It's not enough. She wants the diner and the whole fucking village to explode.

No: she wants a *target*. Not a wall. Not a booth.

She wants the person who's responsible to suffer for it all.

Chapter 36

Holly and Brian hold each other.

They're huddled in a mound of soft, loose snow that rises to their necks. Only their heads are visible. The storm is done. There's a whispery breeze and a trace of flurries, but otherwise the night is eerily serene. They each have a chin on the other's right shoulder, with their ears pressed together and their chests squeezed tight, so they're both staring off beyond the other's back.

Holly sees a vast dark landscape around them. A gently rolling field of pristine snow with a distant, shadowy edge . . . possibly the forest. She remembers grabbing Brian outside the cooler, but she can't remember getting here, wherever the hell they are. She doesn't feel his warmth but she does feel him breathing. He's alive. They're alive. They're finally together.

They slowly pull away, sloughing snow off their backs until they're far enough apart to see each other's faces. At first, they don't speak or even look surprised. It's almost too real, after everything they've been through, to find themselves quietly and calmly eye to eye. Holly starts trembling. Brian does, too. They shove away the snow until their legs are mostly free, and then they kneel close together again like two lost kids.

"We didn't freeze," Brian says.

"Not yet," Holly answers.

Their voices sound intimate and loud all at once, clear enough to hear a quarter mile off if anyone or anything were anywhere in sight. They're incredibly alone. Holly feels it in the old, primal corner of her brain that tells her being lost is close to being dead. The snow might have stopped, and the wind might have softened, but they're crashing from exhaustion and exposure to the cold.

"What happened?" Brian says.

"I held you when you changed."

"We both changed together?"

"I guess," Holly says. "The owner of the diner . . . was she dead? Did you see her?"

Brian shakes his head. "I only saw snow."

They stand and look together at the broad, empty landscape. A breeze blows serpentine snow along the surface, but otherwise the ground is uniformly smooth. Not a mark. Not a print. Like they floated from the sky. If she didn't know better, Holly might have thought they'd been here for hours, in a state of amnesia, while the storm erased every last trace of their arrival.

Brian looks dazed. "Was any of it real? Maybe when the car skidded off the road . . ."

"Look," Holly says. She unzips her coat and shows him the hidden blood. "From the old man's arm."

"It was real."

"It was real."

She wants to say something useful or insightful, but

her memories are scattershot, reality is fuzzed, and she can think of very little aside from being cold. They're suffering from shock, physically and mentally. She's almost grateful that her mind isn't functioning correctly and the horror of the night is partially a blank.

Holly looks at him and focuses intensely on his face.

"Jesus fucking Christ," she says. "I'm so glad you're here."

"We found each other."

"Yeah."

"We're together."

"We're alive."

It doesn't seem enough after what's happened. The monster's gone, at least for now. The storm has mostly passed. But they might as well be huddled in the parking lot again. They were together then, too, and slowly fell apart . . . and everything they did or failed to do led to *this*. At best, they've calmed the maelstrom enough to look around and wonder what the hell will happen to them next. At worst, people died for no good reason, and they're doomed to another year of swallowing the blood.

They hug again for a full minute in the dark. Holly cries as if her body knows more than she's aware of. Brian cries, too, for his own hidden reasons. Pretty soon, they're quaking from the penetrating cold, and they both pull away and reassess their surroundings. Now is not the time to make sense of what they've been through. All that matters now is immediate survival.

Holly checks her phone and the battery is finally dead. Brian left his phone shattered in the diner. It's a crapshoot, choosing which direction they should go. They're in the middle of a nondescript, several-acre field. With no memory of being the monster and no sense of time, it's impossible to know how far they might have come. The sky has partly cleared but it's hard to see the stars with the low, scrappy clouds racing overhead. Even if the north star were visible to help, they can't determine where they're standing in relation to the village.

They weigh their options based entirely on long-range clues. Two directions lead to woods that appear to grow hilly. Another looks ominously foggy in the distance in a way that makes them both irrationally scared. The last direction also leads to dim, wooded hills, but the bushes and the trees there are softer somehow. Subconsciously, that way feels promising and friendly. With nothing else to go on, they go on that alone.

They hike across the field in concentrated silence, driven by an unspoken need to press on, as if hesitating or pausing would freeze them on the spot. Holly doesn't think ahead and doesn't look back. They reach the tree line and find the woods thinner than expected, mostly birches and a smattering of tall, skinny pines, but the ground rises quickly to a much steeper angle, and they're panting after ten long minutes of the climb.

"Look," Brian says.

"What?"

"There's a light. Over there . . . like a pulse. Can you see it?"

Holly sees it. The pulse is yellow-orange, vague and intermittent but impossible to miss in the monochrome forest. It's hard to know exactly how far it really is, because it might be enormous or it might be very small.

They automatically and synchronously head toward the light.

"Radio tower?" Holly says. "A beacon on a building?"

"It's moving," Brian says. "It's probably a truck. Look, it's driving off. We'll never get there in time."

Instead of losing heart, they quicken up.

"If it's a truck," Holly says, "there's got to be a road."

Chapter 37

"Where do we go from here?" Deputy Fickett asks Kendra.

He sounds calmer than anticipated, having examined the walk-in cooler for himself and returned to her side at the middle of the counter. She expected him to stagger back and look for reassurance, but the grisly sight appears to have hardened his resolve. Fickett's solid on his feet, stands beside her like a peer, and has the deadpan intensity of someone in authority. His question doesn't flail. It aims for direction.

Another deputy is standing guard directly outside. Beyond him in the road, police trucks idle with their flashers turned off. The streetlight is dead. The diner's unlit. Keeping everything dark is the one sensible decision Kendra has made at this point. The whole catastrophe, for now, is hidden in the shadows.

The secret won't last. Fickett has already confirmed that help is en route from the department down in Hilldeclaire. Plus, the snow has stopped falling and the night is turning clear. In a few more hours, daylight will spread, and all will be exposed to a thousand-eye glare. The villagers. The tourists. Media and mayhem. News about Vance, Cookie, the damaged property and vehicles—including Kendra's own—and the two missing strangers nobody could catch will race around Pinebuck. Everyone will turn their attention to the sheriff. Residents, reporters, fellow cops, and out-of-towners will be clamoring for answers and arrests and explanations.

Kendra looks outside, envisioning the first light of morning and the unsuspecting patrons coming to the diner. First, they'll be annoyed it's closed. Later, they'll be horrified. The place will sit dormant for a year, maybe less, before reopening with someone else's name on the sign. Tourists won't know the difference. Even locals will accept it.

But Kendra can't imagine ever eating here again. Merely driving past the place will probably be difficult, flooding her with memories and visions—good and bad—of everything that's terribly, irrevocably lost. Even prior to tonight, there were places she avoided, like the spot on Jasper Lane where she last saw the Skylars, and everywhere she and Taz used to feel in love. Tomorrow, there'll be other locations on the list. The road beside the park, where her truck got demolished. The giant metal Christmas tree, standing like a monument to poor Vance Rickman.

But Cookie's will be worse than any of the others. The place she always visited for comfort and companionship. It hasn't fully hit her yet, but Kendra feels it coming like a storm with an incremental, neverending snowfall. They won't get to talk again. They won't share a meal. They'll never get together for another crap movie night.

Fickett seems to notice when she fights down a sob. She feels as if she's literally swallowing her tears, and her tears have the density of hot, gritty sand.

"I'm sorry," Fickett says. He puts a hand on her shoulder.

Kendra nods thanks and genuinely means it, but she stiffens up fast, and Fickett takes his hand away. She looks around the diner, trying to concentrate on details—an upside-down table, a shard of broken glass balanced on a napkin box—instead of feeling dazed by the broader disarray.

"This doesn't feel human," Fickett finally says. "It's like we're dealing with a monster."

"We are," Kendra says.

She sees a plastic squeeze bottle toppled on the counter. Dark maple syrup oozes from the mouth. Kendra stares as if the blob is actually a map.

"All night," Fickett says, "we've been answering emergency calls, chasing strangers, and navigating a blizzard. But the trouble keeps moving and the trouble keeps changing. I say we sit tight, regroup, and wait for backup. We're worn out and fried. Way past the redline."

"It's not my job to sit tight," Kendra says. "And you didn't get hired to wait around for backup."

"Sorry, Sheriff. I only meant—"

"Sally Denver saw a woman with Tanner."

"What?"

"I saw Tanner earlier tonight and told him to call me if he saw anything weird. Anybody lost. Anybody different. And then a little while after, Sally Denver saw Tanner with a woman she didn't recognize. She said the woman seemed hurt. Now I can't reach Tanner when I call him on the radio."

"You think Tanner's in danger?"

"No," Kendra says.

"You don't think he's involved in any of this."

"If he had this woman Holly in the plow and didn't tell me . . ."

"But it could have been any woman, right? Someone Tanner knew? Then again," Fickett says, "you heard it all from Sally."

"Meaning what?" Kendra asks.

"Sally's got her struggles, but she's always been herself. Even when she's acting like a kindergartener now, she's a trustworthy kindergartner. That part of Sally carried right through. If she had a bad feeling, I wouldn't write it off."

"What's your take on Tanner?"

"He fixed my mudroom's roof. Hasn't leaked all winter."

"I'm not asking for a handyman referral."

Fickett shrugs. Kendra keeps staring at the tipped plastic bottle.

"Awkward," Fickett says. "Uncomfortable to talk to. But most people in Pinebuck have had him in their house. When he came to fix my roof, I trusted him enough to leave him with my house key."

"Tanner helped a lot when we were looking for the Skylars."

"I remember that."

"He also eats mayonnaise and syrup."

"Come again?"

"He mixes maple syrup and mayo on his plate. Dips his French fries in. Tonight, he dipped his finger. There's odd and then there's something else . . . a worse kind of odd. Like everything about him is mayonnaise and syrup."

Fickett looks repulsed but mostly just confused. Even Kendra isn't sure of what she's trying to express. The whole conversation has a dreamy functionality, somehow detached—and somehow not—from the visceral reality of standing in the ruins.

This is shock, Kendra thinks. *But that doesn't mean I'm wrong.*

"If Tanner had someone in his plow, he should have told me."

"Cookie always trusted him."

"Cookie made mistakes."

Fickett looks gut-punched. Neither of them speaks. She regrets having said it and resents having needed to. The cooler in the back with its dark, open door has the feel of something primally and permanently bad. She can't see inside from where she's standing at the counter, but her mind tunnels in, the chaos focuses, and everything converges to a pinpoint of action.

"I'm going to find Tanner. He's the only lead we've got."

"You're just going to drive around and hope you get lucky?"

"He's plowing fresh snow," Kendra says. "There's a trail."

Chapter 38

The snowplow's cab is literally freezing.

The heat vents are off, the windows are open, and ice crystals form on the windshield. Despite the cold, Tanner feels feverishly hot. He's taken off his coat and flannel, but even stripped down to his white thermal undershirt, his skin prickles with an oncoming sweat. His eyesight ripples. His head's a sizzling mess. He rubs his face and has the feeling it's another person's body. A cadaver at the wheel. Unfamiliar meat. He watches it control the truck—stiff, automatic—while his mind keeps panicking and broiling in his head.

The plow is on an isolated rural road that connects two others, which are equally remote. All around are whitened trees, snowy fields, and heavy gray hills. No houses, no traffic. A dark, dead zone in the deepest part of night. There isn't a hint of the village halo. Not a solitary bulb blinking on a tower. The stars are coming out with the sky partly clear, but they may as well be ice chips, scarcely even glimmering. The only light anywhere is coming from the truck. Anything beyond it seems nonexistent.

He can't remember traveling the whole way here. His body slows the truck independent of his thoughts and makes a five-point turn to clear the unplowed lane. Back in town, he'll give a final pass to all the major roads, throwing down salt everywhere he goes.

After that, he'll be done. The blizzard's almost over. His body will be home soon, deadened with exhaustion, but his overheated thoughts won't let him sleep. He'll be forced to look ahead to some imaginary storm while tonight disappears as if it never even happened. Nothing ever lasts. Nothing really keeps. Not the weather, or the Skylars, or his memories and thoughts. He dreams of what's coming and it's suddenly behind him, and the more he wants to be a certain way, the more he isn't.

His life has always felt a little like this. Dreaming how it ought to be, then watching how it really was. His mind doing one thing, his body something else. Now and then, he was able to imagine so intensely that his life seemed genuinely under his control. But he never quite believed it. He couldn't make it stick. He'd will himself to be a certain kind of man, but then he'd watch himself behave like someone else entirely. Tanner on the inside, Tanner on the outside. Which of them was real? Which of them was *him*?

He never quite knew who he was or how to be. His family told him one thing, his peers something else, and every other voice and person in the world had a different idea of what he got wrong. He watched himself in different homes and attitudes and jobs the way a person doing shadow puppets watches and experiments. But all he ever made were ordinary shapes. Snowplow driver. Handyman. Loner.

He didn't have the flair of someone like Vance, who built a Christmas tree sculpture everybody loves. He didn't have Cookie's confidence or humor. He visualized himself as someone intimate and warm, except he couldn't make friends, he couldn't get laid, and he couldn't ever move beyond casual connections.

People viewed him with indifference, if they noticed him at all. He was the guy who fixed toilets. The stranger in the plow. The man you said hello to before you turned away.

But then a year or so ago, Tanner tried something different. Instead of reimagining himself as someone better, he began to reimagine everybody else. What if *that* man behaved or thought a certain way? What if *that* woman felt what he expected her to feel? He'd been doing it for years in fantasies and dreams . . . but what if it were true? What if it were real? The stronger he believed, the more it seemed to work. He had to concentrate and practice, and it wasn't always perfect, but he started feeling comfortable and confident and strong. The world bent around him. People changed shape.

He interacted more with tourists, trying little conversations that he scripted and rehearsed. More and more, the interactions went as he expected. When they didn't, he'd replay the scene the way it should have happened . . . imagining the people acting right instead of wrong. He did it month after month. Tourist after tourist. He gave people help, directions, and opinions. He offered people rides. He made them into anything he wanted them to be for just a few minutes. Then a few minutes more.

Eventually, like anyone imagining and shaping, he dreamed of making changes that wouldn't go away. He fantasized for half a year, planning and preparing. He scripted it. He saw the storm. He visualized the shapes. He went through every step so often in his head that by the time he found the Skylars, it was all like a memory of something he had done a thousand times before.

They changed for him. They perfectly conformed before his eyes, and when they looked at him, they saw what Tanner dreamed himself to be.

Someone in control.

A shaper, not a shape.

But then he *doubted.*

Once he doubted, they began to doubt, too, and then they looked at him and only saw his ordinary shape. A loner and a loser. A man you turn away from. He'd tried to make the Skylars and the world flow around him, like water in a pool responding to his moves. Instead, it all froze, and he was powerless and trapped, like a wide-awake brain in an icebox corpse.

Tonight, it's just the same. Nothing's worked. Nothing's flowed. Tanner sees himself barreling insanely through the snow and can't control his body or his feelings or his thoughts. He's going too fast and ought to slow down, because it's hard to see the ditches bordering the road with the huge wave of snow curling off the plow. But he's helpless, only capable of witnessing the scene and almost wishing he would crash. Wishing it would end.

Suddenly there's movement, way beyond the headlights. A pair of dark shapes in the field—maybe deer—coming through the drifts in the direction of the road. Small at first. Vague. Only visible at all because there's nothing else around them and they pop right out against the blank, white snow.

It isn't deer. It's people. Two of them together, struggling to the road and waving at the truck.

Tanner's whole body jolts, as if he's waking out of sleep and finding he's exactly where he dreamed he ought to be. He stops the truck and watches out the passenger side window. The couple gets closer, floundering and fighting through the field's deep snow. It's happening. It's real. Suddenly he's calm and perfectly controlled, and anything he wants to do, his body really does.

He has two stun guns. Batteries charged, safeties off. He puts one on the seat, nestled at his thigh, and keeps the backup handy in the pocket of the door. The handle of his military knife extends toward him unobtrusively from a sheath secured to the underside of the plow-control console. The zip ties are in the glove box. Everything is set.

He unbuckles his seatbelt, leans way across the cab, and swings the passenger door open. The overhead light turns on, which makes the couple outside seem darker than before. But then they're over the snowbank and standing at the running board, wonderfully aglow as if they're on display.

It's the same woman he picked up earlier tonight. Tanner assumes the man is her boyfriend. They're the very two people he regretted having lost. And here they are together, desperate for a ride, having flagged Tanner down and rushed straight toward him. He doesn't question the unlikelihood. He manifested this. His mind simply flows, following the turns, the same way the plow had moved through the dark.

He waves them into the cab but they're already climbing up. Did his beckon cause the climb, or did their climb cause the beckon? It all just happens like they're living in his brain.

"You again," he says, smiling easily and well. "I see you found your boyfriend. I worried when I lost you. How'd you wander out here? Let the lady have the seat . . . you can squeeze in between us. I'll tell you, it's a lucky thing I saw when I did. You would have frozen solid, walking to the village."

The cab goes dark when the woman shuts the door. Now there's nothing but the glow coming from the dash and the headlights glaring off the snow out front. The woman's in the passenger seat. Her boyfriend crouches in the middle of the cab, right next to Tanner with the console in front of him.

"I've already met Jane. What about you?"

"I'm Brian."

"Good to meet you, Brian. I'm Tanner. There's nothing in my thermos or I'd give you both a drink."

"Can you turn up the heat?" the woman says.

"You bet."

Tanner shuts the open windows and cranks the dial. He casually moves his hand to the stun gun beside him. He needs to pass it over his lap, from the left to the right, in a smooth, subtle handoff he's practiced countless times. With the Skylars, he diverted their attention to the plow and didn't move the gun until they both looked away. But the couple here now seems distracted already. Shivering and hunched. Numb from the cold. Focused on the warm air blowing from the vents. Tanner moves the stun gun, easily and quickly, and holds it unseen close to Brian's hip.

His thumb is on the button. His empty left hand tightens into a fist.

But something feels wrong and Tanner hesitates a bit. He's slightly off-script, having transferred the gun without the planned diversion. He falters like an actor who's been improvising words and suddenly draws a blank on the next real line. Neither of them notices. Why can't he move?

He finally understands the part he has wrong. His left hand is clenched and ready for a punch . . . but the punch should come *after* he releases Brian's hair. Tanner unlocks his fingers. Now he feels ready. Everything is right again, flowing and familiar.

He grabs Brian's hair, jerks his head sideways to open up the neck, and jams the stun gun hard against the unguarded flesh. Hits the button. Starts counting.

One Mississippi . . .

Brian grunts and jolts, instantly explosive, every muscle in his body jumping and recoiling.

Two Mississippi . . .

Tanner holds tight, gripping Brian's hair and pressing on his neck so the volts keep flowing. Brian's grunt becomes a wail, like a lockjawed scream—the sound of someone wordlessly, mindlessly in pain.

The woman's reaction is predictable and clear. Her surprise at the noises, her assessment of the danger, her sudden lunge forward to counter the attack. Tanner leans back and releases Brian's hair. *Now* he makes a fist with his empty left hand. All he has to do is throw a little jab. It's a lightweight blow, except the woman's lunging forward, doubling the force with her own moving face. He hits her in the nose with his two biggest knuckles. Instinctively, she lifts a hand to cover up her face. That's when Tanner cocks back and throws a real punch. He drives her palm against her nose with a wet, fleshy pop and knocks her whole body back toward the door.

Then he's back to gripping Brian's hair and zapping at his neck.

Tanner makes it easily to five Mississippis.

Everything's proceeding just as he imagined.

Chapter 39

Holly's too dazed to know she got punched.

Everything's a roar blooming in her head. She can't think clearly, her senses are exploding, and it's all too much to process at once. There's a horrifying sound, part growl, part scream, and a lot of crazed motion right beside her leg. Her eyesight's blurry, her hands feel slick, and something in the truck has a bad, familiar smell.

Blood, she thinks. It's flowing from her nose to her lips. Holly tastes it and her mind starts snapping into focus, and before she's really clear, she's ready to attack again—mad enough to rip Tanner's face off his head.

"Stop," Tanner says.

Brian's fallen silent in the dark space between them. Holly stares. Her adrenaline is lit gasoline. She understands Tanner hit Brian with a stun gun. Now he holds a knife under Brian's chin. It's a half-foot blade. A combat weapon. He grips Brian's hair so his head doesn't tip. Brian's conscious, but his eyes have a faraway look, and his body seems boneless and pitifully inert. He doesn't look badly injured. He's paralyzed with fear. The blade is vertical, its point pressing upward at the spot where the soft, pale bottom of the jaw meets the neck.

Holly freezes. The blood runs freely from her nose.

"Open the glove box," Tanner tells her.

"No," Holly says.

He doesn't move the knife. He simply tilts Brian's head so the pressure of the blade is stronger on the skin.

"I know you're hiding from the cops," Tanner says. "I'm worried that you're dangerous. I don't want to hurt you but I don't feel safe. This is strictly self-defense. Now open up the glove box."

Holly stares for several seconds, thrown by what he's said. It's possible he's scared and telling her the truth. A man who tried to help her earlier tonight and helped Mrs. Denver when they found her in the road—is it crazy to imagine he's an ordinary guy who's heard about the mayhem and murders of the night?

Still, it all feels wrong. The stun gun. The knife. The speed of his attack. More than anything, he makes her feel instinctually queasy with his dead-fish eyes and taut, veiny neck. But her thoughts are too frantic, and the knife's at Brian's throat, and she can't risk challenging or angering him more.

She pops the glove box open.

Fuck, Holly thinks.

"Take them out," Tanner says.

"You use a lot of zip ties and weapons plowing roads?"

Instead of answering, he leans away and twists Brian's head. He keeps the knife securely under Brian's chin, turning him around so his back is facing Holly. Brian's kneeling on the floor and his arms hang limp. He offers no resistance and doesn't make a sound. Not a whimper, not a groan. He's helpless. Catatonic.

"Tie your boyfriend's wrists."

Holly sniffs and the blood feels phlegmy in her sinuses.

"Look at it from my point of view," Tanner says. "I can't let you go. I can't drive away. I have to think the two of you will jump me if you can, so I have to keep the knife underneath his chin. We're stuck like this until the situation changes, and the longer it goes on, the more I can't predict. Tie him up and we can all breathe easier together."

Holly hesitates, furious and bristling with defiance, but she can't disagree that the three of them are stuck. She decides to play along and bind Brian's wrists. As soon as Tanner moves the knife, she'll wrestle it away. She reaches for the zip ties. They're heavy-duty nylon. She slips Brian's hands into the preformed loops. His arms are so slack, he may as well be sleeping. Tanner watches closely over Brian's shoulder, making sure she pulls the loops genuinely tight.

"Now his ankles," Tanner says. "Use the different set of ties."

Brian's kneeling with his heels splayed out behind him. The knife never drifts from underneath his chin. Holly roots around the glove box and finds the different ties. They're single loops, big enough to fit around boots. She folds at the waist, feeling bulky in her coat, and her hair straggles down and dangles at her cheeks. Blood keeps dripping from her sore, cloggy nose, pattering her thighs and the backs of her hands. She loops Brian's feet and cinches them together.

Tanner forces Brian halfway around so he's staring out the windshield.

"Tie your own ankles," Tanner tells Holly.

"Put the knife down," she says. "Look at him. He's terrified."

Tanner doesn't move but his scalp seems to vibrate.

"Please," Holly says.

Tanner doesn't answer. He's as cold and unyielding as the blade at Brian's throat. Holly binds her own feet and shivers at the sound when the zip tie's grooves tighten into place. Tanner makes her toss the final tie into his lap.

"Turn away from me," he says, "and hold your wrists behind you. I'm letting go of Brian's hair. The knife isn't moving. Any sudden move, I'll jab it through his chin. But once you're both tied and everybody's safe, we can all drive away."

Holly does what he says. Tanner binds her wrists with his one free hand and zips the loops tight, snug enough to pinch. Holly—fully bound, staring outward at the snow—sees an odd, dark shudder at the edges of her vision. She's afraid now, straining at the ties until they hurt. Her pulse feels dangerously rapid and intense. It's difficult to breathe with her nose so bloody, and her mouth starts fogging up the window glass. She shuts her eyes. Something in the middle of her shrinks like a withering balloon she can't reinflate.

She turns and looks at Tanner and he's weirdly far away, as if the space inside the truck has widened and distorted. When he moves, it's like he's moving out of sync with her perception—like she's looking at a time-delayed movie of his face.

"I already called the cops and told them where we are," she says. "How's it going to look when they find us this way? Tied up and bloody. Threatened with a knife. However you're justifying this—"

"Where's your phone?" Tanner says.

"It died before you picked us up. You can't check the calls."

"You're lying."

"Want to bet?"

"I want to see your phone."

Tanner turns the knife so the length, not the point, is under Brian's chin. Easier to keep it in position, Holly thinks, while he shifts his attention more aggressively to her. Brian stares blankly at the snowplow console, as helpless as a child who's been heavily sedated. Tanner leans forward, keeps the knife at Brian's neck, and pats Holly down, searching for the phone.

Suddenly the cab is sickeningly small. The three of them are crammed uncomfortably together, and there's no room for Holly to avoid being groped. She strains against her bonds, her fingertips are numb, and the zip ties lacerate the skin around her wrists. Her hair is in her face. Her nose keeps bleeding. Every time she breathes, she swallows more blood. Something in her mind tilts off-center, and her thoughts spin wildly and recklessly away.

She forgets about Brian. She forgets about the knife. She struggles and erupts and fights like hell.

Tanner grabs her throat. Holly twists and struggles but he bears down hard, and without her arms and legs, she can't shake him off. His hand's a tight pincer, squeezing on her arteries. She doesn't really choke but her oxygen is stopped. She's speechless and immobilized, writhing like a worm, with the same deep panic she suffered in the ice. It's primal. Irreducible. A desperate need to breathe.

She understands how Brian must have felt during the Bad Date.

He's killing me, she thinks. *There's nothing I can do.*

She thrashes on the seat and tries to free her neck until her vision, her resistance, and her thoughts blur away.

BRIAN'S HEAD IS a crackly buzz.

It's taken him a while to realize he was shocked. He never saw it coming, and the pain was so intense, he hadn't thought of anything but cowering away. When it stopped for several seconds, his body blazed and blared until a longer zap hit him with obliterating force.

After it was over, he'd have flopped like jelly, but Tanner held him up with a fistful of hair. He can't remember anything for minutes after that. He's spent the time mindlessly inhabiting his body. Everything is ache. Everything is shock. His heartbeat feels like a high-tension quiver. His muscles have relaxed after spasming and flexing, leaving him as slack as a loose bag of meat. He's drooling some. His eyes focus only on the distance, and nothing outside looks tangible or real.

He knows his hands and feet are bound but can't remember how. He never saw the knife but knows it's at his throat. He can't remember anything that Holly and Tanner said. Most of his perception is deep inside his body, so interior it's closer to a memory or dream. He felt the same last year when he was bludgeoned with a brick. He felt it when the snow engulfed him in the storm. He felt it when he woke in unfamiliar places with long, blank gaps where his self should have been. There's a sense that he's imagining the horror show around him, and he can't get away because it's all inside his head.

We're in danger, Brian thinks. *Someone's hurting us again.*

It's not surprising or unusual or new. Someone's always threatening or hurting them tonight. Whenever they escape, there's another kind of danger, and he's given up believing it'll ever really end.

He has a flicker of a memory that Holly called the cops. Except her phone is dead. He thinks it's dead. Maybe she was lying. What little he can see beyond Tanner, through the windshield, is monochrome and featureless. There's a long, straight road extending out of sight. He doesn't see any flashing lights in the distance.

No one else is coming. Not in time to help.

The monster will, he thinks. *The monster always comes.*

He recognizes something building in his body. Not exactly strength—more like density and tension. His muscles are contracting, his skeleton is straining, and he feels as if his nerves are heating and connecting. The vibrating wire ringing in his skull has thickened up and tightened to a compact coil. He's a battery. He's a magnet attracting wild energy.

Brian turns his head partly to the right, and the friction from the knife slices him a little.

Tanner's choking Holly one-handed in her seat. His knuckles stand out. His jaw is firmly clenched. Holly's mouth gapes open, her lips and teeth are bloody, and her eyes look doped and weirdly out of sync. She loses consciousness and sags.

Tanner frees her neck, watches her intently, and slaps her on the cheek to wake her back up. Holly gasps, but her breath sounds thin and insufficient. Her body flops and twitches with involuntary spasms. Before she sharpens up, Tanner's choking her again. His hand makes two-second squeezes on her throat, pumping on and off like he's playing or experimenting . . . seeing what it takes to keep her partially alert, as if he wants her to be foggy and aware all at once.

Tanner's face is close to Brian's, less than one foot away. He has a child's fascination in his unblinking eyes—a spellbound and absolutely focused curiosity. The kind of look a person might have before an orgasm. Right before a fantasy or wish comes true. He keeps the blade securely under Brian's chin and squeezes Holly's neck until she fully passes out again. Tanner lets her go and stares a long time. Holly doesn't move. She's all the way gone.

Brian strains hard, twisting at the wrists until it feels as if the ties or his bones might snap.

Tanner waits and waits. Ten slow seconds. Then he brings Holly back with a crisp double slap, lets her sharpen up, and starts choking her again.

The monster should have come by now. Someone should have changed. But the storm's truly over, and the snow isn't blowing, and the mad, violent energy that usually surrounds them is entirely and uselessly confined to Brian's head.

He turns away from Holly in a roar of white noise. His body feels numb and out of his control. All he sees is Tanner pressed up beside him, and the details are ultra-sharp and startlingly clear. The tight, woven pattern of his white thermal undershirt. The stubble on his cheek. The hollow of his ear. The veins and tendons in his neck are vividly pronounced, like soft rubber tubes underneath the skin.

Tanner seems to have forgotten Brian's crammed beside

him. He's totally engrossed with squeezing Holly's throat. His upper half rotates slightly at the waist, so his strangulating arm has a little more reach. His other arm drifts from its earlier position.

The knife drifts, too, away from Brian's neck.

HOLLY CAN'T REMEMBER why she's battling to breathe.

Is she passing out or waking up? Fading or reviving? Her body seems to move but her limbs feel stuck. Her vision comes and goes. Everything is wrong. One second she's aware of Tanner squeezing at her throat; the next she can't remember anyone is with her. The only constant is the sad and debilitating fear of knowing that she's dying and can't make it stop.

Suddenly she's breathing. Holly coughs and wheezes, but the air comes slowly, almost like her lungs have forgotten what to do. Her throat burns. The zip ties sting around her wrists. Tanner's hand is off her neck and resting on her chest, and his face looks warped and blurry in the dark.

Her gaze falls to Brian in the middle of the cab. He hasn't changed position but he's different somehow. He's sitting on his heels with his hands pinned behind him but instead of looking powerless, he radiates danger. She's chilled by his eyes. They're alien and cold, too focused and intense to notice Holly watching him. Brian stares at Tanner. Tanner looks at her. Their faces form a triangle—Tanner, Holly, Brian—and a bad, hot charge is sizzling between them.

Tanner lets his knife drift away from Brian's neck. Holly

notices but doesn't have a second to react before the tight little scene viciously explodes.

Brian headbutts Tanner squarely on the temple. Holly hears the crack of bone on bone, followed by a thump when the knife hits the floor. Brian springs off his heels with his hands tied behind him. He smashes Tanner hard against the plow control console, shoving with his head and chest and snarling like an animal. The console breaks and tilts off its mount. Tanner's in a terrible position to maneuver in the very cramped space between the two seats. He tries pushing Brian but his elbows are pinned, and his head is at a sharp, wicked angle near the dash.

Holly hasn't totally recovered from the choking. She gasps for air, her eyesight sparkles in the dark, and when she tries sitting forward, she's overwhelmed with dizziness and feels as if the truck is rolling and revolving.

The knife . . . where's the knife . . . I've got to get the knife.

She concentrates and stamps the floor blindly with her heels, hoping she can trap the blade underneath her boots.

The men are a ferocious knot pressed against her legs. Tanner's addled and surprised but it won't last long, and he's the only one whose hands aren't tied behind his back. He forces Brian sideways and they're separated briefly, just enough for Holly to glimpse Brian's face. His eyes are crazed. His teeth are bared. He's scarcely recognizable.

He lunges into Tanner. Not to headbutt.

To bite.

He goes for Tanner's neck, between the shoulder and the ear. She can't see exactly where his teeth sink in, but she can tell he has a solid grip and won't let go. This isn't something halfway or tentative or quick. Brian bears down. Burrowing and snarling. All his force and weight are focused on the spot where his teeth sink deeply into vulnerable skin.

Tanner's face contorts from the strange new pain. He makes an agonized sound, like a low, gurgling growl, and his head jerks sideways against Brian's mouth. It's similar to Brian's own reaction to the stun gun—an instinct to clamp and contract where it hurts. He pins Brian's face between his shoulder and his cheek, but he's jammed against the dash and folded at the waist, and he doesn't have the leeway to get himself free.

Holly tries tangling Tanner's arms with her boots. She isn't much help. Her position's too cramped, she's afraid she'll kick Brian, and her mind's too startled by the savagery in front of her. The bite sounds wet. Brian's slavering and gnawing into thick, tough flesh. Blood starts burbling at the corners of his mouth. Tanner squeals. His undershirt darkens, his complexion loses color, and his body seems to shrink and soften and collapse. Brian bites harder, twisting with his jaws until a huge flow of blood gushes through his teeth.

Holly looks at Tanner and a weird thing happens. She sees him as a child or a puppy getting tortured—the squinty face, the woundedness, the high-pitched whine—and all she wants to do is make it stop. *Make it stop.*

She plants her heels on his forehead and pushes him away. Tanner's heaved up and back toward the driver's seat. Brian goes with him, hanging by his teeth, until a chunk of Tanner's neck finally tears free.

A PIECE OF bloody flesh drops from Brian's mouth. It has the taste of raw steak and the feel of raw chicken. Slippery and elastic. Viscerally fresh.

Tanner's upper half settles on the driver's seat. His head's against the door, his legs are sprawled across the cab, and he's pressing both hands against his ripped-open jugular.

Brian tastes blood. He spits a little out. His mind isn't blank so much as primitively pure, as if he's satisfied an appetite that doesn't have a name.

He understands how Holly must have felt after the Bad Date.

I killed him, Brian thinks. *Nothing can undo it.*

Tanner's still alive, but he won't last long. Brian knows it in his gut. He feels it in his teeth.

He finds the knife on the floor and holds it up behind his back. Holly twists and reaches backward, finagling her wrists until the blade fits snugly in her zip tie's loop. She rubs the heavy nylon up and down the edge until her hands pop free. Then she frees Brian, too.

Instead of cutting their ankle bonds, Holly drops the knife, squeezes past Brian, and stretches up the length of Tanner's limp body. She's on top on him. They're face-to-face like lovers in the dark. Brian grabs the knife, ready to attack again but mostly just watching in a calm, quiet trance.

Tanner's bleeding badly. He grips his neck and doesn't try to shove Holly off. She lays her palm on Tanner's hand, keeping pressure on the wound, with her other hand cradling his head to keep it still. Tanner stares at her. He seems to be a whole different person—someone desperate and defenseless and incapable of violence.

"Don't hurt me," Tanner says. "I'm sorry. Please, I'm sorry."

"Why did you do this?" she says. "Why did you do this to us?"

Brian listens hard, waiting for the answer.

"Help me," Tanner whispers.

"The pressure isn't working," Holly says. "You're bleeding out. There's nothing I can do and no one else is coming. You're dying. Understand? You've got to talk to me, okay?"

Her voice is low, almost tender, and it softens Brian's edge. He puts the knife down and leans toward Tanner in the dark.

"Why'd you hurt us?" Holly asks.

"Hurt," Tanner says. "I don't know, I don't know. I dunno what's happening."

"You tied us up. You strangled me."

"Therestwo of me," he slurs.

"That's bullshit. It's you. It's all just you."

Tanner half faints and slowly flickers back.

"I didn't see it like this. You didn't change. You should have changed."

"What do you mean?" Holly says. "Tell me what you mean."

"I'm scared," he says.

"I know."

"Lisssen," Tanner says. "I'm not the right shape."

Brian watches closely from inside his body. The three of them are bloody. One of them is dying. They're all in different shapes now, and everything has changed, and he can't imagine any other outcome together. Whatever came before, whatever happens next, they're part of something monstrous, and everybody fits.

Chapter 40

Kendra finds the target she's been seeking all night.

After following the roads that are most freshly plowed, she's driven from the populated center of the village to a dark, rural lane miles out of town. Half the road is clear, almost to the asphalt. She drives a quarter mile, crunching over salt that hasn't yet dissolved, and then her headlights reflect off something in the distance. It's shadowy and big. Dead ahead.

Tanner's plow.

She speeds right up instead of hanging back and hits the brakes hard, thirty feet before the plow.

The high beams illuminate Holly in the road. She's standing with her empty hands dangling at her sides. Her face is bloody. Actually, a lot of her is bloody. Brian sits beside her, pressed against the snowbank, and doesn't seem to care that Kendra has arrived. His face and hands are bloody, too. No sign of Tanner.

Kendra draws her gun and steps out of the truck. She doesn't see weapons, but she isn't taking chances. Her headlights cast her own shadow in between them—a distorted silhouette, menacingly different from the version of herself who looks like a cop.

"Whose blood is that?" she asks.

Neither of them answers or reacts in the slightest. Kendra wonders if the blood is partially from Cookie. Her hand with the gun starts tightening and trembling.

"On your stomach. Spread your arms and legs. Slow. Do it now."

Holly lies down but Brian doesn't move. He might be injured after all, or suffering from shock, but Kendra doesn't care because he fooled her once already with his goddamn act of seeming like a victim. She approaches him, keeping Holly partly in her sights. He's a mess up close, even worse than she expected, with blood on his chin like he's an animal that's recently devoured something fresh. She says his name twice before he finally responds.

"Sorry," Brian says, without explaining why.

"Are you hurt?"

"No."

"I'm cuffing you. Kneel and turn away. Hold your hands out behind you."

He does what she instructs. Kendra takes her eyes off Holly for a moment. She squats, keeps the gun at Brian's back, and grabs the cuffs. She's about to snap them on when she sees Brian's wrists. Several inches are exposed and the skin looks raw, as if he's already been struggling with a different set of bonds. She cuffs him anyway and double-checks they're properly secured.

"Tanner!" Kendra calls.

Tanner doesn't answer.

"Where's the snowplow driver?"

"In the cab," Holly says.

"I don't see him in the cab."

"He's there. He's on the seat."

Kendra walks sideways and slowly to the plow. She keeps them both in her periphery. The stillness is surreal. Her truck's idling engine is the only sound she hears, and all around them, past the headlights, there's nothing in the fields except the dark, blank snow and the darker woods beyond.

She steps onto the running board and opens up the door. The automatic light inside the cab turns on. Tanner's head lolls out. His face is upside-down. He's sprawled across the driver's seat, drenched with sticky blood, and there appears to be a chunk missing from his neck. Kendra checks his pulse and verifies he's dead, aware of how furious her own pulse is. She steps back down and looks at Holly and Brian. Then she walks around the plow and opens the passenger door. She finds a stun gun. A giant knife. Pairs of severed zip ties.

A picture forms, logical and sharp in Kendra's mind. Tanner tied them up. They freed themselves and killed him. But her thoughts don't linger on the how or the why.

At the moment, Kendra doesn't give a fuck about Tanner. He wasn't at the diner. Cookie would have mentioned that. *I think I have your girl* was all Cookie said.

It was Holly. No one else.

And I *have her now.*

Kendra shuts the door and turns from the plow. Her shadow moves behind her in the headlight glare, and suddenly and eerily, she feels as if the rest of her—the self she always knew—is no longer here.

She grabs Brian's arm and pulls him to his feet.

"Get up," she tells Holly.

Holly stands and wobbles. Kendra walks them to her truck, staying close behind, and feels a cold energy intensify inside her. She opens the door and puts Brian inside. Once he's in the back with the door shut and locked, she steps away and faces Holly from the road beside the truck.

Kendra knows the rules of handling a gun. She's told them to her deputies and told them to herself.

Keep your trigger finger outside the guard until you're ready.

Never point at anything you aren't prepared to shoot.

Identify your target and anything behind it.

All of which flashes through her mind very clearly . . . especially with Brian in the truck behind Holly, the gun held between them, and her finger on the trigger. She knows it's wrong. Her body seems to operate without her.

"My friend said she had you in the diner," Kendra says.

"Is she dead?"

"Were you there?"

Holly doesn't answer. A strong smell of blood floats up between them, and the gun keeps rising all by itself.

"Tell me everything that happened," Kendra says.

"You won't believe me."

"I just found my friend torn to pieces in a cooler. Now the two of you are here with a mutilated body. You need to understand the situation right now."

Holly takes a very long time before responding.

"I know the situation. I'm a stranger covered in blood. We're miles from the village in the middle of the night. You're a cop and I'm refusing to cooperate fully. Maybe I'm aggressive. Nobody would blink."

"You're giving me ideas?"

"They're already in your head."

"You know what's in my head? Tell me what I'm thinking."

"I can tell you what you're feeling."

"I doubt it," Kendra says.

Holly stares at her face instead of at the gun. Her hair's a frigid wreck, her cheeks are deadly pale, and yet her eyes are so alive and fiery and clear, they burn into Kendra like wicked little suns.

"You want to hurt me," Holly says, "but it's more than that now. You've spent your life believing you're a certain kind of person. Now you find yourself here and it's a whole different story. Maybe you'll forget yourself. Or suddenly you'll change. Or you were *always* someone capable of things you never dreamed."

The gun floats between them at the level of their stomachs.

"You're right," Kendra says. "That's exactly what I feel."

Chapter 41

Deputy Fickett finds Kendra hiding behind the police station.

She leans against a cinder block wall near the dumpster, looking at the tips of the daylit pines. The sky is winter blue. The new-fallen snow is blinding in the light. But Kendra's in a spot where the sun doesn't reach, and the shadow and the cold feel like night.

Fickett walks up and says, "You want to be alone?"

"You can stay," Kendra says. "I need a break from everyone else."

She's had a frenzied and increasingly intense several hours. After tracking down the plow, Kendra waited there for backup, and every new arrival added something to the scene. Flashlights. Road flares. Nitrile gloves and photographs. A body bag for Tanner. Questions and opinions.

Ever since, Kendra's ricocheted between her own department, additional officers from Hilldeclaire, the medical examiner, a tow truck driver, the mayor, prominent locals, less-than-prominent locals, reporters, witnesses that may or may not have witnessed anything, and lots of different voices in her own noisy head. She appreciates Fickett coming out to find her. Otherwise, she might have just frozen here alone.

"Can I get one of those?" Fickett asks.

"You don't smoke."

"Neither do you. I thought you quit."

"I thought I did, too."

Kendra hands him a cigarette and lights it once he has it on his lip. She looks to see if Fickett actually inhales or only blows smoke to keep her company a while. He actually inhales. He doesn't even cough.

"This all keeps up," he says, "we'll have to raid the evidence room for something more potent."

"Maybe there's a noose."

"Jesus," Fickett says.

"That's probably more like it. I'll be crucified for this."

"Why? It's not your fault."

"I'm supposed to be preventing this kind of thing. Instead, I spent the whole night flailing and reacting. Getting angrier and angrier. Wishing it would end."

"Well, eventually you *did* bring it to an end. You can't prevent everything from happening," he says. "A lot of this job is picking up pieces."

"You're right," Kendra says. "Now we need to figure out how they all fit."

They talk the night through, step by step, based on everything they know from witnesses, evidence, and Holly's and Brian's individual accounts.

Fickett says, "Maybe this is more than one puzzle. We've got property damage from the storm. We've got the whole bloody mess with Tanner in the plow. And we have two people dead from what could only be an animal. Three separate deals with separate explanations."

"Assuming that's true, and that's a lot to assume, Holly and Brian just happened to be there for every twist and turn?"

"I don't see Brian wrecking trucks with his hands, and I don't see Holly tearing off limbs. The only thing they *could* have done is bite Tanner's neck. Which they claim was self-defense. That's a real possibility. It almost makes sense to look at them as victims."

"Victims who insist a monster is responsible."

"Three other tourists say the same thing."

"Members of the press, good people of Pinebuck," Kendra says. "A thorough investigation has yielded irrefutable proof of the existence of . . ."

"Say a bear," Fickett says.

"You don't believe that."

"I don't believe monster."

"Every yahoo with a gun, bow, or social media account will be out in the woods hunting innocent bears," Kendra says.

"Say monster, then. The tourism board can sell shirts."

Coincidentally, they both flick their cigarettes away. The butts hit the ground in opposite directions, extinguishing with faint little hisses in the snow.

"I appreciate you talking this through," Kendra says. "But all these explanations sound like excuses."

"You did everything you could and things went bad. But you found your missing couple and the storm's finally over."

"The aftermath isn't."

"Everything's an aftermath of something," Fickett says. "Didn't Cookie always say you ought to let things go?"

"She also told me not to worry. Look how that worked out."

Fickett's mostly in the shade, but the sun hits his head like a miniature cap made of bright, winter light.

"My niece had a monster underneath her bed," he says. "The monster was invisible, so it didn't matter if my sister checked and gave the all clear. It was *there*, my niece said. Every day. Every night. She avoided her room. She left it little gifts, like peace offerings. She talked to it, and threatened it, and tried to figure it out. Eventually she just started sleeping in her bed again."

"The monster went away?"

"She learned to live with it," he says.

Water melts off the eaves and drips down between them. The temperature is freezing so it has to be the sun, or maybe subtle warmth is rising from the roof, or maybe there's a force she doesn't understand about the way snow melts or holds itself together. Elements converge in Kendra's field of vision. Falling water. Bright snow. Fickett's face, deeply shadowed, like an inkblot reminding her of something else entirely.

"Give me your truck keys," she says.

Fickett hands them over. "Where are you going?"

"There's one more piece I need to follow up on. Cover for me, will you? I don't want reporters trailing me out."

"Right," Fickett says. "Something bad?"

"I don't know."

"You're worrying again."

"I'm thinking like a monster."

Chapter 42

Brian looks at her and says, "I don't remember biting him."

"You will," Holly says. "When you try feeling normal."

They're in a holding cell in the Pinebuck police station. Cinder block walls, concrete floor, fluorescent overhead lights. The bars are cold gray. There's a steel toilet without a lid. The other cells are empty, giving the impression of an uneventful day. Holly and Brian sit hip to hip on a cushioned bench that's bolted to the floor. They've been allowed to shower and their hair's still damp. Their grisly clothes were taken as evidence, and now they're dressed in ill-fitting sweatpants and T-shirts a deputy rummaged from a storage closet. The shirts read *Pinebuck P.D. Softball 2013.*

"How much do you remember of the rest?" Brian asks. "From inside the snow."

"Nothing," Holly says. "Like it wasn't even me."

They were questioned by the sheriff. Independently. At length. No doubt they'll be questioned much more and tell the whole thing to many more people. They know what to say and what to leave out because the worst stuff is hidden by their own lack of memory. Their stories line up as well as they can hope.

As far as they can tell, there isn't much against them. Almost everyone they hurt or killed and everything they damaged suffered the effects of superhuman force. Surviving witnesses will say they saw a creature, not a person, and anyone who spotted them as ordinary people saw them getting chased or threatened or attacked. That leaves only Tanner, whom they killed in self-defense . . . assuming there's enough to implicate *him*.

Still, the trouble is enormous. There are no guarantees. Regardless of the evidence or lack thereof, they know how terrible the whole thing looks, and they're expecting to be held and scrutinized and doubted.

For now, they're left to doubt and scrutinize themselves.

"Maybe if we talk it all through," Brian says, "we'll fill each other's blanks. Remember for each other."

"We never really did that after the Bad Date," Holly says. "We shared an awful night, but then we didn't really *share* it."

"I couldn't imagine what you were going through."

"I couldn't imagine what you were going through, either. I didn't want to ask."

"Why?"

"You needed so much help at first. Once you seemed stable—"

"You didn't want to see me fall apart."

"I didn't want *myself* to fall apart," Holly says. "Everything was telling me to keep moving forward. I was doing so well. At least, I told myself I was. All my old fears and insecurities and weaknesses . . . They seemed to go away. They just felt silly. Once I tackled an assailant and killed him barehanded, I thought, well, *shit*. I can handle winter blues. I can face down challenges at work no problem. I didn't want to lose that and start going backward."

"And I was in a tailspin and couldn't stop falling. I didn't want to pull you down with me," Brian says. "I was counting down the days, thinking you should leave."

"You wanted that?"

"No. But I hated being bad for you. I had a realization after therapy one day. For a whole year, we each lived with the only person who remembered the worst night of our lives. No one could have helped us more to put it all behind us. But no one could have hurt us more with nonstop reminders."

"We were the best thing for us and the worst thing for us. And here we are again. Trauma number two."

They sit a long time, staring at the cell's dull metal bars, with the overhead lights buzzing at their heads.

"Evidence or not," Holly says, "we're to blame."

"I didn't mean to kill Vance. You didn't mean to kill Cookie."

"But we knew we were struggling for the past twelve months. We didn't do enough to pull ourselves together."

"We couldn't have predicted we'd turn into a snow monster."

"We should have guessed *something* would eventually explode. I'd love to think we've learned how to deal with this better, but I'm pretty sure tonight made things worse."

"It's different now."

"How?"

He pauses so long, it's like he didn't hear the question. She watches him and waits, hanging on the answer.

"When I went back to work," he says, "everybody *knew*.

And they were all really kind. They didn't make a thing of it or treat me like a child. But obviously, everyone was looking at me differently. They saw me as the guy who got his head bashed in."

"Same with me," Holly says. "I was suddenly the person who had crushed someone's skull."

"And that's exactly how the two of us were looking at each other. I was the victim. You were the killer. One of us was weak, and one of us was strong. But now," Brian says, "we've both been . . . *both*."

"You're saying that we're horrifying mirrors of each other."

"I'm saying that we're balanced. No one's weaker. No one's stronger."

"No one's in the lead."

"Or getting dragged behind."

They've been sitting side by side for such a long time, they can't feel their legs touching anymore. It's like their bodies are conjoined or entirely apart.

"Jesus," Holly says. "A lot of people died so we could have this healthy relationship insight."

"We almost died, too," Brian says. "Now we have to live with it."

"So what are we supposed to do?"

"I don't know," Brian says. "But the two of us should talk more. Like seriously talk."

"I'll wake you up when I have nightmares."

"You have nightmares?"

"All the time," Holly says with a faraway gaze, as if her mind, even now, is falling into shadow. "Don't assume I'm always doing great, because I'm not."

"And don't assume I'm helpless, even when I am."

Brian holds her hand. Holly grips back.

He looks at her and says, "We're like a one-of-a-kind support group with only two members."

"Fucked-up Anonymous."

"Not anonymous."

"You're right. We're identified."

"Known."

Chapter 43

Kendra arrives at Tanner's place, parks along the road, and plods up the unplowed driveway.

The squat, tidy house is well-maintained but unremarkable in almost every detail. The trim is white. The siding's taupe. She can't name the style. The landscape is flat and clear and bordered by the woods. The nearest neighbor is a quarter mile off, and very few drivers ever come this far unless they're purposefully driving where there's nothing much to see.

Kendra's come on purpose to see things through. Because there's no going back. She has to go through. If the night taught her anything at all, it taught her that. When you start at point X and you're forced into Y, you can't return to X because it's different. Or it's gone. She's been trying to recover who she was last winter, but too many things have permanently changed. Of course she's lost her confidence and doesn't feel secure after losing her relationship and fucking up her job. Wishing in reverse is as futile—and as stupid—as expecting Cookie's diner to ever feel okay again.

Has anything about her survived along the way? What's the throughline connecting who she was *before* to who she is now after everything that's happened?

I've been frozen, Kendra thinks, *but I've tried to keep moving. I've always kept clawing at the goddamn ice.*

Which brings her out here, where Kendra's never been, to the isolated place where Tanner used to live.

A little structure stands a short distance from the house. It resembles a minor shed, with corrugated steel siding, a metal chimney, and a small square door on one end. Kendra knows it's a woodburning furnace—not uncommon in Pinebuck—that Tanner would have loaded once or twice a day. Underground pipes send the heat into the house to convection units, radiators, water tanks, whatever. By now it must have burned through its last load of wood.

Kendra lets herself into the house using keys she found in Tanner's plow. It's cold inside. The lights are off. She flicks the nearest wall switch and looks around the living room. *Living* is a stretch. The room is so generic, it appears uninhabited. Very neat and clean. Standard fixtures. Common furniture. The kind of room that's featured in a Home Depot catalog where everything is mint and perfectly arranged.

She looks around the dining room, bathroom, and kitchen, turning on the lights as she progresses through the house. She checks the cabinets and the closets. She peeks in the refrigerator. Eventually, she notices the pictures on the walls. They're photographs of Tanner. Every single one. Smiling awkwardly or staring dead ahead in various settings. Different outfits. Different poses. Many different ages, from childhood to recently. A lot of them are studio shots, like family pics for holidays, but every single photograph is Tanner on his own. They're on every wall in every room, Tanner after Tanner—a personal museum of his slightly changing face.

"What the fuck," Kendra says.

The Tanners gaze back. Oftentimes, from wall to wall, they're gazing at each other.

She's instinctively delayed investigating his bedroom, feeling in her gut that something's waiting for her there. But she walks in now, turns on the light, and doesn't see anything that raises alarms. A plain wooden bureau. A tiny TV. A crisply made bed with a patternless comforter.

Kendra thinks of Fickett's niece and checks beneath the bed.

There are casters on the feet, so Kendra rolls the frame toward the middle of the room. A metal trapdoor emerges on the floor.

Handyman Tanner. What's your project here?

Kendra's heartbeat strengthens and her eyesight narrows. She slides back the barrel lock, squeezes on the handle, and takes a long breath before opening the door.

When she does, she smells Lysol and months of old urine, like the air inside a restroom that's never really cleaned. The overhead light in the room is insufficient, and the space below is dim and difficult to see. Gradually, the details sharpen into focus. There's a room, maybe seven feet across in both directions. A thick steel ladder on the wall straight beneath her leads ten feet down to a concrete floor. In the center of the floor is a round chrome drain. She sees an air vent, presumably for oxygen and heat, but with the furnace out of fuel, the air blows cold. She can tell the room below is even colder than the house.

Kendra kneels, pokes her head inside, and cranes to see

the recessed portion of the room. The light is so diffuse, she only sees shapes until her eyes have time to readjust further. There's a rectangle—possibly a small, narrow cot. At first, she can't discern what's lying on the cot because the shapes are pressed together, darkly jumbled up, and part of her resists making sense of what she's seeing.

Mitch and Becky Skylar hold each other tight. They're naked and they're shivering. Whatever they've been fed for the past seven weeks has barely been enough to keep the two of them alive. They're skeletal. Their skin is sickly white but also blotchy. Maybe raw from the cold. Maybe bruised or abraded. Mitch has grown a beard. Becky's legs are unshaven. Her fracture boot is missing and her cast looks filthy. Their unkempt hair is greasy on their heads.

They look at her without a sound. They're like another species.

They've been here the whole time since Kendra last saw them. Forty-eight days that were always like night. Now that Tanner's dead, they'd have stayed here longer if she hadn't kept looking and found the trapdoor. In another few hours, they'd have died of hypothermia, and even now, there's no guarantee they'll survive.

But she did keep looking, and she will get them out.

She wants to say, *I'm here. It's over now. You're safe.*

They watch her from the dark.

"I'm here," Kendra says.

Acknowledgments

Boring fluff, a reader may say about acknowledgments pages. But those of us who always read them know they aren't always the equivalent of a dull acceptance speech. Sometimes, they're more like Jack Palance doing one-armed push-ups on the Oscar stage (check YouTube). I'll try to entertain.

Stories are shapeshifters. This one, like the monster in it, appeared out of nowhere. Elements swirled together and became something weird. My first reaction was to wonder—enthralled and anxious—what the hell it *was*.

Every book I've written has started with a simple combination. I have to be choosy and wait for something special. Most combinations don't have the juice. Warm air and low moisture result in pleasant, undramatic weather. But cold air crashing into sweltering humidity . . . now we've got a storm. That's what I look for in a starting idea: a volatile mix that defies safe forecasting. A little cloud that keeps growing, rumbling, and shooting lightning bolts until I'm standing in the middle, hoping to harness the energy and scared shitless that I'm comically, badly unprepared.

Two lovers, separated in a blizzard, and a snow monster that *belonged* to them somehow. I knew, in my gut, this combination was kinetic enough to fuel a whole book. So I charged right in, got overwhelmed, and lost my bearings. For a while, I thought it was an audiobook told entirely through cellphone dialogue. But I kept *seeing* too much of the blizzard, the dark landscape, the characters' faces. I was visualizing Holly and Brian's past. Sheriff Kendra Book appeared with a cigarette. Tanner fired up his plow. The story didn't want to be an audiobook . . . it wanted to be a movie. I followed that direction until my film agent essentially said (kindly), "Everybody and their mother writes unasked-for screenplays. Write a book."

Which I hadn't done in several years.

Around 2016, my writing had turned exclusively to horror and weird fiction, and my agent at the time didn't feel he was the best champion of that kind of stuff. So I originally self-published my novel *Ghostlove* as a podcast, and then I did a different podcast of strange stories called *Equinox Society Radio*. A new agent, Stacia Decker, liked my work and got me two deals with Audible. My creative mind had found a rejuvenating sense of play with audio, film and TV scripts, and amateurish visual art, all of which I did instead of writing novels.

And then, suddenly, the snow monster revealed itself as an unwritten book. What a thrill! After years of exploring different paths, novel-writing felt new to me again—as full of possibility as when I'd first started writing as a teen.

That winter and spring, I wrote and wrote (and wrote) until the story found its shape. Almost, anyway. I went through a few deep revisions with my agent, and a couple more with my eventual editor, and then, after all that time and many shifting currents, I finished the book you're holding now. I wouldn't have gotten here if I hadn't followed the peculiar forces of the story itself. And I'd have been lost without a rescue line, crashing blindly into snowbanks, if not for the help of many good people.

Thanks to my wife, SarahNicole (sic), aka Coley. Crazy love. Bended knee. Like anyone who shares a life for more than a quarter-century, we've sometimes lost our way and made shocking mistakes, but our shapeshifting story is two people always reaching for each other. We've made a family, faced monsters, summoned storms, and reinvented ourselves over and over. What a world together. I love you, Coley.

Thanks to our son, Jack, once a fascinating sponge, now an ocean with his own fantastic waves. It's really something to raise a child to adulthood and discover, endlessly, that they're way more interesting, vital, and delightfully strange than anyone you know. "Force of nature" is a tired term, so let's go with *galactic lightning hawk.* He's giving me extremely good creative advice these days. You're going to know his music someday. I love him.

Thanks to our family dog, Bones, a spirited companion, a vigilant Watcher at the Window, and a master of subtle communication. We love eat. We love walk.

Thanks to my dad, who's always cheered me on, and who used to tell me tantalizing details of horror novels I wasn't yet old enough to read. I remember him talking about some book he was reading (maybe *The Talisman*?) in which an evil power exploded a bunch of sheep . . . and the sheep's smoldering legs were *still standing*. This horror book's for you, Dad.

Thanks to my mom, who's always supported me, and

who once handed my adolescent self a musty library book and had me read a story. It was Shirley Jackson's "The Lottery." A life-changing day. She doesn't much care for horror overall, and would prefer that I write more literary fiction, but when you take your kid to Lottery Day, well . . . you knew the rules, Mom.

Thanks to my Aunt Catherine, a true raconteur, a composer of unforgettable letters, and a godsend of a godmother.

Thanks to my agent, Stacia Decker. After getting me two audio deals (and another for a paperback that didn't have an acknowledgments page), this is my first chance to praise her in public. If I were to write a book about a marvelous literary agent—one who cared for her author's well-being, improved his work with keen revision, answered emails eerily fast, and was great to know as a person—someone might say, "Oh, that's fiction." And I would say, "Friend, all of it is true." Stacia is someone whose virtues have offshoot virtues, including humor, patience, razor wit, chicness, mysterious depth, and devotion to dogs (hello, Penelope). When I'm buried in snow, Stacia lifts me out by the hair.

Thanks to my editor, Taz Urnov. The day we met on Zoom to discuss publishing this book together, I recognized her as the type of person I always hope to meet. In short, someone too vivid and unique to be reduced to a "type of person." Taz has the energetic charge of a good story and the open warmth of a good human. Her smarts, enthusiasm, and care brought this book out of the cold and provided the extra fire it needed.

The first time Taz read this book, she yelped at a certain

moment (featuring a frozen arm) and inadvertently scared her dog. I'm told that double startlement inclined her to offer me a book deal, and so I must acknowledge Taz's dog with apology and gratitude. Thank you, Leopold.

All hail Hell's Hundred! Soho Press created a horror fiction imprint because they love good horror, and many readers do, too, and they wanted to bring more monstrosities out of the ground and into the clear, dark light. Shout-outs to Bronwen Hruska, Rachel Kowal, Johnny Nguyen, Lily DeTaeye, Rudy Martinez, and everyone at Soho Press for their hard work and care. You've given me a home: a rare and wonderful gift for a horror writer.

Thanks to Janine Agro for the amazing cover design. My hope was "the kind of horror cover that would have disturbed and fascinated me as a child in the 1980s." Janine nailed it.

Thanks to Steve Feldberg at Audible for opening new story doors at a pivotal time in my career.

Thanks to Roshi Shivalila-James, RN for her friendship and medical expertise on the visceral specifics of chomping someone's neck.

Thanks to all the horror readers, viewers, listeners, writers, filmmakers, and shadowy night-folk who keep this mutating genre gorgeously alive, year after year. Special affection to my Equinox Society audience for their warm connections with my podcasts, my internet signals, my books, and me directly.

And thank you, dear stranger. I appreciate you being here.